PRELUDE
TO
MURDER

PRELUDE
TO
MURDER

A Julia Kogan Opera Mystery

Erica Miner

LEVEL
BEST BOOKS

First published by Level Best Books 2023

This novel is entirely a work of fiction. The names, characters and incidents portrayed in it are the work of the author's imagination. Any resemblance to actual persons, living or dead, events or localities is entirely coincidental.

Erica Miner asserts the moral right to be identified as the author of this work.

Author Photo Credit: Stephen Dorian Miner

First edition

ISBN: 978-1-68512-442-7

Cover art by Level Best Designs

This book was professionally typeset on Reedsy.
Find out more at reedsy.com

"Touch the country [of New Mexico] and you will never be the same again."
—D. H. Lawrence

"Those of us whom God has willed to sing and dance and play will perform on the street corner if there are no more theaters."
—John Crosby, founder, Santa Fe Opera

Foreword

By David Holloway, Santa Fe Opera Apprentice Program Director
Emeritus

Reading *Prelude to Murder*, I am reminded of the opportunity I had showing Erica Miner around the Santa Fe Opera so that she would have a complete sense of the wonderful atmosphere of the place (the only opera company in the world with its own swimming pool).

Erica and I have worked together as colleagues, she in the orchestra pit as violinist, and I onstage singing in the operas, at both the New York City Opera and the Metropolitan Opera in New York. Erica's firsthand knowledge of operatic repertoire, violin parts, and further, her dramatic understanding of the operatic works, gives special insights to the particular productions that are the setting for this mystery. But even more, one gets a sense of the valued, ultra-important contribution of a top-notch violinist to the job of concertmaster in a major opera company.

The operas in this story are not ordinary, when one starts out with Alban Berg's *Lulu*, traversing Gounod's *Roméo et Juliette*, then Donizetti's *Lucia di Lammermoor*, and finally *Salome* by the great Richard Strauss. There is plenty of death and mayhem in all of these operas, even without this added mystery, and they all have been in the repertoire of the Santa Fe Opera.

This is a wonderful read, but Erica also brings so much more to the story than merely solving the crimes. She really shows the inner workings of the theatre and the relationships between individuals functioning in their many varied jobs at this unique major opera festival; and she paints a portrait of the atmosphere of the company against the matchless background of majestic mountains, compelling history and intriguing spirituality that can only be found in New Mexico's "Land of Enchantment."

Baritone David Holloway, who himself was an apprentice singer at the Santa Fe Opera in the late 1960s, has over a fifty-year connection with the company. Having served as Director of the Santa Fe Opera Apprentice Program from 2005 to 2017, he now has been named its Director Emeritus. David has sung with the Metropolitan Opera, as well as all of the major opera companies in the U.S., and for ten years was leading baritone with the Deutsche Oper Am Rhein, Düsseldorf/Duisburg Germany.

Praise for Prelude to Murder

"*Prelude to Murder* provides front row seats to a thrilling and evocative musical mystery in the further adventures of Julia Kogan, a young violinist with the Metropolitan Opera. Julia leaves New York City for a three-month guest appearance with the Santa Fe Opera, where there's enough ambition, intrigue, and jealous wrangling to ensure plenty of suspects when murder takes center stage. A Shakespeare-quoting detective, a pragmatic NYPD lover, a falsely accused friend, and a wealth of opera lore, combined with Julia's parallel journey of self-discovery, will surprise and fascinate the neophyte as well as the opera buff."—Lori Robbins, award-winning author of *Murder in First Position*

"Erica Miner has created a world few people know or have access to: a mystery with music beyond the words on the page. If all music aspires to the human voice, this author has found hers from the start. Bright and hot by day in the desert sun, violinist Julia Kogan has cold feet and colder nights in her next adventure in Santa Fe. Readers will enjoy a tasting flight of opera, a hint of the paranormal, and the promise of romance. Erica Miner's *Prelude to Murder* is an introduction to a new voice for those who enjoy music with their mystery."—Gabriel Valjan, Agatha & Anthony Awards nominated author of the Shane Cleary Mysteries

"Erica Miner is the Agatha Christie of the opera world."— Richard Stilwell, international opera star

"I read and finished *Prelude to Murder* the second time and loved it all over again. Very beautifully written. You made me want to go to Santa Fe! And

especially to see an opera there! Such color and beautiful scene painting...
lovely!"—Aaron Paul Lazar, *USA Today* bestselling author

"*Prelude to Murder* is a tantalizing peek behind the curtain of the world-renowned Santa Fe Opera. There's plenty of mayhem on the bill, rich spirituality, sumptuous history, and metaphysical frights, too. So much to enjoy in Erica Miner's new novel. But it's the music that steals the show. Concertmaster Julia Kogan, on loan to Santa Fe from the Metropolitan Opera, returns (after *Aria for Murder*), and finds herself smack in the middle of a clever and dramatic mystery set against bloody arias and deadly recitativo."—James W. Ziskin, Anthony, Barry, and Macavity Award-winning author

"Erica Miner's *Prelude to Murder* is a delightful read. In addition to being an engaging mystery story with the characters we first met in *Aria for Murder*, this new book provides rich details of the Santa Fe Opera Festival and its exquisite setting. Whether or not you are a regular reader of mystery stories, I recommend this book to all opera fans. Throughout the pages of *Prelude to Murder* Erica Miner has given us countless treats; it's like being given morsels of candy throughout, as she sprinkles in fascinating background and performance details of numerous operas. I encourage everyone to dig in and enjoy!"—Pat Wright, Host of *Opera for Everyone* podcast, and KHOL radio show, Jackson Hole, WY

"Fans of clever, elegant mysteries have something to cheer in *Prelude to Murder*, the wonderful new Julia Kogan opera mystery. Author Erica Miner brings Santa Fe and the world of opera to breathtaking, passionate life as violinist Julia arrives for a summer gig with the world-famous Santa Fe Opera. It's bad enough that she'll be working under one of the opera world's most demanding conductors. But when a fellow musician is arrested for murder, Julia and her boyfriend, NYPD detective Larry Somers, find themselves caught up in the investigation. Miner brilliantly weaves the violent, dramatic stories of real operas with the fictional murder at the core of her novel. Richly detailed and intricately plotted, this twisty story of a detestable diva will capture your intellect and your heart. Congratulations to Miner on having written such a fun, wonderful mystery!"—Mally Becker, Agatha Award-nominated author

"Erica Miner's *Prelude to Murder* will thrill opera lovers, mystery lovers and nature lovers. Miner's personal experience and insight into the inner workings of an opera house rings true on every page. You will be transported by the sights and sounds of The Santa Fe Opera and its incomparable surroundings, while a hint of the paranormal will keep you guessing as you uncover each layer of this haunting story wrapped in adobe pink."—Tina deBellegarde, Agatha-nominated author

"Miner skillfully interweaves the backstories of Julia and her mentor, which hold the key to the killer's motivations. And her scene-setting in the opera world, replete with divas, wannabe stars, and snarky stagehands, makes for a delicious read."—Lynn Slaughter, award-winning Silver Falchion finalist

"Richly drawn characters in the mysterious world hidden behind the curtain. Will Concertmaster Julia Kogan uncover the killer, or become the next victim? Quick pacing coupled with historical elements make this an enjoyable read. Who will survive the curtain call?"—James L'Etoile, award-winning author of *Black Label* and the Detective Nathan Parker series

Characters

- JULIA KOGAN, young Metropolitan Opera violinist, new concertmaster of Santa Fe Opera
- LARRY SOMERS, NYPD detective; Julia's significant other
- KATIE MA, Julia's perennial stand partner from the Met
- ALAN REYNOLDS, Santa Fe Opera General Director
- STEWART BLATCHLEY, Music Director of Santa Fe Opera
- SALMAN KIPINSKY, stage director for *Lulu*
- MATT KIM, assistant concertmaster of Santa Fe Opera Orchestra
- STELLA PEREGRINE, SFPD detective
- CONSTANTIN GRABOWSKI, Stella's partner
- MARIN CRANE, mezzo-soprano, Julia's friend from the Met
- EMILIA TOSTI, Italian soprano diva
- GORAN ŘEZNIČEK, baritone, Emilia's leading man
- DEBORAH ALLEY, Emilia's understudy
- STEVE CAÑON, head stagehand
- MAGDA KERTÉSZ, costume director
- SÁNDOR KERTÉSZ, tenor, Magda's brother
- DANIEL HENDERSON, wig and makeup director
- ROB CHEEVER, apprentice program director
- LORELEI FORMAN, Marin's understudy
- ANDREW STILLMAN, opera impresario
- ADAM CONRAD, *comprimario* tenor in *Lucia*
- NICK PLEASANCE, Chief Medical Investigator for SFPD

Prologue

The magical hues of the spectacular bloody sunset wrought by the Jemez Mountains to the west of Santa Fe disappeared beyond the horizon. Against the backdrop of the majestic but fearsome red clouds of the Sangre de Cristo Mountains to the east, the New Mexican high desert terrain resembled a moonscape: dark, unforgiving, and desolate.

A shadowy figure came into view, dragging a shovel. In the ghostly silence, the figure dug a deep hole next to a scrubby chaparral, heaving aside the dry desert dirt with a vengeance.

'No se preocupe. Cuando llegue el momento, me conocerá a mí, y mi obra.'

Don't worry. When the time comes, you will know me, and my work.

At the base of these peaks, in the summer of 1610, Governor Don Pedro de Peralta and his band of kinsmen had imposed their will on what the early Native American inhabitants called the "Dancing Ground of the Sun." On the site of an ancient Pueblo Indian ruin called *Kaupoge*, "a place of shell beads near the water," Peralta and his men assembled the plan for a city they would call *La Villa Real de la Santa Fé de San Francisco de Asís*—The Royal City of the Holy Faith of Saint Francis of Assisi.

The Spaniards were well aware of the region's sacred name given by the natives. They acknowledged the "Dancing Ground" title; then they went on to create havoc, foisting their beliefs—and their catastrophic diseases—upon the hapless natives.

In 1598, they had established *Santa Fé de Nuevo México*, a province of

New Spain. What did they care for the ten thousand years of occupation by the nomadic people who designed mud houses entered with ladders that opened on the roof that later developed into the Pueblo style? Who grew corn, squash, melons and beans and established their own legitimate society?

No Corn Dance, Harvest Dance, no drumming and chanting, will change anything. Pageantry means nothing. None of it matters—except revenge.

Comanches, Apaches, and Navajos fought back against the Spanish in the Pueblo Revolt of 1680, the source, according to legend, of the Sangre de Cristos' bloody name. Out of necessity, alliances were formed. True to the spirit of Santa Fe, multiculturalism required the acceptance of all their differences, but barely. As time went on, the native cultures and traditions survived, as did those of the Spanish. But the Native Americans' resentments toward their tormentors, *los conquistadores*, remained: festering, embittering, chafing their psyches.

A monument at the main plaza's center, built in 1868, honored not the fallen, who sacrificed all to the interlopers, but rather those who had died in "battles with the Indians in the New Mexico Territory." How this must have rankled the Indigenous people.

What developed into the country's second oldest city had become a melting pot, simmering over four centuries like a tapping lid to absorb waves of settlers of different persuasions; but for the natives it was a cauldron ready to boil over, its cover about to burst forth from the excess pressure.

The figure stopped, wiped off a bead of sweat, and looked around. The remoteness of the locale, in the shadow of the volcanic rock faces of abandoned twelfth-century Puye cliff dwellings and their few remaining petroglyphs, assured a well-hidden site for the grave.

I must do what I must do. They must be punished. I will let no one interfere.

With a vicious twist of the wrist, the figure flung away one last shovel of dirt and walked off, leaving the hollow void gleaming in the eerie light of the Super Moon.

It doesn't matter how long it will take. I can wait forever. The Moon will give me patience.

Named because of its close proximity to Earth, most people considered this luminous orb auspicious, but it was known to affect any person's emotions in stark, profound, incomprehensible ways.

I am done for now. But I'll be back.

Chapter One

Mia Tosca idolatrata, /Ogni cosa in te mi piace
You are my idol Tosca, /All things in you delight me
—Puccini, *Tosca*, Act 1

Beams of early summer sunlight spilled over the white duvet tucked around Julia Kogan's bare feet as she buried her nose in the Santa Fe Opera brochure that had occupied her thoughts for days. Her emotions fluctuated between wild excitement and utter panic. Tomorrow, she would be heading for New Mexico, "Land of Enchantment," to begin a stint as the first of the first violinists: the concertmaster of the opera orchestra. They were starting off with *Lulu*, a rarely performed twentieth-century opera, which she would be playing for the first time.

That was the exciting part. But *Lulu*, which also was one of the most challenging operas to play, contained some of the most challenging violin solos in the repertoire. Julia wasn't sure she was ready for the pressure of performing in such an important position under the vigilant eye of Stewart Blatchley, one of the opera world's most demanding conductors, who recently had been elevated from the position of chief conductor to the first music director in the company's history. Thus, her panic. At the moment, however, she tried to summon up a more positive outlook.

"What's a 'high desert,' Larry?"

Julia's boyfriend, Larry Somers, buried in the blankets beside her, stirred. "The opposite of 'low desert,' I guess. Why?" He reached over and gently stroked the smoothness of her calf.

Julia read aloud from the brochure. "'The Santa Fe Opera shines in the high desert, mystical and magical, taking you to a timeless place where the experience is unlike any other.' Huh. You know what this makes me feel like? A New Yorker."

She stretched out her hand for her latte cup, Dean and DeLuca emblazoned in a small, tasteful white font on the black porcelain, and took a sip. The familiar, blissful taste always gave her spirits a lift. She had heard the coffee in Santa Fe was outstanding, but somehow, she doubted it would compare with the flavor of the blends made with New York's unique-tasting water.

Outside the window of her fourth-floor Upper West Side Manhattan walk-up, traffic made a dissonant music that she rarely heard consciously. She tried to imagine creating music in the silence of a southwestern desert surrounded by mountains.

"You are a New Yorker. We both are." Larry sat up a little, appropriated the cup, took a sip, and handed it back, frowning. He preferred less sugar than she did. "Even if Santa Fe is considered one of the world's great centers for the performing arts—"

"You think it means 'high altitude' desert? Because Santa Fe sits at seven thousand feet?"

"I'm not sure. I do know the desert's a place of extremes, hot by day and cold at night. And the place where Christ met Lucifer for the first time."

"Oh, great. That certainly makes me feel better. Speaking of the Devil, how close is Santa Fe to the Los Alamos National Laboratory?"

"Not that close. Twenty-four miles." Larry yawned and ran a hand through his thick hair, the sunlight playing over a rugged body somehow stark against the soft duvet. "Why?"

"You know I'm chemically sensitive. If there's still any fallout around—"

"That's why I didn't schedule a stopover in the test flats."

"But do you think it gets in the air? Maybe comes down as rain?" She knew she was being overly finicky, as she often was about her health. She also knew Larry could handle it. "What if I get short of breath from the altitude and screw up my playing—"

"What's happening, Julia? Are you having second thoughts about going to

Santa Fe?"

"They wear cowboy boots to the opera there, Larry."

"Of course they do. It's the southwest. The opera campus used to be a dude ranch. Anyway, it's too late. You've signed the contract."

She knew he was right. Her apprehension had little to do with cowboy boots and everything to do with fulfilling the conductor's exacting requirements.

"I've heard the music director has fired people with no notice and for no reason."

"No worries. Blatchley will love you. It'll be a great experience for you."

Julia smiled. "And for you."

"Me? That's different. Somebody once said opera can be deadly for non-opera people."

"That was a joke."

"Personally, I think Santa Fe will be a walk in the park compared with New York. Plus, it's hot and dry during the day, brisk in the evenings," Larry said. They both hated how humid New York summers could be. "And all that history. Now there's something I can relate to."

"History? You mean like practically every building constructed in the last six hundred years has a ghost of a murdered person haunting it? Unexplained phenomena occurring all over the place? Flickering lights, mysterious slamming doors, sounds of children crying—"

"Let me stop you right there." He covered her concerned pout with an affectionate kiss. "You'll be fine. We'll be fine. It can't be worse than opening night at the Met."

Julia frowned, remembering the night of her debut performance in her first season as a fledgling twenty-two-year-old violinist at New York's Metropolitan Opera. Julia's mentor, conductor Abel Trudeau, had been shot and killed on the podium before her eyes. Abel had been like a father to her; trying to do her job without his benevolent caring and guidance had been a constant struggle. Worse, when she somehow became entangled in the murder investigation, she also got caught up in an ominous web of jealousies and rivalries she never knew could exist at the venerable institution and ended up the target of a ruthless killer. Yet, despite the hazards and impediments, Julia had completed the Met season with her self-respect—and her life—intact.

Larry, almost twenty years older than Julia, had been the NYPD detective assigned to the murder case. The unlikely pair had become friendly as a result of their working together toward the goal of exonerating Sidney Richter, Julia's closest colleague at the Met, who she was convinced was framed for Abel's murder. Larry had started out concerned for Julia's safety and welfare but had come to care for her in other ways. Now, they were an item.

Once Sidney had been cleared of all charges, Julia had felt free to soar to the heights of musical accomplishment of which Abel thought her capable. She had performed so exceptionally that Santa Fe Opera music director Blatchley had offered her the position of concertmaster for the company's summer season, while the Met was on hiatus. Julia jumped at the opportunity.

"Besides," Larry said, "How often does a twenty-three-year-old get a chance to be the most important violinist of a major opera company?"

"Abel always told me I would be a concertmaster someday. But what if I'm not ready?"

"Abel would say you're more than ready. He would be incredibly proud of you. As am I." Larry beamed at her. "Once you start playing that violin of yours in Santa Fe, they won't know what hit them. Plus, I get to tag along for their most erotic and murderous opera season in years. Berg's *Lulu*, Donizetti's *Lucia*, Richard Strauss's *Salome*. Each opera bloodier than the last."

Julia was secretly proud that Larry had been expanding his operatic horizons since the two of them had first started working—and sleeping—together.

"You're right," Julia said. "Very high body counts. In *Lulu*, the painter slits his own throat. Dr. Schön gets gunned down by Lulu. She and Countess Geschwitz are knifed by Jack the Ripper. And St. John's severed head in *Salome* could hardly be more gruesome. Crosby would have been thrilled."

Julia and Larry held huge respect for John Crosby, who founded the Santa

Fe Opera in 1957. "The crazy guy who wants to start an opera company," as one Santa Fe resident described him. Against all odds, he had established the company in the middle of the desert, framed by New Mexico's mesas and mountains.

Though Crosby had passed away in 2002, the company's reputation was now at an all-time high, and Julia felt privileged to have been tapped for such a major role in it. But at that moment, her thoughts turned back to her immediate fear. "What if Blatchley hates my playing?"

"Nonsense. He'll love it." He flipped to a page showing a stunning photo of the opera's John Crosby Theatre in front of a New Mexico sunset. "And who wouldn't love playing here?"

"I hadn't thought of it that way," Julia said, mesmerized by the stunning image.

Larry reached under his pillow and pulled out a rectangular plastic box. "Here's something to commemorate your embarking on this important new chapter in your career."

Julia eyed the package, intrigued. "Sweet. But you didn't have to get me anything."

"Don't just look at it, open it."

Placing the brochure on the night table, she slid the cardboard sleeve off the box and gasped. "A Fitbit! You sly dog, you knew I've been wanting one. And in purple, my favorite."

Larry aided Julia in her struggle to remove the wrappings and tape that sadistic designers always included in their packaging, lifted out the device, and clasped it around her wrist.

"This will motivate you to walk up and down hills and all around the Santa Fe campus," he said. "It even has a flashlight. Perfect for snooping around backstage in the dark."

Julia felt uncomfortable, remembering the trouble she'd gotten into for nosing around hidden stairways and hallways at the Met during Abel's murder investigation. "There'll be no snooping. But thank you. This is one fancy piece of jewelry. I love it."

After her terrifying experience at the Met, when she barely survived a brutal attack on her life with the help of her friend Katie's tiny gold cross necklace, the only jewelry Julia wore was a small gold Star of David necklace. But growing up, Julia had admired her Aunt Zsófia's delicate, half-heart-shaped gold locket. When Zsófia had passed away, her daughter, Julia's cousin, had gifted it to Julia. Now Julia wore Zsófia's treasure constantly, the gold star peeking out from behind it. But Julia often fantasized about what had happened to the other half.

"Now let me up," she said. "I have to practice those fiendish solos. You wouldn't want me to self-destruct like Lulu's character does—after she destroys every poor slob unfortunate enough to fall under her spell."

He pulled her back onto the bed. "I had a different kind of practicing in mind."

"For an opera buff, you can be absurdly unoriginal," she said.

He wrapped his arms around her. "Reliable as a fine watch. That's what you love about me."

Chapter Two

O welche Lust, in freier Luft den Atem leicht zu heben!
O what joy, in the open air to breathe with ease!
—Beethoven, *Fidelio*, Act 1

Mountain views on all sides, more glorious than they had imagined, the mysterious Sangre de Cristo range to the east, the majestic Jemez peaks to the west, filled their eyes and captured their imagination as Julia and Larry drove from Albuquerque Airport toward Santa Fe.

Through the open window, Julia breathed in the smell of *piñon* trees, made pungent by the summer rain. "It's intoxicating. Like honeyed tree sap. Sweet, woodsy, and fresh. So purifying."

"And cozy, like a campfire," Larry added.

Forgotten were Julia's initial spaciness from the extreme change in altitude from sea level to thousands of feet above and her unrelenting anxiety over the anticipated stresses of her new job. Her attention was focused on the natural wonders surrounding her.

"It's as magical as everyone says. Such an air of mystery about it. Two hundred miles of Precambrian crystalline rock over five hundred-seventy million years old—"

A sliver of lightning tore through the sky. Julia gave an involuntary gasp and waited until it was followed by the inevitable clap of thunder. Thunderstorms usually frightened her, but in this environment, they seemed more like a natural wonder.

She spied the main building of the Pueblo Inn on the left. "Oh, there's our turnoff. Wow, there's absolutely nothing around here."

"Unlike Manhattan's thousands of buildings and throngs of people, New Mexico, our home away from home for the next three months, is all wide-open spaces. We'll get used to it."

There were no *piñon* trees, not a cactus in sight, only scrubby native chaparral and sparse vegetation. But Julia found the Spanish Pueblo Revival-style buildings awe-inspiring. They looked like contemporary versions of ancient Anasazi cliff dwellings: low-slung, square- and rectangular-shaped adobe-pink boxes with flat roofs and strange-looking wooden posts protruding from the walls.

A concierge led Julia, holding tight to her violin case, and Larry, wheeling their luggage through a leafy garden across an "Enchanted Courtyard" dominated by a large, chunky fountain.

"The design shows the influence of New Mexico's Indigenous Puebloan Ancient Ones and of Colonial Spain. The turret-like structure attached to the main building, our *Kiva*, represents Anasazi religious practices and symbolizes the watchtowers that were found all across the Southwest," the concierge said. "The mysterious, all-important presence of the Ancient Ancestors' ghostly spirits is very keenly felt—the Tiwa of Taos, Picuris Pueblos, and Puye."

Julia's friend Marin Crane, a mezzo-soprano from the Met who had been engaged to sing at Santa Fe, had filled in Julia about the local ghost lore, informing her that Santa Fe was considered one of the most haunted places in the U.S. The thought of spirits' surveillance made Julia significantly more uneasy than the prospect of electrical storms.

"Do you think we'll have one of their ghosts in our room?" Julia whispered to Larry.

"Maybe you should request one."

"Very funny."

Their room was decorated in the typical Southwestern style Julia had seen in her research about the southwest. A heavy, wooden king-sized four-poster bed festooned with a colorful Navajo wool coverlet and matching throw pillows and draped with thick homespun curtains dominated the space. Above the bed, the inscrutable faces of two sepia-toned Native American photo portraits looked off into the distance. Immense exposed rough wood ceiling beams, which Julia had found out were called *Vigas*, completed the effect.

"The bed's got curtains," Julia said after the concierge had left.

"Good. We can take refuge behind them when the ghost comes by tonight."

Hiding her unease, Julia peeked into the bathroom, where a traditional pueblo ladder served as a towel holder.

"Oh, look, *Latillas*," she said. "Puebloan mud houses had no doors, so they entered them via ladders opening on the roofs. They used them to climb from one level to another. That eventually developed into the pueblo style, using the more long-lasting brown-earth adobe, which the Spanish learned how to use from the Moors."

"You've done your homework," Larry said, opening up his carry-on. "I'm impressed."

"I probably should have researched less and practiced more. I'm getting *Lulu* anxiety."

"Maybe our ghost can help you."

"Your jokes are as tarnished as a Navajo silver necklace exposed to a southwestern storm."

"You're right. I should respect your feelings more. I apologize."

"You can make up for it with a kiss."

Julia and Larry shared a cuddle. Then Julia moved to the window and gazed out at the light rain that had begun to fall. She had envisioned a Santa Fe of dust-covered roads and cowboys and Indians on horseback. She never had expected to be surrounded by mountains enveloped in mist, inhaling the scent of *piñons* in the rain-soaked air.

It truly is a "Land of Enchantment."

* * *

At night, the room was quiet, perhaps too quiet. Despite the bed's relative comfort and its hefty curtains blocking out any ambient light, Julia felt restless. She generally was a light sleeper, but somehow, this was different. She wasn't sure if it was the time change, the altitude, or nervousness over starting her new position, but something didn't feel right. She lay listening to the rain and glanced over at the LED clock on the night table. Four a.m.

She tried to conjure one of the more difficult violin passages from *Lulu* in her head, but it was much too complicated to visualize. Sighing, she turned over and, as she tried to go back to sleep, felt a sensation, as if someone had plopped down next to her on the bed. She felt next to her for Larry; he was in his usual position, which never changed during the night.

Again, she felt the imprint of a body, but this time it moved closer.

Don't open your eyes, don't open your eyes.

Was it the ghost of one of the Native Americans pictured on the wall, come down to avenge his ill-treatment at the hands of Spaniards or Anglos, angry that the population of Native Americans in the region had dwindled to a mere two-and-a-half percent? A Spanish missionary killed in the bloody wars with Comanches? A wounded soldier from the Mexican-American War? A Pueblo Indian rebel? A crypto-Jew, persecuted by the Catholics?

Julia had a hard time reconciling any of these. Her Russian-Hungarian-German-Jewish ancestors came to America in the 1920s and never went beyond New York, as far as she knew. Then she remembered that Spanish Jewry had found a tenuous foothold in the American West and had made their mark as merchants, philanthropists, and artists in Santa Fe. They were discriminated against, however, and those who refused to become Catholic converts, or *"conversos,"* sometimes had to observe their religion in secret as "Crypto-Jews." Perhaps one of them was trying to get her attention, make her more aware of her roots?

That's crazy, Julia. Let it go.

She would have had to see the ghost to believe in its presence, so Julia fought off her curiosity and followed her gut feeling, i.e., to keep her eyes closed and not tell Larry about it.

It must be the altitude making me spacey. Now I understand what "high desert" means.

That morning, she rose before Larry and went to the front desk to request a room change. Larry was wise enough not to ask any questions.

Chapter Three

Un nobile esempio è il vostro...al cielo attingete dell'arte
il magistero che la fede ravviva!
It is a noble example that you give...you draw from heaven
the mastery of art to revive the faith of men!
—Puccini, *Tosca*, Act 1

Julia's heart raced as she and Larry drove north on Highway 285 toward the opera campus. Some of her palpitations might have stemmed from her adjusting to the altitude or perhaps from her paranormal experience the night before. But more likely, they were a result of her nervous anticipation of the day ahead: meeting the general director, music director, and new colleagues, and, most importantly, proving her mettle.

They turned on Opera Drive, passed by the OPERA TRAFFIC KEEP RIGHT sign, and wound along the one-point-six miles toward the campus. Julia gazed out across the Tesuque Valley, surrounded by the mountains. The blue New Mexico sky seemed to go on forever.

Larry pulled up to the curb in front of the entrance to the box office. "See you later."

"What? You're leaving me here? To face this alone?"

"It's your show, your chance to shine. Go forth and impress people."

Larry blew her a kiss and pulled away. Julia shrugged off her nerves and followed a path lined with adobe-pink pavers to the entry portal, where "The Crosby Theatre" was spelled out in gold-toned capital letters on the wall of the open-air structure. With its soaring roof and ship-like baffles, the architecture evoked images of Wagner's *Flying Dutchman*, an opera that had fired up Julia's imagination when she had played it at the Met the previous season.

Overcoming her distress, she approached the building and stopped at the security gate.

"I'm Julia Kogan, here to see Alan Reynolds. He's expecting me."

The security guard looked up at her. "The general director? I'll buzz him."

"Thank you. Oh, and my colleague is parking the car. His name is Larry Somers."

As the Guard tapped Larry's name onto his touch screen, Julia admired her surroundings. The plaque honoring John O'Hea Crosby and his parents, Laurence Alden and Aileen O'Hea Crosby, was impressive, but what struck her most was the newness of everything, especially when compared to the Met. The theatre clearly was meant to show that Santa Fe Opera was of the twenty-first century.

A tall, lanky man, his sand-colored hair peppered with grey, approached her. "Welcome to Santa Fe, Julia. I'm Alan Reynolds."

Julia shook his hand. "Thank you. I'm honored to be here."

"The honor is ours. Your reputation precedes you. Stewart is anxious to meet you."

At the mention of the music director, Julia made a concerted effort to restrain her anxiety. "You have such a beautiful environment. Even the birds' chirping sounds musical."

"Southwestern birds sing more sweetly here. The music inspires them."

Julia was surprised by how affable and unpretentious he was, how comfortable he made her feel, a huge contrast to her nemesis at the Met, General Manager Patricia Wells, whose disdain and overt lack of respect for the musicians made their lives miserable. Julia sensed she was going to have a much different experience at the Santa Fe Opera.

* * *

Alan guided her past the box office and adjoining Opera Shop, down to the central plaza and theater exterior. Julia pointed at several enormous white structures off to each side resembling twist-up ice cream pops.

"What are those huge, gauzy things?"

"Baffles for keeping out the wind and rain," Alan said. "Mostly to prevent your instruments from being harmed during our heavy storms."

Julia had never heard such a concern expressed for the orchestra at the Met. "Amazing."

"This is actually our third theatre, constructed between the 1997 and 1998 seasons. It replaced the second one that was built after the fire in 1967."

"Did they ever find out what—or who—started it?"

"No. It remains a mystery—"

"Wow, that security guard." Julia turned to see Larry approach. "I've seen my share of heavy interrogations at the NYPD, but this one was over the top."

"Alan Reynolds, meet Larry Somers. Larry is a detective with the NYPD."

"Nah, I'm just Julia's chauffeur," Larry said with a wry grin. "Also, her greatest fan."

"As you were saying, Alan, about the fire—" Julia said.

"Never mind," Alan said dismissively. "Shall we go inside?"

Julia disregarded Alan's abrupt change of topic when she had her first glimpse of the theatre. Open at the sides and at the rear, its sweeping stage and mountain views from every vantage point left Julia wide-eyed.

Alan pointed upward. "That clerestory window up there adjoins the two roofs, allowing natural light in, like those found in the upper levels of Gothic churches and cathedrals."

"It looks anything but Gothic," Julia said. "It's all so new, so... contemporary."

"We've always had a modern spirit. That's our hallmark," Alan said. "The size and curvature of the roof make it capable of collecting rainwater, which goes directly into tanks below the theatre. Crosby knew the importance of having water sources in the desert. Some local ranchers swore that the rainouts in the early performances were responsible for ending a sixteen-year drought. They became big opera fans."

"Is it true when Crosby wasn't conducting or studying a score, he was directing traffic?" Larry asked.

"Or watering the birch trees. The gardens were his greatest pleasure. Most days, he was out there in his Bermuda shorts and straw hat, clipping away."

Julia gestured toward the stage, where stagehands were assembling a set. "One of my close friends from the Met, Marin Crane, is singing the role of Countess Geschwitz in *Lulu*," Julia said. "She told me the characters who share this world of destruction are all doomed. Such a creepy and disturbing story." Julia suppressed a shiver.

"Would you care to see the dressing rooms and shops?" Alan asked.

Julia nodded eagerly, then leaned over and whispered to Larry. "I can't believe we're getting a personal tour of the backstage."

"Perks of being a concertmaster," he whispered back. "Enjoy it while you can."

Chapter Four

Ma dee luminoso...tal astro qual sole brillare.
Per voi qui ciascuno dovrà palpitare
But your luminous beauty should shine here...like the sun.
Every heart here should beat faster for you
—Verdi, *Rigoletto*, Act 1

O n the way downstairs, Julia peeked in the Chorus Dressing Room to see a large space crammed with costumes, wigs, hats, and shoes neatly organized on shelves labeled with opera titles. She was especially impressed with a cylindrical canister holding an enormous cache of swords with red leather straps.

"Those are for *Roméo* and *Lucia*," Alan said. "Shall we look at the costume shop?"

As they entered the high-ceilinged, well-lit space, which rivaled Grand Central Station in size and breadth to Julia's awestruck eyes, dozens of costume worker-bee teams were cutting, stitching, and draping. Seamstresses kept electric sewing machines humming.

Julia gaped at endless racks of vibrant-colored costumes, stacked bins of accessories, and enormous worktables too numerous to count. She surveyed the sea of tables heaped with bolts of cloth separated by dark and light shades and textures and countless bins of fabric pieces in all sizes, colors, and textures, with teams of assistants expertly sorting, measuring, and cutting them. Julia felt a momentary twinge of nostalgia as she pictured her Aunt Zsófia peddling away at the ancient Singer sewing machine brought from her native Hungary.

"Who handles all this?" she asked Alan. "A wardrobe person, or costume person?"

"Costume director. Wardrobe is costume maintenance and running of the shows. Costume is building and altering costumes for the shows. It is piles of work," Alan said. "But our costume director, Magda Kertész, is exceptional, very organized. She knows every inch of fabric, every detail of each costume. Let me introduce you to her."

Alan led Julia past a row of huge steel drums that were hard at work, churning and agitating, and an immense cylindrical kettle that sported a sign reading, "FLAMMABLE, KEEP FIRE AWAY." Julia was getting a keen sense of the dangers inherent in an opera's inner workings.

"Those are for washing and dyeing," Alan said. "Ah, here's Magda."

A petite, sixtyish ebony-haired woman who, despite her diminutive stature, projected a steely strength, both physical and mental, was putting finishing touches on a mannequin's slinky sequined 1920s-era black dress.

"Magda, this is Julia Kogan, our new orchestra concertmaster from the Met Opera. And her companion, Larry Somers." Alan turned to Julia. "Magda came to us from the Met, too."

"Many years ago, before you were born, Júlia." Julia felt a *frisson* of nostalgia to hear Magda pronounce her name as Aunt Zsófia always had done, with the Hungarian-accented "ú."

Magda noticed Julia's admiring expression. "Black dress is from *Lulu*. Would look very good on you. You may borrow if you like. Or any costume. We have very liberal policy."

"Thank you," Julia said, blushing. "I love your accent. Hungarian?"

"*Igen.* Yes. *Te magyar vagy?* You are Hungarian also?"

"My mother Olga came from Hungary, but she died when I was five. My mother's sister, my Aunt Zsófia, taught me a few words." Julia hesitated. "But I have no one to speak it with."

"You can speak with me. And with my brother, Sándor, too. He is tenor. He sings role of Alwa in *Lulu*. You must introduce yourself."

Magda eyed Julia's gold half-heart locket, which gleamed under the shop's fluorescent lights. "That is beautiful piece."

"It's vintage," Julia said. "It belonged to my Aunt Zsófia. Her daughter gave it to me when Zsófia died. The other half has been lost."

"I have seen similar ones in old city of Budapest," Magda said. "And one matching yours at Radiance Gallery on West Palace Avenue near Santa Fe Plaza."

"Matching?" Julia thought for a moment. "Actually, that makes sense. My aunt's husband was Mexican and came out here after she died. So, the other half might have ended up here."

"You must go to gallery to see if piece is other half of yours, yes?"

"I definitely will. *Köszönöm.* Thank you."

"*Szívesen.* Regretfully, I must get back to work now. Much to do before opera opening."

"Of course."

Magda went back to her draping. "You were a big hit with her, Julia," Alan said. "Not many people here speak Hungarian."

"She loves languages," Larry told Alan. "She studies all the librettos at the Met."

"Stewart will be happy to hear that. It's very unusual for an orchestra player," Alan said. "Speaking of which, he's waiting for us in the dressing room."

At the mention of the music director, Julia suddenly felt apprehensive, but she did her best to hide her trepidation. Touring the opera house was a nice perk, but sooner or later, she would have to face her intimidating new boss.

Chapter Five

Regardez donc cette petite...Je suis là...voilà
Just look at that young girl...Here I am, at your service!
—Bizet, *Carmen*, Act 1

The sign on the door, "Music Director, Maestro Blatchley," made the blood course through Julia's veins and pound in her eardrums. All of her insecurities converged at once. She felt completely deficient and inexperienced, terrified she wouldn't be able to live up to her new boss's standards. She took a few deep breaths to quell her nerves.

Alan rapped lightly on the door, then opened it and ushered in Julia and Larry. A chestnut-haired, impeccably dressed man sat at the piano, practicing a passage from a piano score of Alban Berg's *Lulu.* He stopped playing, turned, and rose. Julia eyed his flawlessly tailored suit and diamond-studded Rolex and suddenly felt self-conscious, not having dressed formally.

"I'm so honored to meet you, Maestro."

"Please, call me Stewart. It's a privilege I afford my concertmasters." Stewart regarded Larry. "And this is...?"

"My apologies," said Julia. "Please meet my companion, NYPD Detective Larry Somers."

Stewart offered his hand, eyebrows raised. "I wasn't aware we needed police protection."

Larry shook Stewart's hand. "Oh, I'm not working. I'm just here to support Julia."

"Then you will be a valuable asset. Most of our players bring family members along."

"Oh, we're not…family," Julia said.

"Ah. I see." Stewart indicated a chair near the piano. "Please, sit, Julia."

Alan caught Stewart's glance. "Would you like to see the rear stage area, Larry?"

"Absolutely," Larry said. "Take good care of her, Maestro."

"Looking after the orchestra players and protecting their creativity are my most important tasks."

Larry followed Alan out the door. Stewart sat on a sofa, Julia opposite him.

"We pride ourselves on our orchestra, Julia. A critic once called it the best feature of our company. That makes your contribution as concertmaster here all the more important," Stewart said. "I'm very demanding of players, and they are exacting in their expectations, both of themselves and of me. That is what makes our experience here unique. Intimate and close-knit."

His *politesse* seemed forced, high-and-mighty, so different from Abel's avuncular, benevolent attitude. Julia worried he would be far more demanding than he had let on.

So much for niceties. Now we get into the nitty-gritty.

Stewart glanced at his Rolex. "Now, if you'll excuse me, Julia, it's time for my coaching. I look forward to hearing your solos. I'm sure you will exceed my expectations."

Julia shook Stewart's hand, left him to his piano, and quietly closed the door behind her, convinced she didn't have a prayer of fulfilling his expectations.

* * *

At the back of the theater's exterior, Alan showed Larry an elevator-like structure that moved up toward the stage between two staircases.

"'B-Lift,'" Alan said. "It raises scenery to stage level from the storage area three floors below. "It may look treacherous, but everyone here is extra cautious," Alan said.

"Good thing there's that netting to keep stuff—or people—from falling through," Larry said. That's the cop in me talking."

Chapter Six

Sie ward geschaffen, Unheil anzustiften...Zu morden—ohne dass es einer spürt.
She was created, evil to instigate...to murder—without leaving any clues.
—Berg, *Lulu*, Prologue

A t the theatre the next morning, the orchestra personnel manager, Sarah, greeted Julia.

"I can't tell you how blessed we feel to have you here. Let me show you the orchestra's digs." Sarah led Julia down a long hallway. "Practice rooms. Orchestra women's lounge." She opened the door to an airy, carpeted space with rows of lockers and benches and indicated one at the end of a row. "This one's yours. As concertmaster, you get the best location."

"Julia!" A young Asian woman holding a violin case and bag strode briskly toward Julia.

"Trust you to get here at the last minute, Katie," Julia said.

Despite her protestations, Julia was thrilled to see the young woman, who always brought a surge of buoyant energy to Julia's disposition. "Sarah, this is my Met violin colleague Katie Ma. My former foster sister, roomie—"

"And best friend." Katie dropped her bag in a locker, gave Julia a brief hug, and pumped Sarah's hand. "Nice to meet you. I'm ready for anything, even *Lulu*. Lead me to it."

"Five minutes to rehearsal. Orchestra to the pit, please," called the P.A. system.

Katie grinned. "Well, that sounds familiar."

"It's like we never left the Met," Julia said.

In the pit, Julia sat next to a dark-haired, friendly-looking Asian man. "I'm Matt Kim, your associate concertmaster, Julia," he said. "I'm looking forward to turning your pages."

"We'll see how you feel about that after the first rehearsal," Julia said, smiling.

Matt returned her smile, then gave her a sober look. "I heard what happened to your mentor, Abel Trudeau. I can't imagine how you must feel."

Julia took a moment, then said, "I'm okay now. They caught the guy who did it."

"Glad to hear it," Matt said.

Katie offered her hand to Matt. "I'm Katie Ma, one of Julia's Met Opera co-conspirators, here to steal your secrets and root around for skeletons."

"No skeletons here, Katie." His voice became hushed. "Though they say John Crosby's ghost is still hanging around the place."

Katie's eyes widened. "Ooh, that sounds spicy. Doesn't it, Jul?"

"But no worries. Someone always leaves on a ghost light—a light bulb on a post in the middle of the stage—to appease Crosby and the ghosts living in the theatre," Matt added.

Ghosts in hotel rooms, and now in the theatre?

They were interrupted by Sarah, who spoke from the podium. "Please welcome our new concertmaster, Julia Kogan, plucked from the ranks of the Metropolitan Opera Orchestra."

Sarah descended the podium to the approving sound of shuffling feet. Once Julia had gotten the "A" from the first oboe and tuned the orchestra, her responsibility as concertmaster, Stewart snaked his way through the pit, nodded to Sarah and Julia, and mounted the podium.

"Good morning, all." Stewart shook Julia's hand and addressed a small-statured, barrel-chested singer exploring his paces onstage. "Good morning, Sándor."

"Good morning, Maestro."

Julia looked up at the stage. "That set looks dark and foreboding, Matt," she whispered.

"As dark as the desert sky and sun are dazzling. Totally appropriate for this opera."

"Is that the costume director's brother up there?"

"Yes. Too bad the poor guy has to die onstage so violently." Matt lowered his voice. "Speaking of which, be forewarned. The guy behind you, Lenny, he's been coming here for years and resents you being chosen over him. He may try to sabotage you. Be on your toes."

Julia glanced behind her to see a skinny, long-limbed man feverishly practicing.

Let him try to ruffle me. I'm ready for it.

"Act Three, final scene, please. Let's start right off by killing Lulu." Amidst snickers from the ranks, he opened his score. "Harold, it's five seconds to downbeat. Where the hell is Emilia?"

Julia looked up to see a petite dark-haired woman flounce onstage, followed by a disheveled man wearing glasses and a second, equally unkempt man waving his arms.

"Ma...quel direttore non sa niente," the woman complained to the bespectacled man in a high-pitched, heavily Italian-accented voice. "This director, he knows nothing."

Matt leaned over and whispered to Julia. "That guy with the book is the stage manager, Harold. The other one is the director, Salman Kipinsky. And in case you didn't know, the screaming lady is none other than Emilia Tosti, Italian soprano from hell."

Harold gestured helplessly. "But I thought you loved working with Salman, Emilia."

"That was before I found out he knows nothing," Emilia retorted.

Stewart waved from the podium. "Good morning, Emilia."

"Buongiorno, Maestro," Emilia narrowed her eyes in the dim light. "This *direttore* tells me murder must take place offstage. Ridiculous."

"Let's rehearse the music and worry about that later," Stewart said. "Where is Goran?"

Goran Řezníček, a large, imposing man with wild-looking curly locks, strode to Emilia, kissed her on both cheeks and gave her a reassuring hug.

"Emilia, my darling."

"Goran, I cannot stomach working with this impostor. What am I to do with him?"

"Let him direct, my sweet."

"If I do," Emilia said, seething, "It is only under protest."

Julia watched from the pit as the mini-drama took place onstage. Even by Met standards, Emilia's capricious, Italian-accented diva behavior seemed over the top.

"Good morning, Maestro," Salman said, then addressed the three singers. "Before we begin, may I remind you of the great Russian teacher and director Stanislavski, who said—"

Emilia rolled her eyes. "Does he think we are beginners?" she said with a disdainful pout.

Salman regarded Emilia with a cold stare. "*Lulu* is 'a wild journey of love, obsession, death, bloodshed and betrayal,' written in a context of darkness." He turned to the tenor. "Sándor, resume your position on the floor. Places, everyone. Now, Emilia—that is, Lulu..."

Emilia faced Salman with a disparaging look.

"You are Garbo, Dietrich, Louise Brooks. Your formidable psychic force causes you to destroy everyone in your path. Those who fall in love with you suffer or die. You have undone Dr. Schön, but you don't know that Goran is Jack the Ripper."

Emilia remained silent. Salman turned to Goran. "The so-called 'Whitechapel Murderer' cut his victims' throats before he eviscerated them with medical precision, showing knowledge of human anatomy. Thus, the parallels between Jack and his alter ego, Dr. Schön. Jack's music is less harsh than Schön's but more menacing. The man Lulu murders is the one who murders her. And still present after his death."

Matt leaned over and whispered to Julia. "Kind of like John Crosby, right?"

Julia shuddered.

"Marin," Salman said, "You must convey the distressed attributes of the countess. When you sing '*Im Ewigkeit*' after Goran stabs you, it is your *Liebestod*, your tragic love death."

Julia, elated to see her friend appear onstage, waved in Marin's direction.

"This music is difficult enough without your being distracted, Julia," Stewart snapped.

Julia heard a soft chortle from behind her and snuck a peek at Lenny, smiling crookedly.

Maybe Matt is right. I'd better watch out for this guy.

Emilia whispered to Goran. "She sings too loud. Always tries to upstage me."

Marin frowned. "I heard that, Emilia. In case you've forgotten, I'm your lesbian lover. Try to be a little kinder, would you?"

Salman suppressed a groan. "Let's just sing, shall we?"

"Das ist nich deine schwester," Goran sang to Emilia. *"Sie ist in dich verliebt."* [That's not your sister. She clearly is in love with you.]

"You could have fooled me," Marin muttered under her breath.

"What did you say?" Fuming, Emilia turned to Salman. "You see? She is sabotaging me."

"Could we continue, please?" Salman begged. "Lulu and Jack, offstage, final dialogue."

Emilia's nostrils flared, but she allowed Goran to shepherd her off into the wings.

"Nein, nein!" [No, no!] came Emilia's bloodcurdling cry.

"Lulu, mein engel!" [Lulu, my angel!] Marin rushed offstage, then returned, slowly backing up, eyes wide in horror, as Goran stalked onstage wielding an oversized stage knife, which he plunged into her. Then he washed off the knife with wine from a bottle on a table, wiped the knife on his coat, and sang: "I am just the damned luckiest of men!"

Salman was ecstatic. "Excellent, excellent."

Julia couldn't take her eyes off the action until she caught Stewart's disapproving glare.

Meanwhile, Emilia had returned to the stage. "Hours wasted because of his terrible incompetence," she shouted. "Murder must be onstage!"

Salman finally lost his patience. "It's the way John Crosby conceived it," he growled. "Take it up with him."

"But John Crosby is dead."

"Precisely," said Salman.

"Oh!" cried Emilia. Fuming, she marched toward the wings, where she ran into Magda.

"How am I supposed to stand in these shoes for three hours? They pinch my feet!" Emilia shrieked at the costume director. "Where are shoes you were supposed to order from Italy?"

"I am sorry, Emilia. They still have not arrived. I will check with wardrobe director."

Emilia gritted her teeth. "See that you do. *Nézd meg.*"

Julia was surprised to hear the Italian soprano speak Hungarian, but when she looked up at the podium, she was mortified to see Stewart glaring at her.

"It seems you find the stage more interesting than your music," he said.

Julia heard a soft snicker behind her. Ignoring Lenny, Julia kept on playing.

Salman was furious. "Your attitude will make you even more enemies than you already have, Emilia!" he shouted. Turning on his heel, he stomped offstage in the opposite direction.

"Harold," Stewart called out, "Tell Emilia if she shows up at the dress rehearsal less than thirty minutes before downbeat, she will be replaced. Where is her understudy? Deborah!"

An attractive young woman sitting a few rows back stood up. "I am here, Maestro."

"Be ready to jump in in case Emilia does anything else stupid."

Deborah's smile radiated hope and anticipation. "Yes, Maestro."

Harold stood rooted to the stage, his expression helpless.

Chapter Seven

Là...là...nol ravvisi?...Quest'occhi l'han visto...
There...there...can't you see it? I saw him with my own eyes...
—Verdi, *Macbeth*, Act 2

"She's a tough one," Julia said to Marin at the cantina during the rehearsal break.

Marin grimaced. "Emilia? She tries to be. But mostly, she's paranoid. She thinks everyone's out to get her. Specifically other singers. Me in particular."

"She's a soprano. Why should she feel threatened by you, a mezzo?"

"The size of her ego dictates that she be in the limelight at all times. She's made it clear. There's only one 'I' in 'Diva.' Sometimes, this profession can be really nasty, you know?"

"How do you manage to sing this music, Marin?" Julia asked. "It seems impossible."

"I learned to connect with these doomed characters. Ironically, mine is the only one in the opera who loves Lulu unconditionally. Me and Emilia. As if."

After the grueling rehearsal had ended, Julia trudged to the exterior of the theatre for a whiff of fresh air and some solitude. Standing by the fence behind the B-Lift opening to the back of the stage, she gazed into the distance beyond the hillside dotted with brush and chaparral, squinting from the intensity of the New Mexico sunlight. Then she blinked. Someone was out there, darting among the bushes. Male or female, she couldn't tell, but whoever it was wore Bermuda shorts and a wide-brimmed straw hat.

The ghost of John Crosby? No, no, that's ridiculous. I must be hallucinating.

Julia closed her eyes, then opened them. The figure was gone. She shook off a shudder.

"Whoever you are," she muttered aloud, "Could you please get rid of Blatchley? Or at least get him off my back?"

Sighing, she took one last look at the empty landscape and went to find Larry. One thing she knew for certain: she would never tell him what had just happened.

* * *

Julia had seen photos of the miraculous Santa Fe sunsets emblazoning the expanse over the opera house, but the reality was even more stunning. The night sky was lit with ribbons of orange and rose. Even the dazzling crystal chandeliers rising toward the Met ceiling at the beginning of performances couldn't rival the magnificence of this unique outdoor setting.

As the heavens darkened, the third act of the opening night of *Lulu* progressed to its violent end. Julia thought the blood-red sky seemed ironically appropriate. A sudden gust and the resultant whoosh of the white baffles outside the theatre resisting the wind made her uneasy. But a flash of lightning sent tremors through her; a small streak could portend a huge storm about to hit. Rumbling in the distance grew closer and then resounded with a violent crack.

"That was the thunderclap from hell, right on cue," Matt murmured to her. "We're in for it. Good thing we have clips on our music to keep it from taking off in the wind."

Then, just as Jack the Ripper appeared onstage, a bolt of lightning slashed through the sky, along with another huge clap of thunder. The heavens opened in torrents of driving rain.

Julia gasped. "Lightning and thunder striking exactly at Jack the Ripper's entrance?"

"That's the kind of magic that happens here," Matt whispered.

Julia could do without that kind of "magic." Thunder and lightning accompanying murderers' entrances onstage. Strange apparitions in the late afternoon sun. What was next?

The downpour ceased as suddenly as it had begun. Julia braced herself for the brutal *dénouement* and Marin's declaration of love for the recalcitrant, unlovable Emilia.

"Let me speak only once, for the last time, to your heart! Have pity on mine!"

Marin fell into a delirious faint. Goran/Jack pointed to Marin/Geschwitz: "Who is that?"

Emilia/Lulu: "My sister! She is insane!"

Julia knew the rest of the dialogue by heart from studying the libretto. Jack tells Lulu he has no time, nor enough money, to stay all night. Even half of a token payment is too much. He starts to leave. Geschwitz tries to protect Lulu, her beloved. "Poor creature," says Jack.

Julia stole a furtive glance at the stage and steeled herself for the final horror.

A weary Lulu leads Jack offstage. He insists they not bring any light; the moon is bright enough. Lulu swears this is the last time she will enroll herself in this enterprise. The two move off into the darkness as Marin languishes onstage.

Julia knew the violence was mere play-acting, but she couldn't help gasping at Emilia's far-too-realistic shrieks emanating from the wings: *"Nein! Nein! Nein, nein!"* [No! No! No, no!]

Goran returns to the stage, declares, "That was a piece of work!" and plunges his stage knife into Marin. "Lulu! My angel! Let me see you once more!" Marin cries as she staggers into the wings.

Jack pours wine from a bottle onto the knife and his hands to wash off the blood and wipes the blood on his coat. He returns his knife to his inside pocket as the final, anguished chords resound to Marin's last offstage words: "I am close! Stay close! For eternity!"

But as the curtain fell, Julia heard more shrieks emitting from the wings. Shrieks that were too hair-raising to be part of the staging. Shrieks that could be heard over the roaring applause from the audience. Shrieks that weren't Emilia's.

And she knew something was terribly wrong.

Chapter Eight

L'impresa compier deve il delitto, poichè col sangue s'inagurò
The enterprise by crime must end, since with blood it was begun
—Verdi, *Macbeth*, Act 1

T he next moments seemed suspended in time. The curtain swished to a close. The audience kept applauding in anticipation of the curtain calls, but there were none. Stewart had left the pit to go onstage for his bow. After a minute or two, the applause stopped, and patrons began murmuring among themselves.

Puzzled, Julia looked to Matt, but he seemed equally bewildered. Then her cell phone buzzed softly: a text from Marin. *"Julia, help! In trouble. Come to wings."*

Alarmed, Julia turned to Matt. "I have to go. Could you give my violin to Katie so she can put it away?"

"Sure, but what's—"

"I'll tell you later. My case is on the 'Violins & Violas' shelf. The dark blue one with the purple ribbon tied to the handle."

"Not to worry, I'll make sure it's safe."

She hurriedly thrust her violin at him. "I know you will."

Clutching her phone, she raced out the door.

* * *

Behind the curtain, the screams had stopped, but the scene was chaotic.

Salman and Harold simultaneously accosted Goran. "Where is Emilia? Where is Marin? Why haven't they come onstage for their bows?"

"I don't know," Goran said, panicked. "It's not like Emilia to forgo her shining moment."

Then Marin staggered on stage, breathing heavily, her face ashen, a large knife dripping with blood gripped in her palm.

"Marin," Goran said, "What the hell—"

Salman accosted her. "Where is Emilia? Why isn't she here?"

Marin opened her mouth to speak. No words came out at first. Then, finally: "She's dead."

"Well of course she is," Salman said. "But if she thinks she can keep the audience waiting while she milks her moment, she has another thing coming. Now go tell her they will leave if she doesn't get here immediately—"

"N-no, she...she can't," Marin stammered. "She's...really...dead."

"What?" Goran rushed off. A piercing cry, "Oh, my God," came from the wings. Salman and Harold raced toward it. Marin stood motionless. Then, she slowly followed them.

* * *

Alan, who had gotten a cryptic text from Salman to cancel the curtain calls, appeared onstage in front of the closed curtain. "Ladies and gentlemen, there will be no curtain calls tonight. Please accept our apologies. Thank you."

Alan watched as the audience members, some grumbling, some murmuring in confusion, exited the theatre. He gestured toward the orchestra. "Curtain calls are canceled. But don't go anywhere."

After he surveyed the confused musicians' expressions, he rushed backstage.

* * *

In the wings, Salman and Harold stared, incredulous, at Goran kneeling over Emilia's lifeless, blood-soaked body. Marin's eyes glazed over. The knife tumbled from her hand and clattered to the floor. Salman confronted her. "My God, Marin, what have you done?"

Marin struggled to regain her composure. "What have *I* done?" She stared, trancelike, at the red stains on her hands and dress. "I haven't done anything. I just…found her, like that. Blood everywhere…." She fell to her knees.

Goran rose and faced Marin. "Where did that knife come from, Marin?"

"I don't know. I went offstage to sing my last line and found it there. Next to her…body."

She began to sob. Goran squeezed her shoulder. "Marin, calm down, for God's sake."

Stewart appeared and strode over to them, red-faced and ready for a battle. He stopped short when he saw the bloody scene before him. "What is going on here?" he said, tight-lipped.

"Clearly there's been a murder," Salman said.

"What?" Stewart peered at Marin's bloodstained clothing, saw Emilia's body, and gasped.

"Marin found her," Goran said.

"Or perhaps," Salman said grimly, "Killed her."

"Call 911," Stewart said.

Hands shaking, Harold extracted his cell phone from his pocket and dialed.

* * *

Julia rushed in to see Marin on her knees, weeping. "Marin, what happened?"

"Julia! Oh, Julia!" Marin moaned. "I didn't do it, I swear. I didn't do it."

"Do what?" Lifting her eyes from Marin's tear-stained face, Julia caught sight of the knife at Marin's feet and Emilia's bloodied form on the floor. "Oh, my God!"

Alan approached from the wings, taking in the scene before him. His face paled.

Harold hurried to Alan's side. "Thank God you're here. Things are pretty out of hand."

"I can see that," Alan said. "It's good you texted me. The police?"

Harold nodded. "On their way."

The sound of clicking heels drew everyone's attention to a striking figure striding toward them from the wings. The taps on her cowboy boots reverberated loudly on the bare floor as she approached. She wore a Santa Fe Police Department badge and a video body cam on her jacket.

"Who's in charge here?" she asked in a husky voice, her steely eyes surveying the scene.

"I am." Alan walked over to her and extended his hand. "Alan Reynolds, general manager of The Santa Fe Opera. And you are...?"

"Detective Stella Peregrine, SFPD," she said, shaking his hand.

Stella's eyes fixed on Emilia's body, the knife, Marin and Julia next to her. She slipped a latex glove onto her hand and carefully picked up the knife, placing it in a labeled plastic evidence bag and sealing it. She turned toward the wings, where she had entered.

"Grabowski, get over here."

A short, wiry, tousle-haired man in his early thirties appeared. Stella handed the evidence bag to him and turned back to Alan. "This is my partner, Constantin Grabowski."

Alan shook Constantin's hand. "Alan Reynolds, general manager of the Opera."

"When did this incident occur, Mr. Reynolds?"

"At the end of the opera. There's a murder scene. Actually, several murder scenes in this particular opera."

Stella raised her eyebrows. "Oh?"

"But this...incident happened during the *dénouement* at the end."

"I see." Stella looked around at the group surrounding her. "Who found the body?"

Salman pointed an accusing finger at Marin. "She did. Marin Crane. She was holding the knife, too. She had it in for Emilia."

"Let's not get ahead of ourselves. There'll be time enough for that when we interrogate everyone," Stella said. She leaned over Emilia's body and scanned the damage. "Multiple deep stab wounds to the abdomen. Looks like she bled out." Stella turned to her partner. "CSU?"

Constantin nodded in the direction of the stage. "They're here with CMI."

The Chief Medical Investigator and his team pushed through the gaggle of company members gathered onstage. Stella turned to M.E. Nick Pleasance. "Thanks for getting here so fast, Nick."

"Light traffic night." Nick knelt beside Emilia's body. "Stab wounds are very fresh."

"It just happened. At the end of the opera, I'm told."

Nick grimaced. "They say opera can kill you."

"Evidently," said Stella, fighting a smile. With company members standing around, many looking shocked, the grim humor she might indulge in to deal with the horror of violent crime was absolutely not appropriate here. "Samuel Johnson called opera 'an exotic and traditional entertainment.' Looks like much more than that."

"Well, what did he know?"

The two professionals exchanged sardonic smiles. In the background, CSU techs were photographing the scene and collecting DNA and prints, some of which would be sent to the forensics lab in Las Cruces. Ultimately, it was Stella's responsibility to make a case, so she watched them for a moment to make sure the team was on the ball. They were a good crew, but they didn't get a case like this very often.

"Good news is, we have the weapon." Stella nodded toward Constantin. "Make sure they send it to the lab ASAP."

Constantin handed the evidence bag to a tech. Nick continued examining Emilia's body.

"Who else is still here, Mr. Reynolds?" Stella asked Alan.

"Pretty much everyone. Stagehands, costume and wig people, and singers are all onstage. Musicians are in the pit."

"And the conductor?"

"I'm right here."

Stella acknowledged Stewart. Then she turned back to Alan. "We'll need as much space as possible to question them."

"Stieren Hall, where the orchestra rehearses, should be spacious enough.

There's also an orchestra lounge," Alan said. "I'll call the personnel manager and ask her to meet us there."

"Grabowski, gather up everyone onstage for questioning," Stella said. "Nobody leaves."

The techs continued their work. Stella narrowed her eyes at Julia, still clutching the quaking Marin, impressed at the young violinist's gentleness and look of concern as she watched Julia help Marin up off the floor.

Julia reached in her pocket, pulled out the handkerchief she always used to protect her chin from the hardwood violin chinrest, and thrust it at Marin. "Here, use this for…the blood."

Marin mechanically wiped her hands. Stella plucked the handkerchief from Marin's grasp. "Grabowski, bag this hankie. Ms. Crane, come with me. Lead the way, Mr. Reynolds."

Julia dutifully trailed behind Goran, Salman, Stewart, and Harold, who were following Alan, Stella, and Marin. She opened her phone and texted.

"Larry. Come to the orchestra lounge. Need you…It's happened again!"

Chapter Nine

E tu va, fruga ogni angolo, raccogli ogni traccia
And you, search every corner, track down every clue
—Puccini, *Tosca*, Act 1

W hen Stella took a close look around the orchestra lounge, she saw a generous-sized room with several large grey sofas, two of them placed back-to-back, and one positioned a few feet away. Grey metal lockers lined two of the walls, along with a bulletin board with posted announcements, mailboxes, and a spacious galley with numerous cabinets, a sink, and a coffee machine. One set of cabinets was placed above a countertop beneath a window that looked out over a hillside.

Stella watched the group file in. "Nice space you've got here, Mr. Reynolds."

"The orchestra people are spoiled," Harold said.

"No, they're not." Sarah came to Alan's side. "They work tirelessly, and they're here all the time. It's the least they deserve."

Julia was astonished—and gratified. Compared to the condescending attitude of the Met's general manager, it was refreshing to hear someone from management express appreciation of the orchestra musicians' contribution to the company, even in the present grim circumstances.

"Ms. Peregrine, this is our personnel manager, Sarah Gruen," Alan said.

"Pleased to meet you, Ms. Gruen." In a semi-darkened corner at the far end of the lounge beyond a row of lockers, Stella spied a table and two chairs. "Okay to use that space?"

"Whatever you need," Sarah said. "Although if you need space behind closed doors—"

Stella spied a printed sign posted on one of several rooms Sarah had pointed out, some with small windows in their doors:

"'DANGER! Harp Tuning Room,'" Stella read. "'DANGER?' What's with that?"

"Just a bit of orchestra musicians' humor."

"I see." Stella resisted another smile. Still not appropriate. But good to know musicians dealt with stress in a similar way to her own.

Another room was labeled "Orchestra Library." Yet another, "Percussion Room."

"Would you like to use one of these to interview Ms. Crane? It would be more private."

Stella nodded. "Yes, I think that would be best. The table in the corner over there will work fine for the others."

"Of course. Which room would you prefer?"

"Any one will do. Your choice."

Sarah unlocked the Orchestra Library door.

"By the way, Ms. Gruen—"

"Please, call me Sarah."

"Sarah. How do the maestro and orchestra get on?"

"He has a super relationship with them, on and off the podium. He's not only a true artist, but also likable and bighearted. He looks out for them, too."

"Please ask him to be available for questioning."

"Of course."

Stella motioned to Marin and escorted the singer into the Orchestra Library.

"I'll stay here in the lounge, Detective, in case you need me," Sarah said.

"After I show your partner the way to Stieren Hall, Detective Peregrine," Alan added, "I'll come back and wait here in the lounge in case there's anything else you need."

"Thank you both."

Alan turned to Constantin, who shepherded a large group of other company members. "Please follow me."

As the group filed out, Stella faced Goran, Salman, Harold, Stewart, and Julia. "All of you wait here until I'm ready for you."

The five found spaces on the sofas, sat down, and took out their cell phones. Julia gazed at two French doors with an "Exit" sign hanging over them and texted Larry again.

* * *

Stella and Marin sat down opposite each other at a table in the Orchestra Library. "Okay, Ms. Crane, can you tell me what happened?"

"What...happened?" Avoiding Stella's gaze, Marin stared down at the bloodstains on her now-wrinkled costume and twisted the material in her shaky fingers. "I...I can't remember."

"Surely you can."

Marin barely managed to talk in fits and starts. "I remember...at the end of the act, I was...I was trying to...to sing. Goran, the baritone. He...huddled together with E...Emilia..." Marin almost broke down. "Then...he sang, 'Wer ist das?—Who is that?' And Emilia sings, 'Meine schwester—my sister.' Referring to...me."

"Go on," Stella said.

Marin stared into the distance. "Goran murders Lulu...in the story, offstage, with a fake knife. I hear screams. Then Goran comes back onstage, stabs me with the same knife. I run offstage to see Lulu one last time. When I get there...I see...oh, God."

"What did you see?"

"Blood. Blood, everywhere. And this big knife. A real knife. Covered with...blood."

"And you picked it up. Why?"

"I don't know. I was...scared."

"Did you see anyone else lurking around at all?"

"No, no one. All I could see was...blood." Marin began to sob uncontrol-

40

lably.

"Let's take a break. Don't go anywhere. I'll be back."

Stella peered at Marin's helpless form. She suspected the singer was not about to move anywhere anytime soon.

Chapter Ten

Ora a te...pesa le tue risposte
Now, as for you...weigh your answers well
—Puccini, *Tosca*, Act 1

As Julia waited her turn to be interrogated, text messages came in rapidly on her phone.

Larry: "Julia, where are you?" [*"Orchestra lounge. Waiting for you."*]

Katie: "Julia, I'm holed up in Stieren Hall with the orchestra. What's happening? Are you okay? They won't tell us anything." [*"Not okay. Emilia's been murdered. I'm waiting to be interrogated."*]

Katie: "WHAT?? I'm coming straight over." [*NO. They won't let you. Wait till I find you later. I CAN'T BELIEVE THIS IS HAPPENING AGAIN."*]

Katie: "OMG. Need to see you ASAP." [*Nothing I can do. WAIT FOR ME."*]

Larry: "Opera house on lockdown. Will have to wait for you outside."

* * *

Stella left Marin hunched over the table, closed the door behind her, and approached the two back-to-back sofas where Stewart, Harold, Goran, and Julia waited to be questioned. She approached Alan, who had returned and was seated on the third sofa and gestured toward Goran, who was still in costume. "Is that the baritone?"

"Yes," Alan said. "Goran Řezníček."

Stella motioned at Goran to follow her to the table in the corner at the far end of the room, where she placed the chairs opposite each other. Goran politely pulled one out for Stella and sat down in the other as she pulled out her iPad Mini.

"You were Emilia's leading man?"

"Not the only one. In this opera Lulu had many men," Goran said. "I play the one who murders her. Pretends to, of course. With a fake knife."

"Could you explain how that plays out?"

Goran repeated the final scenario, much as Marin had described it.

"When you went offstage to 'murder' Emilia, did you see anyone else back there?"

"No. I did the deed. She screamed, '*Nein, nein!*'—that's 'No, no!' in German. Then I came back onstage to 'stab' Marin. After that, she staggered offstage to Lulu's aid—Marin and Emilia are lovers in the story, by the way, though honestly, *die liebe brennt.*"

Stella frowned questioningly.

"That means, basically, 'no love lost.' Between them."

"I see." Stella scribbled notes in her device. "And then?"

"The next thing I knew, Marin was screaming her head off. Then she came back onstage with a *real* knife. We were all in shock."

"Aside from their 'issues,' do you know any reason why Marin would want to harm Emilia?"

"We all respected Emilia's voice, her talent. I myself adored her. But frankly, everyone had conflicts with her. She was difficult to work with. Almost all the time. And she complained about everyone and everything. Grated on everyone's nerves. But Marin harm Emilia? I don't think so."

"Conflicts?" Stella tapped notes into her device. "What kind—and with whom?"

"She didn't like her wigs, for one, and then there were complaints about her costumes, her shoes. You might want to speak with the costume director, Magda, about that. Shall I go on?"

Stella entered a note about the costume director. "Please do."

"The first time Emilia performed here, a particularly strong gust of wind from the Sangre de Cristo Mountains blew a clump of gravel into her mouth while she was singing. You can well imagine how she reacted to that."

"What about this time, the *Lulu* rehearsals?"

At the dress rehearsal, she criticized Salman Kipinsky—the director—mercilessly," Goran said. "Basically, said he was incompetent. That he knew nothing. '*Quel direttore sa niente,*' she said, right to his face. Who else but Emilia could get away with telling the director—'*direttore*'—he knows nothing—'*niente?*'"

Stella tapped into her iPad: "*Talk to director, Kipinsky.*"

"I see," she said. "How did he respond to that?"

"Well, he didn't like it, of course. Said something about her attitude making even more enemies than she already had," said Goran.

"Sounds like she had loads of them."

"Perhaps. Emilia didn't want to share the limelight with anybody. But she pushed Marin's buttons in a huge way. And Marin made sure everyone knew it."

"Did Marin ever threaten Emilia directly?"

Goran hesitated for a long moment. "I...I might have heard her say something vaguely to that effect at some point. But I'm sure she didn't mean it."

"Do you remember what it was?" Stella asked.

"No, not specifically."

"Do you know anything about the relationship between Marin and that violinist, Julia?"

"Just that they knew each other at the Met. They seemed pretty close."

"Is that why Julia was backstage, taking Marin's side?"

"I couldn't say for sure. But I suppose it makes sense."

"I see. Don't go anywhere in case you remember any details. Thank you for your help."

"Of course, Detective."

When Stella rose, Goran gallantly leapt up, pulled out her chair, walked back to the sofa, and sat down. Stella looked over at the others who were waiting and, noticing Julia was frantically texting on her phone, sent a text to Constantin.

"I'd like to know what Julia has to do with all this. Find out who knows her."

Then Stella gestured at Salman. "You're next."

* * *

Alan had asked head stagehand Steve Cañon to guide Stella's partner Constantin to Stieren Hall to interview other company members.

"Cañon. That's an appropriate name for around here," Constantin said as Steve led him down one flight of stairs and then another.

"I'm supposedly descended from the first Spanish conquerors, diluted over the centuries into your run-of-the-mill Hispanic dude," Steve said.

"Not exactly 'run-of-the-mill' if Santa Fe's founders are your ancestors."

"No way of knowing that for sure, but thanks for the compliment."

Steve guided Constantin to a terrace leading to an enormous, contemporary-looking room with high ceilings. "That's Stieren Hall," Steve said. "Where the orchestra and singers rehearse. Anything else I can do? Would you like me to show you the properties shop and the scene shop later?"

"Sounds like a good idea, thank you."

"No worries." Steve indicated the entrance and followed Constantin inside.

The hall was an immense space: a long and vast gallery with windows that reached almost to the top of the high ceilings. A set of a dozen or so tall screens stood at one end.

After he had instructed the waiting group to seat themselves in the chairs that looked as if they had been lined up from a recent orchestra rehearsal, Constantin scanned the faces of those assembled.

"Who wants to be first?"

Steve waved his arms. "Steve Cañon, head stagehand, at your service."

Constantin indicated two chairs and pulled them to the far edge of the stand of screens, out of earshot from the others. He and Steve sat down.

"Did you see anything unusual backstage, Steve? Anyone who shouldn't be there?"

"Nope," said Steve. "It's generally mobbed back there. But not at the end of this opera."

"Why not?"

"Well, there's no chorus, and the set is what they call minimalist. Very little to move around. When it's near the end, we—I mean the stagehands—generally hang out by B-Lift— that's the elevator at the back door of the house that moves up and down—so we can be ready to move out the sets when the show finishes to make room for whatever comes next. We don't come back to the stage until we get the call."

"Then you weren't there when the incident occurred?"

"Nope," Steve said. "And we didn't think anything of the screams. We knew they were part of the show. We didn't get the call, so we came back when we heard the applause."

"Didn't you think it odd that you didn't hear the call?"

"Not really. It was opening night. There often are glitches, kinks that are ironed out later."

"What happened then?"

"We came onstage to strike the set. Then we saw Marin in the wings and all that blood. She kept screaming. That's when we knew something was amiss."

"And all hell broke loose?"

"Well, strangely, no. Everyone stood there onstage, gawking. We were all kind of in shock. Then these management types came rushing in—director, stage manager, conductor. And that violinist, Julia. Seems she and Marin are friends, and Marin sent her an urgent text."

"Marin actually had her phone?"

"Even singers can't live without them. They always manage to find a pocket somewhere in their costume. Ringer off, of course."

"Do you know Julia?"

"Not really. Though personally, from what I've of seen her, I wouldn't mind knowing her," said Steve. "That is, if her boyfriend wasn't watching her like Papa Bear."

"Her boyfriend?"

"Yeah. He's a NYPD cop."

"Off duty, I presume."

"Yeah, along for the ride while she plays in the orchestra. Nice work if you can get it."

"Generally, would you say the stagehands work as hard or harder than the rest of the company/"

"It's the singers who work the hardest. They're the ones who work the magic. I once left my post to go listen to a soprano. I even sang along. There's no greater joy than hearing a big 'ol stagehand clumsily singing along with Mozart. Two octaves down, of course. She sang like an angel. More like a 'magic flute' than a mere mortal. That's what it's like around here."

"I see. Thanks for your time. Stick around."

"Sure. No biggie."

Steve walked back to the group waiting in the chairs and sat down. Constantin tapped some notes into his smartphone, mumbling.

"NYPD cop. Humph."

Chapter Eleven

Ohne Zweifel, wird er wieder tausend Fragen an mich stellen
Without doubt, he will have a thousand more questions to ask me
—Beethoven, *Fidelio*, Act 2

Salman sat opposite Stella, nervously fidgeting with his ascot.

"You're the director, Salman Kipinsky?"

"Yes. That is correct."

"Is it true Emilia and Marin were at odds with each other?" Stella said.

"Yes, yes," Salman said. "Extremely."

"Care to explain?"

Salman avoided Stella's gaze. "Marin was always accusing Emilia of acting like she was the only diva in the company and made it clear how much she resented being eclipsed by Emilia's importance—or should I say, sense of entitlement."

"You mean Marin wanted the spotlight? Maybe even take it away from Emilia?"

Salman kept his eyes down. "Exactly."

"Is it true you threatened Emilia during the dress rehearsal?"

Salman raised his eyes. "I'm sorry, I didn't hear the question. Could you repeat that?"

"I asked if you threatened Emilia."

Salman's distraction turned to panic. "What? You're seriously asking me that? Who told you I threatened her?"

"Answer the question," Stella said.

"Her attitude made me mad. Do you know Stanislavski?"

"The Great Russian director? Yes, I've heard of him."

"I tried to emphasize to the singers what he said about the importance of theatrics for singers. Every word they sing must reach the audience. Their bodies must be liberated from all tension not integral to the drama. They are communicating music to the audience straight from the heart and should be interpreted as such," Salman said. "Emilia, she…she disparaged me, humiliated me, in front of all of them. And…" He lowered his voice to a near whisper. "I…might have said something about her making more enemies than she already had. But I did *not* threaten her. In rehearsal, the conductor, Blatchley…"

Stella wrote the name in her Mini.

"…He threatened to replace her. He…he told Harold to tell her as much."

"Why would he do that?"

"She was habitually late. He'd had enough."

"I see." Stella rose. "We're done for now. But don't go far."

After Salman had walked off, Stella watched Julia for a moment. The young violinist looked nervous and exhausted. Whether or not that indicated possible involvement or even guilt associated with the murder, Stella wasn't sure. It was beginning to look like Julia had reason to stand up for Marin—perhaps even conspire with her. She tapped a note into her device: *"Ask Constantin about Julia. Interview her next."*

Stella approached Alan, who was seated on the sofa closest to the Orchestra Library, and sat down next to him.

"Mr. Reynolds, if you don't mind…"

Alan looked up from his iPad, on which he was perusing a digital version of the soon-to-be-defunct *Opera News*.

Aware of others close by, Stella spoke softly. "Is it true Emilia gave everyone grief?"

"There's no denying she was a diva in every sense of the word and not hugely popular. She was…how can I put it? Difficult. Rubbed people the wrong way."

"From what I've heard about her character in this opera, *Lulu*, it seems like

Emilia was typecasting. In fact, the opera itself sounds downright perverted."

"You think *Lulu* is bad? They once did an opera here by Penderecki—"

"Who?"

"Krzysztof Penderecki. Very *avant-garde* mid-twentieth, early twenty-first century Polish composer. He wrote this opera based on a Huxley novel, *The Devils of Loudun*. It was so sadistic, so sensationalistic, depraved, and obscene that it made *Lulu* seem like the story of a saint."

"Thanks for putting things in perspective." Stella shuddered at the thought. "Clearly Emilia was no saint, Mr. Reynolds," she said. "But how did *you* feel about her?"

"Detective Peregrine," Alan said, snapping shut the cover of his digital device, "Let me tell you something about being general director of an opera company. Since opera first began, people in my position have been dealing with artists who have a huge sense of self with a capital 'S.' It goes with the territory. I'm used to coddling people like Emilia. Stroking their egos, dealing with their self-esteem and self-image issues. It's my job to make sure they perform optimally because, ultimately, it's my responsibility to make sure we fill seats. We have an expression in German, *"Die liebe brennt,"* which in opera language means, 'No love lost,' with a wink and a nod. I neither liked nor disliked Emilia. I simply put up with whatever behavior she felt compelled to inflict upon me for the greater good of the company. Does that answer your question?"

"Totally."

"Excellent. If you need anything else, please don't hesitate."

"Thank you."

Alan went back to his reading. Stella motioned Stewart to follow her to the corner table. They sat down. She regarded the flawlessly turned-out man, his tailored suit and diamond-studded Rolex.

"Is it proper to address you as Maestro?"

"Yes," Stewart answered. "That's fine."

"Then, Maestro, tell me. Did you have a difficult time working with Emilia?"

"Everyone did. I was no different, except that my main concern was how she performed. Nothing else."

"And yet you threatened to replace her."

"It wasn't exactly a threat. I was stating a fact. Emilia is habitually late," Stewart said. "*Lulu* is one of the most important operatic works of the twentieth century. Presenting it skillfully is one of the best ways a company can demonstrate its musical and theatrical capabilities. Singers are secondary in light of the enormity of such a work. Thanks to our founder John Crosby's foresight, our company had the honor of premiering the complete opera after the composer's widow had died and the Act Three music finally was released. That was huge."

"I've heard Crosby was an amazing force."

"Yes, he was." Stewart paused. "Diva tantrums are one thing, Detective, but when it comes to chronic lateness, I make it clear that it will not be tolerated. That kind of behavior undermines the other singers, the conductor, the director, and everyone else involved in trying to create art on the stage. The orchestra included."

"Tell me more about the orchestra."

"Our orchestra is our greatest asset. Some of the most accomplished players, both nationally and internationally, have been coming here for decades to play great opera and work with distinguished conductors. It's my responsibility to protect their creativity, to give them the best possible experience," Stewart said. "Our company is unique. The theater's intimate sound allows the orchestra to hear the vocalists well, thus leading to better overall balances between stage and pit. If a singer is singing about the moon, you look out into the mountain night sky and see the moon shining down on the theater. And we don't stint on orchestra rehearsals. It all comes together brilliantly. When we reconvene at the beginning of the season, it's as if we had just finished the previous season's closing night."

"Isn't it kind of unusual to start right off rehearsing with the singers onstage rather than in the rehearsal hall?" Stella asked.

"Generally, yes," Stewart said. "But given the extreme complexity of *Lulu*, I wanted to give the singers as much opportunity as possible to rehearse onstage with the musicians. There's so much more work involved than in traditional operas, getting all the notes at the right length and pitch when it's all so dissonant."

"I've heard that the opera has had great significance for your company."

"It has. First came our 1963 American premiere production of acts one and two. Then, when Berg's widow finally died in 1977, and every opera house in the U.S. literally stampeded like elephants for the chance to premiere the complete opera with the third act included, people presumed the honor would go to the Met," Stewart said. "It was John Crosby's determination and savvy that convinced the publishers to give that premiere to Santa Fe Opera. Of course," he continued, "After the initial premiere in Zurich in 1932, there had been the Austrian premiere in 1962, and the European premiere in Paris in 1979..."

Stella paused. That kind of information was above her pay grade. "Going back to the orchestra. Can you tell me more about your relationship with them?"

"Just as important as sculpting the character and timbre of the music we create without having to spell things out with too much verbiage," Stewart said, "It is my responsibility to get to know the players well enough to aid the visiting conductors in relating well to the players and vice versa. But they are thoroughly professional, and keeping the peace is generally not a challenge. It all comes together brilliantly."

"Yes. I'm sure it does. What can you tell me about the violinist, Julia?"

Stewart raised his eyebrows. "She is talented but young and relatively inexperienced. I'm hoping she'll be up to the task of being concertmaster, the first, most important violinist. I am trying to mold her, to guide her into reaching her best potential. I fear her extreme sensitivity might prove to be an obstacle. But we shall see."

"So, you're protecting her creativity?"

"Yes. Hopefully, I will succeed."

"How far would you go to protect everyone else's interest?"

"All the way to the general director, if necessary."

"I see."

At that moment, Alan looked up and exchanged glances with Stewart.

Stella furiously tapped notes into her device.

Chapter Twelve

Fia lunga, tal notte
It's going to be a long night.
—Verdi, *Rigoletto, Act 3*

In the Orchestra Library, Marin was seated on the edge of her chair. She had removed her wig and was slowly and compulsively pulling the hairs out of it. When Stella opened the door, Marin jumped.

"Did I startle you, Ms. Crane?"

"I...I didn't see you coming."

Stella set a steaming cup of coffee before the trembling singer. "Here," she said. "This will help." She delicately took the wig from Marin and set it aside as she resumed her own chair.

Marin stared at the cup, not drinking.

"So," Stella said. "I'm hearing Emilia was pretty hard to get along with. And people are saying you were jealous of her. Is that true?"

Marin's breathing started to come in shallow gasps. "No...I mean...yes, I had a hard time getting along with her. Everyone did. She was so full of herself."

"But what about you, specifically? Did you feel like you wanted to share her limelight? Or maybe even take it away from her?"

"What? No, no, I would never—"

Stella sat back in her chair. "It's an emotional opera. In the heat of the drama, you lost it. Or maybe even planned it, kept a knife backstage because you couldn't bear it any longer."

"I couldn't do anything so vile, not for anything!" Marin cried. "Yes, I resented her stardom. And the despicable way she treated me. But I could never kill anyone! Ask anybody. Ask Julia!"

"I'll do that, Ms. Crane. Meanwhile, sit tight."

* * *

Constantin had interviewed another stagehand and was busy questioning Magda.

"What is your job at the Opera?"

"I am costume director. I make sure all stage people have attire in shape to look best."

"How well do you get to know the singers?"

"We are, as you say, up close and personal with them. We know each one. We have to. I have conversations with them before they come here. About their special needs."

"What kind of needs?"

"In meetings, singers confide, how you say, self-esteem difficulties, sometimes with voice, sometimes with appearance. If they do not feel confident about voice or new role, it spills out in closed room with very quiet, intimate atmosphere where they have to talk about their character and their body. We are close to them in terms of self-image."

"Anyone else work directly with you on that?"

"Daniel Henderson. Wig and makeup person."

Constantin tapped a note into his phone. "What was your relationship with Emilia?"

"Strictly professional," Magda said.

"No conflicts?"

"We all had difficulties with her. She was diva in every sense. Fussed over everything, demanded everything, expected to get what she wanted. She complained if something not fitting right. She complained if special ordered shoes have not arrived from Italy. But it is my job to make singer comfortable onstage, whatever character they play, even if director wants

55

them ugly. Everyone understands that is how it goes in opera."

"If that's how it goes, then why would someone kill her?"

"Who can say? In excessively stressed environment, emotions run high one moment, low next moment. Tempers flare. Rivalries common. Affairs, too. Some people do not control emotions."

"I gather you're not one of them?"

Magda looked Constantin in the eye. "I learn to keep my passions in check. Otherwise, I get into trouble." Her face darkened. "I survive Communist-era Hungary. I escape to America with my little brother, Sándor. He is tenor." She pointed toward Sándor among the group still awaiting interrogation. "Every day we are grateful to have job in opera."

Constantin added a note to his phone: *Sándor.* "Where were you when Emilia was killed?"

"With wardrobe supervisor and wig person in dressing room area. At end of show we wait for singer to return to dressing room so we can remove costume and wig, send for clean."

"Did you see or hear anything unusual? Anyone lurking around who didn't belong there?"

"I see only stagehands and singers," Magda said. "I hear screams, but that is part of final opera scene. It did not seem anything wrong."

"Thank you," Constantin said. "Please tell Sándor to come over here."

Magda rose, walked over to Sándor and whispered to him. He exchanged grim glances with her as he moved toward Constantin.

The detective tapped a note into his device: *"Ask Reynolds for tour of costume shop."*

* * *

In the lounge, Stella gestured to Julia, whose eyes were fixed on her phone screen. Stella cleared her throat to get Julia's attention. "Come with me, Julia."

"What?" Julia tapped a quick text into her phone. *"Larry. I'm dying out here."* She looked up at Stella. "Sorry, I was—"

"You Millennials, always glued to your screens. Think you can tear yourself away?"

Clutching her phone tightly, Julia rose and followed Stella to the table at the far end of the lounge. Stella regarded the pretty, petite young woman as they sat across from each other. She was possibly the youngest person in the company. And she was pale, shaken.

"What is your connection to Marin Crane?"

"We're friends," Julia said. "We worked together at the Met."

"Could you elucidate?"

"I first encountered Marin at the Met café during a Met rehearsal of Offenbach's *The Tales of Hoffmann*. We sat down over coffee, and a friendship began," Julia said. "I was so impressed at the way Marin sang the role of Hoffmann's sidekick, Nicklausse, that I complimented her, which was not easy because innately, I'm very shy."

"How well do you know each other?"

"Well enough to spend time hanging out whenever we're working together."

"Why were you onstage after the last scene of *Lulu*?"

"Marin sent me a text asking me to come."

"Why would she text you when she was in such a tense situation?"

"She needed help," Julia said. "She's here all alone, with no one else to turn to."

"And you didn't come here to Santa Fe alone?"

"My partner, Larry, is here with me."

"The NYPD cop?"

"How did you know?"

"I'm a detective. I investigate, get information. It's what I do. You should know that—if your partner's a cop."

Julia blushed. "Y-yes. Of course."

"What did you see when you got to the stage?"

"Blood. Everywhere."

"What kind of condition was Marin in?"

"She was hysterical," said Julia. "Understandably."

"What did she tell you?"

"She kept saying she didn't do it. Over and over."

Stella murmured under her breath. "Methinks the lady doth protest too much."

Julia, surprised to hear Shakespeare's *Hamlet* quoted by a detective, knew the passage was a way of saying someone who denies something too strongly is hiding the truth. "Excuse me?"

"Oh, sorry, I performed with A.R.T. when I was at Harvard Law. Shakespeare understood people so well. Sometimes he helps me think," Stella said. "Getting back to Marin. Did she ever confide in you about her feelings toward Emilia?"

"Well, actually, she…" Julia stopped mid-sentence. She had heard Marin spout her frustration about Emilia and was afraid Stella might misinterpret Marin's resentments. She fell silent.

"Answer the question, please. What did Marin say?"

"She…she did say once that Emilia felt threatened by her. But from what I had heard, everything threatened or troubled Emilia. Everything and everyone. She was paranoid."

"How did you know? Is that what Marin told you?"

"It was pretty much common knowledge."

"I see. Stick around, Julia. I may need to ask you more questions later."

"Larry is outside. Is there any chance he could be let back in?"

"We'll see about that. For now, please go back and sit down."

Aggravated at the thought of further grilling, Julia went back to the sofa and sank down wearily. She had been resisting the memories of the night at the Met when her mentor, Abel, was murdered before her eyes. But she couldn't hold back the emotional turmoil anymore. She shut her eyes tightly to avoid the images, but the shocking scenario from that horrifying night invaded her senses.

Abel, on the podium, conducting the assassination scene from Verdi's Don Carlo… a bullet striking him…Abel, collapsing from the podium onto the floor…Julia, jumping up from her orchestra chair, rushing to him, holding him in her arms as the life drained from his body, his blood staining her fingers…

The feelings were all too familiar. They were not good. Not welcome. Not at all.

* * *

Stella walked through the orchestra lounge, bypassing the sofas where Julia and Stewart waited, and strode through the French doors over to Stieren Hall. She stood inside the entrance, watched Constantin, who was involved with interviews, for a moment. When he was between interrogations, she waved him over.

Constantin rose and approached Stella. "What's up?"

"Have you heard anything from Forensics?"

"Not yet."

"Let me know right away if you do. Anything interesting from the head stagehand guy?"

"He told me that the violinist Julia's boyfriend, an NYPD cop, came to Santa Fe with her."

"I hope he doesn't try to butt in."

"Doubtful. Those New York guys know their jurisdiction boundaries."

After Stella had walked off toward the lounge, Constantin found Sándor standing by the chairs. Constantin motioned for him to sit. "You're Magda's brother?"

"Yes. We are very close. She has been with company for many years. She always looks out for her little brother."

"I'll bet she knows stories no one else does," said Constantin.

Sándor nodded. "Our grandmother was costume director here in 1963 for first production of *Lulu*. Superbly decadent, as immense tale of psychosexual obsession and death should be. High price of immorality," he said. "Berg's widow refused to release last act. After she died, Crosby was responsible for our company having privilege to premiere complete opera in U.S."

"I've heard the production was legendary," Constantin said. "I would have loved to see it."

"You know much about opera of *Lulu*?"

"Not really. I'm more of a theater and movie buff. I'm familiar with the original Wedekind plays the opera was based on and the film *Pandora's Box* with Louise Brooks. Her performance embodied the film's harsh German Expressionism, with its misogyny, fear of female sexuality, and murky film techniques. The female characters are especially layered, but I am especially intrigued by Lulu. She seems absolutely unique."

"I agree. Lulu represents all frightening aspects of human condition and complexity of female sexuality in oppressive society," Sándor said. "She entices men and women, then destroys them, and eventually herself. Brutally murdered by Jack the Ripper."

"How ironic. Seems like Emilia was playing the role a bit too close to her character. Whoever murdered her managed to replicate Lulu's demise. Judging from her wounds, the killer showed a knowledge of human anatomy similar to that of Jack the Ripper with his true-life victims."

Sándor looked stricken. Constantin steered the interview in a less ominous direction. "Whatever happened to that original production?"

"Sadly, it was among productions destroyed in 1967 fire. But now I embody Berg's spirit onstage in new production. It is great privilege," Sándor said. "Some say Berg's widow refused to release last act because she hated main character, Lulu. Others say she believed my character, Alwa, was her husband's spirit *in persona*, and his dying onstage would cause death of Berg's spirit." His expression suddenly became wistful, far away. *"Durch dieses Kleid empfinde ich Deinen Wuchs wie Musik'*—Through this dress I feel your body like music.' That's what my character says to Lulu."

Constantin sensed Sándor's obvious sexual insinuation referred to someone other than Emilia. "Has Magda told you stories of John Crosby?"

"Many. He loved this company. He would rise at crack of dawn to water birch trees. He was committed to maintaining infrastructure and landscaping. He did everything to make sure his operation was as green as possible, even back then, before it was, how you say, 'in vogue,'" Sándor said. "And he had something to say about everything. In one rehearsal, he noticed silk rose on one woman's chorus costume slightly lower on shoulder than others. He insisted Magda sew it higher up to match."

Constantin was impressed.

"But he also was embodiment of contradiction. His office desk was immaculate, everything in its place—including ashtray spilling over with cigarette butts," Sandor said. "Once, he found wad of chewed gum in swimming pool and threw fit. Did not rest until he found culprit. Then it was—" Sándor made a slashing motion across his throat.

Constantin's eyes widened. "Is it true Crosby's ghost haunts the theater?"

"Yes, it is said. Wearing same Bermuda shorts and straw hat he always wore. Some musicians visit his grave every summer, drink toast, and talk to him about old days."

"I heard he was absolutely devastated over the fire in 1967."

"Yes. He did not want to talk of it. But everyone rallied together to rebuild. Do not forget, without John Crosby, opera would not exist in New Mexico."

"And thank goodness for him." Constantin paused for a respectful moment. Then he asked, "Where were you when Emilia was stabbed?"

"Waiting in dressing room for my curtain call. "I am…my character is… killed earlier in opera. One of many deaths in *Lulu*."

"Did anyone see you back there?"

"Magda. And Daniel, wig person."

Constantin tapped in a note: *Speak to wig guy next.*

"How did you get along with Emilia?"

"I have no problem getting along with her."

"From what I've heard, you may be the only one."

"I get along with everyone. Especially women. I love beautiful women."

"Do you know of anyone who found her especially difficult to work with?"

"Everybody complain about her. Except me. I am just happy to have job singing. With her, or anyone else."

"You seem to be unique in that respect, Sándor," said Constantin. "You're done for now, but stay close by. Could you point out the wig person, Daniel?"

"Wig *director*?"

Constantin nodded. "Wig *director*." Then he texted Stella: *"It's going to be a long night…"*

Sándor waved at Magda, who was sitting with Daniel among the other members, then pointed toward Daniel. The wig director looked back questioningly, his face darkening.

"And...could you ask Reynolds for a tour of the costume shop? I have a feeling there's something of interest there. Something that hasn't occurred to us—until now."

Chapter Thirteen

Sai quale oscura opra laggiù si compia?
Are you aware of what dark work is done down there?
—Puccini, *Tosca*, Act 2

"Sunset and moonrise. Blue skies and towering thunderheads. Light-drenched days and star-filled nights. The smell of *piñon* and the feel of a noontime breeze on the skin. *Al fresco* dining under azure skies with fabulous performances as the sunset yields to stars. A humidity-free seven-thousand-foot altitude. Those New Mexico glories bind together everyone who is part of The Santa Fe Opera."

Alan was escorting Stella to the costume shop, filling her in on details about the company on the way. Stella tried to show interest, but her mind was focused on finding some insights into how company members' minds worked, and she wanted to follow up on Constantin's text.

"Incidentally," Alan said, "We're proud of our state-of-the-art theatre and its unparalleled acoustics. The company still sustains our balanced budget, as we have for decades. I always feel there is much more to be done in the future, of course."

"Of course."

Alan stopped by the crafts and millinery room. "Take a look inside."

Stella stuck her head inside a small but neatly organized space that contained shelves loaded with boxes and two dressmakers' dummies—one female and one male—standing side by side as if awaiting their next engagement. Next to it stood a spacious, mirrored dressing room crammed with costumes and wigs, hats and shoes, neatly organized on shelves labeled with opera titles. They peeked into it briefly.

"That's the chorus dressing room. The choruses here are not huge, maybe about forty people."

"I never imagined you used so many shoes and boots."

"Our costume and wardrobe people have their hands full. They set out shoes and boots at each person's space. It's busy back here."

Then they wound their way downstairs. "The backstage spaces recently underwent a thirty-five-million-dollar overhaul, increasing them by more than ten thousand square feet," Alan told Stella. "Some areas hadn't been modernized since the year after the fire."

When they entered the costume shop, Alan said, "Previously, this was a dark, cramped space with a few tiny windows and no air-conditioning. Imagine that, in Santa Fe. Now it's been expanded by five thousand square feet."

Stella looked around at dozens of costume worker-bee teams, cutting, stitching, and draping. "That must put these people in a better mood to work."

Alan laughed. "I would hope so. We have twice as many fitting rooms now, plus an entire room just for threads, zippers, and other sewing necessities, which they all have access to. We call it 'the vault.'"

Stella eyed the heavy hand irons at each table. Each one had a long, thick cord attached to it at one end and to the ceiling at the other. "What is the story with those irons? They look lethal."

"We need to make sure they don't fall off the tables," Alan said. "As you can see, they're quite weighty."

But Stella's curiosity was more piqued by a door at the far end of the enormous space with a lit sign above it marked, "Emergency exit only. Alarmed."

"Where does that door lead?" she asked.

"Outside to Stieren Hall, the orchestra rehearsal room." Alan pointed out a window. "The costume workers don't like people to access the exit. Foot traffic coming through here disrupts their work. We've only marked it

'Alarmed' to discourage people from using it. It is an exit technically because it has a bar that pushes out. But when this room is full of as many as seventy people, it's better if 'outsiders' don't use it as a through passage."

"Where else does it lead, aside from Stieren Hall?"

"From the exterior, you can walk all the way around to the backstage and eventually to the cantina. You can also access a staircase that goes all the way up to the roof. It's another way to get there other than through the theatre."

"Could you show me how?"

Stella followed Alan to the exit, which was not alarmed, as Alan had explained, and out the door to the exterior. They passed by B-Lift, which Stella thought looked treacherous but didn't ask any questions, up the staircase to the right of it. An immense door at the top was wide open, showing a gargantuan space with forty-foot ceilings, where a foreman was supervising a half dozen workers in loading a piece of scenery held up by Ionic-style columns. On either side of the stage, rows of sawhorses held enormous doors, open storage units stuffed with plastic-wrapped mattresses, and other stage trappings.

"This is only a small cross-section," Alan said. "These people work long, grueling hours. But they are keenly cognizant of how important their contribution is to the greater good."

"Whatever they're doing, they look happy. I hope they're also safe."

"Safety is our top priority."

If safety was a top priority, Stella speculated, it clearly didn't apply to avoiding murders onstage.

* * *

Daniel was portly, cheerful, and voluble. "What would you like to know?" he asked Constantin in a booming, stage-like voice.

"You're the wig director?"

"And makeup director."

"And you work with Magda?"

"The costume director? Of course. Magda and I combine the best of each of our own methods. Have you met her?"

"Yes. She mentioned that the two of you worked together with the singers. Up close and personal."

"I hope it was all good."

"Neither good nor bad," Constantin said. "Where were you when the murder took place?"

"Do you mean the one onstage in the opera or the actual one?" Daniel looked at Constantin's disapproving frown and reconsidered his response. "I was in the dressing room area with Magda, waiting for the singers to come back to remove their wigs."

"Is that a hard job?"

"It's labor intensive, but not as much as actually building the wigs. That's downright dangerous."

"How so?"

"We use some tools that could be considered…well, hazardous. But most of the departments have at least a few of those."

"Could you describe some of these implements?"

"Well, we build the wigs out of human hair by hand, and we use very sharp objects. Needles to tie the hair in, one by one, with thousands of knots. Or tiny little hooks you could do punctures with and hardly even notice. Like the things they used in ancient Egypt to get the brains out of mummies," Daniel said. "If you drop one of those instruments and it goes into your leg or arm, you can really feel it when you have to rip it out. It definitely will tear your flesh."

Constantin winced.

"If that happens, you have to be careful about pushing against it when pulling it out in order not to rip your leg or arm open," Daniel added.

"Is that how you get those cuts on your hands? From working with those instruments?"

"Cuts?" Daniel looked down at his hands. "I suppose so. It's unavoidable."

"Sounds like you have a risky job."

"It is, sometimes." Daniel paused. "We work with loads of toxic chemicals, too. Ninety-nine percent alcohol. Bleaches and colors for dyeing hair. We have to wear gloves with the acetone we use to clean the laces on the wigs. The substance seeps into your body."

"Don't you use masks when you work with that stuff?"

"We should, but we don't always, considering all the fume-y things in the ventilation room." Daniel pointed to some strange-looking wooden boxes. "Those wig dryers actually go to fairly high heat. You could chop off someone's hand and dehydrate it in there."

Constantin swallowed hard. "What?"

"Theoretically. Not that it ever happens. This company is remarkably safe, more than most. We have yearly two-day safety seminars that everyone is required to attend, run by an industrial safety consultant. People in the audience don't know about these things, of course."

"For sure."

"With our schedule—we open two shows, one right after another, tech rehearsals every other night—people get tired, make mistakes. So, we have to be careful and pay attention. We really should get hazard pay."

"How did you get along with Emilia?" Constantin asked.

"Oh, she was a joy to work with. Not."

"Can you elaborate?"

"She gave new meaning to the phrase, 'temper tantrum.' She had one in the room here with me once during a run of *Salome*."

"What about?"

"She was habitually late. The director, someone much more high-powered than Salman, scolded her every time. At the final dress, Emilia came in five minutes before curtain and got onstage just as the curtain opened. The director told her, 'If you show up like this on opening night, you will be replaced.' When I got in there, the stage manager was getting impatient. He said, will you be done in time?' I said, 'I'm trying.'"

"That must have been annoying for you."

"Admittedly, yes. Meanwhile, Emilia couldn't yell at the director, so instead, she had a fit, throwing stuff around, yelling, 'It's not my fault!'—at me. I picked up my stuff, lobbed the head of John the Baptist onto a couch, said, 'O-kay,' and walked out. One of the other singers grabbed me on the way out and said to me, 'I guess I should behave.' I said, 'Yes, you should.' The stage manager made sure the head was unharmed." He chuckled.

"Did you ever lose your cool?"

"No. I got used to it eventually. I still would never put up with that kind of behavior. But it's very rare. Most of the singers are perfectly lovely. Onstage, certain divas still act out their own self-importance, like Emilia does—did. But that so-called ruling of the opera world by divas is mostly a thing of the past. They don't get away with it like they used to. Maybe in Europe, but not here in the U.S. It's the conductor and director who rule the roost. With all the fierce competition out there and the conservatories churning out more and better singers, companies these days prefer to hire someone who seems to be a good colleague as well as able to handle new compositions that require a certain physicality. I do encounter a few nasty types, but I have my ways of getting back at them—if need be."

"Oh? How?"

"Like when we do molds of the singer's head, kind of like a cast, for something like John the Baptist. That can be pretty unpleasant. The properties director has his own way, but I prefer to do it my way, where the entire head is wrapped with sheets covered in plaster of Paris. We wet them, dip, and lay them. When the plaster sets, we take the sheets off and pour plaster inside to create the mold."

Constantin tapped a note into his device: "*Speak to properties director about 'unpleasantries.'*"

"The singer has to sit there for a long time, extremely still, with only straws in their nose to breathe. If they give me grief, I could plug up the straws. Not that I've ever done that, of course."

"Of course," Constantin said dryly.

"Alternatively, when we bring someone in for a fitting to mold a head, we also put a plastic bag over their head. We cut the front out and tape it down. If they don't act nice, I don't cut it out."

"Seriously?"

"Of course not."

"You can't be claustrophobic," Daniel continued. "So, the singer had better be nice. Sopranos especially. Otherwise…"

"Sounds like you're in a good position to get your revenge if you wanted."

"Like I said, I have my ways. But none of them has involved murder."

"Let's hope not."

"I have no reason to lie. Trust me."

* * *

After the mini-tour with Alan, one of the CSU auxiliary officers approached Stella and handed her a report sheet. "Forensics came back. I thought you'd want to see it right away."

Stella looked over the report, frowning.

"You're sure about this?"

"They checked and rechecked at the lab," the officer said. "They're absolutely sure."

"I see. Thanks."

Stella perused the report once more. The words on the page told all there was to know about the murder weapon. The knife revealed only one set of fingerprints.

Marin's.

Chapter Fourteen

Mal qual mai s'offre, oh Dei, spettacolo funesto agli occhi miei!
But, oh God, what dreadful sight confronts my eyes!
—Mozart, *Don Giovanni*, Act 1

I n an opera house, news customarily travels as fast as a California wildfire. Santa Fe's rumor grapevine was no exception. By the time Larry managed to persuade the security guard that Julia needed his support, Julia had already heard that Marin was accused of Emilia's murder and been arrested. Larry appeared in the orchestra lounge to find Julia crumpled up on a sofa, her diminutive body quivering.

"No, no, no. This can't be," she moaned, shaking her head.

Larry sank down beside Julia, his arms around her. "You poor thing. What an ordeal."

She turned her tear-streaked face toward him, her expression grim. "Those bastards have arrested Marin."

"What? Why on earth?"

"That SFPD detective—"

"So, you're the NYPD cop?" Larry looked up. The woman standing before them was in her forties, tall, broad-shouldered, with close-clipped, raven-black hair. Her neat outfit suggested plain clothes, even with the cowboy boots. The badge on her right shoulder read, "Peregrine."

"Yes. Larry Somers," he replied. "My reputation precedes me, evidently."

"'Reputation is an idle and most false imposition. Oft got without merit and lost without deserving.' But then, we are bastards after all," Stella said, eyeing Julia.

Julia looked down but didn't apologize for her earlier remark.

"Am I dreaming, or were you quoting from *Othello*?" Larry asked. He assumed that this Detective Peregrine would be aware, as he was, that people often lashed out in stressful situations. Cops dealt with it all the time.

"What can I say? Shakespeare is universal. But never mind," Stella said. "We normally don't get visits from your kind. I hope you're not thinking of—"

"Investigating? 'Our kind' tend to know better." Maybe she wasn't dealing so well with it, Larry thought. Well, he'd continue to be civil to try and dissipate any tension between them.

"Good." Stella regarded Julia's trembling form. "You probably should take her home. It's been a long night. For all of us."

"I can only imagine how much longer it will be for you."

"I'm sure you can."

Larry helped Julia up from the sofa. "Are you okay to go?"

"Yes…No…I don't know."

"Here. Lean on me," Larry turned to Stella. "She's been through a lot. Adjusting to the responsibilities of being a concertmaster, and now this. She and Marin were close."

"So I've heard," said Stella.

Larry guided Julia toward the exit. "So much blood," Julia said. "So much blood."

"*Who knew the old man had so much blood in him?*" Stella murmured.

"Did you say something, Detective?" Larry asked as he and Julia passed by Stella.

"Talking to myself," Stella said.

Julia shook her head. "I can't believe this is happening again, Larry."

"Let's talk about it later. Right now, you need some rest."

Stella watched as Larry gently led Julia away. Her keen sense of hearing caught Julia's comment. She made a mental note to find out whatever "happening again" referred to.

* * *

Once back at the inn, Julia became increasingly unraveled as the full import of what had occurred that evening began to collide with her shattered emotions.

"Larry, what am I going to do?"

"There's nothing you can do. Except maybe ask for a day off to get over the stress of what you've gone through."

The thought of further jeopardizing what felt like her precarious position in the eyes of the imperious music director heightened the degree of panic that already had begun to consume her.

"I can't do that. I've barely started my job."

"We'll see about that. I'm going to speak with Alan and get you a day off."

Julia shook her head vehemently. "No, no, I can't. And I…I have to help Marin—"

"You have to help yourself first."

Julia felt backed against a wall. She knew Larry was right, but with her relationship with Stewart tenuous at best and very little opportunity to prove her worth so far, she couldn't conceive of absenting herself from the orchestra. And she was frantic with worry about Marin.

A frenzied knock at the door distracted her from these dark, circular thoughts. Larry opened to admit Katie, who rushed to Julia and threw her arms around her.

"Julia! I heard about Marin. Are you in one piece?"

"What do you think? So many pieces, I'm barely holding them together," Julia said. "Another murder, another friend accused. I must be cursed. I can't let this happen to Marin."

"Right now, you have to recover. You've been traumatized. And Blatchley's not exactly making your life easy, either." Katie lowered her voice. "Abel never begrudged the orchestra players a quick look at the stage."

Katie's remark hit Julia like a bolt of New Mexico lightning. Thoughts of her fallen mentor overwhelmed her with grief. She blinked away a tear. "Abel was extraordinary."

And I could really use his help right now.

"Yes, Jul. He was."

Larry's brow creased in tight lines. "I couldn't agree more, Katie. I'm going to ask the general director to excuse Julia from work for a day."

Julia's face darkened. "But I can't—"

Katie tightened her supportive grasp around Julia's shoulder. "Yes, you can. I'm sure Matt is ready to jump in. And I'll be there, too. We'll both support you."

"What about Lenny? This is the perfect excuse for him to undermine me."

"Screw Lenny," Katie said. "I can deal with him. He has no clue as to the power of New York females, especially violin-wielding ones."

"But I have to be there," Julia said. "Plus, I owe it to Marin to find out the truth about what happened. And I need you to help me, Larry."

"Okay, back up," Larry said. "You just experienced a very harrowing incident. Now you're ready to investigate?"

"Marin's my friend. She's been unjustly accused of murder. How can I just go off for some R&R and thoughtlessly abandon her in her time of need?"

"'A,' she's probably got a lawyer to take care of her by now. 'B,' you've been through this investigation thing before with Abel—and look where it got you."

"It got me to his real murderer."

"At what price?" Katie said. "You were almost killed."

"And 'C,'" Larry added, "I'm not allowed to do any probing out here. Didn't you see how that detective was looking at me cross-eyed?"

"She doesn't have to know what you're doing."

"She's a detective," said Larry. "A damn good one, from what I could gather in the few minutes we spoke. I don't see anything getting past her."

"Then what are we going to do?"

"I don't know about you, but I'm staying out of it. And I'm hoping you'll do the same."

"I can't let Marin down." Julia gazed at Larry intently, a look she knew he couldn't resist. "It's not fair."

"Okay, you win. I'll see what I can do to find out how things operate around here. At least what kind of sentence Marin may be facing," Larry said. "But in exchange, you will follow my orders and take a day off."

"He's right, Julia," said Katie.

When it came to Julia's well-being, Katie and Larry were allies. Katie had encouraged Julia and Larry's relationship from the very beginning and cheerfully found other digs when it seemed clear that Larry was going to spend more time at Julia's apartment than at his own place. She was convinced that Larry and Julia were the best thing that had ever happened to each other. In the current situation, Katie and Larry were on the same page.

Julia recognized when she was defeated. "Seems I'm outnumbered."

Larry and Katie flashed each other triumphant looks. "Yep."

Chapter Fifteen

Ah, pietà, pietà di me!...il delitto mio non è...
Il padron con prepotenza l'innocenza mi rubò.
Oh, spare me, spare me...the fault is not mine...
My overbearing master led me astray.
—Mozart, *Don Giovanni*, Act 2

A s a first-time suspect awaiting trial, Marin found herself
imprisoned in the Santa Fe County Detention Center. The fact that
the facility was only a county jail was little consolation. She was
thousands of miles from home, in a town she knew little about, and accused
of murder. If she were sentenced she faced incarceration in the infamous
Grants facility with the serious, so-called Level three-to-six criminals. She
couldn't even fathom what that might be like.

Worse, given the nature of her alleged crime, she was only allowed
visitation by appointment, which meant that Julia—likely the only person
Marin knew who might consider visiting—would be severely restricted by
her rehearsal schedule from finding time to visit. And since Julia was not a
family member, a visit might even be out of the question.

But at the moment, Marin had no time to contemplate visitation. A guard
led her to an interrogation room, where she sat handcuffed to an eyelet on
the table and waited until the DA arrived with a court-appointed lawyer in
tow.

"Ms. Crane, I am District Attorney Henry Cordero of the First Judicial
District of New Mexico. This is your attorney, Elaine Baxter."

Attorney Baxter nodded toward Marin. "Henry, is it necessary for my client to be restrained? She is a first-time offender. Could you please unshackle her?"

"I suppose we could allow it." The D.A. motioned to the guard, who unlocked Marin's cuffs. Henry tapped his foot while Elaine reached over and shook Marin's hand.

"I have read the reports, Ms. Crane," Henry said. "You are suspected of the stabbing murder of Emilia Tosti, a singer at the Santa Fe Opera, the evening of June twenty-ninth. You had a known rivalry with Ms. Tosti. You were heard having heated discussions and disagreements with her previous to the incident and were found holding a weapon that matched the stab wounds on the deceased shortly after she was attacked. The weapon contained your fingerprints and yours alone. Do you have anything to say?"

"Don't say anything, Ms. Crane." Elaine turned to the D.A. "It's all circumstantial, Henry."

"Not. We've learned that Ms. Tosti had stolen Ms. Crane's female lover right from under her nose. People have been murdered for less."

Elaine's face paled. She looked at Marin, wondering if it was true. They'd need to talk about this. Later. Marin, her head lowered, avoided Elaine's gaze.

"You can't deny it's a very high-profile case, Elaine," Henry said. "We would seek the maximum penalty."

Elaine recovered her composure. "You know as well as I do, Henry, there's no death penalty in New Mexico."

"Premeditated murder is still a capital offense in this state, Counselor. Punishable by life in prison, possibly without parole. Even non-premeditated first-degree murder is eighteen years in prison."

Hearing this, Marin jumped out of her chair. "What?"

Elaine gently restrained Marin. "Premeditated or not, you'll have to prove it first, Henry."

"I intend to."

"And even in a felony case, with no criminal record and no proof of drug involvement, the judge could sentence her to probation," Elaine added.

"For murder? You're dreaming," Henry said. "I'd consider a deal if I were you."

"Not gonna happen. Now if you don't mind, I need to consult with my client privately."

Henry motioned to the guard, who ushered him out of the room.

Elaine turned to Marin. "Okay, Ms. Crane, what really happened?"

* * *

Larry left Katie in charge of keeping Julia calm while he went to visit the Santa Fe Police Department headquarters. He found the building itself, located on Camino Entrada not far from the so-called artsy "Railyard" District, non-descript: a brown flat-roofed cinder-block-shaped rectangle with virtually no landscaping surrounding it. But he was somewhat impressed with the tidy, well-organized interior, its displays of historic SFPD photos, certificates of merit and earned honors, and even the SFPD logo-imprinted souvenir glasses and mugs for sale at ten dollars each. The dissimilarity from his much older-looking home precinct in Manhattan was extreme: his home base was not as well-lit, a bit unkempt and disorganized. But it still was as homey as a police facility could be and familiar territory to him.

Julia, whom Katie could not prevent from frantically pacing the hotel room, looked up expectantly when Larry returned. From his expression, she could tell the news was not going to be reassuring. Her face fell.

"Start with the bad news," Julia said.

"What makes you think it's bad?"

"I know you, and your looks," she said grimly. "Now tell me. And don't mince words."

"Okay, then, I'll give it to you straight." Larry paused. "It's a high-profile case. They're going for life without parole."

"What?!"

"You told me not to mince words."

Julia stopped pacing and sank down on the bed, head in hands. "How is this possible?"

"It's not all bad. I talked to your personnel manager, Sarah. She approved your day off."

"I need to visit Marin first."

"Ah. About that..."

Julia bit her lip. "What?"

"They're not allowing her any visitors yet," Larry said. "Even Marin's attorney has limited access. Plus, you have to submit an application, which could take some time."

"That's positively Byzantine," Julia said. "In New York, when I wanted to visit Sid—"

"In case you hadn't noticed, Dorothy, we're not in New York anymore."

Julia moaned. "This can't be happening."

Katie sat next to Julia and grasped her hand. "What's the good news, Larry?"

"The good news is, I've booked us for a night at a historic Santa Fe hotel for some R&R."

"I'd rather rehearse *Romeo and Juliet*," Julia said. "At least that would keep my mind off all of this misery."

Larry sat on Julia's other side and squeezed her shoulder. "I've already paid for the night, and they've enlisted Matt to take your place in tomorrow's opera performance."

"A night away from the scene of the cri...the opera...will do you good," Katie said.

Julia knew that standing in opposition to either Larry or Katie was within the realm of possibility, but trying to wrangle with both of them was useless.

"Okay, I give up," Julia said. "Which hotel is it?"

"It's a surprise," Larry said.

Julia looked up at Larry dubiously. "You know I don't like surprises."

"Don't worry. It will be perfect." Larry smiled. "Trust me."

* * *

Criminal Court Judge Marlo Madison of Division VII, Santa Fe District Court, was no Ruth Bader Ginsburg. She was not an opera fan; in fact, she had never seen an opera. Nor did she feel undue sympathy for female defendants because they were female.

Elaine Baxter had warned Marin of this, so Marin was deeply apprehensive about her bail hearing. Still, she welcomed the chance to get away from her prison cell and catch a glimpse of the flawless, crystal-blue Santa Fe sky from the prison van, if only for a few moments.

The court building on Montezuma Avenue was not far from Santa Fe Plaza. As the van wound through the narrow streets, Marin kept her eyes fixed on the window. Due to an event blocking off the usual route, the van had to pass by famous Santa Fe landmarks she recognized from her tourist brochures: the Cathedral of St. Francis (which she had read of in Willa Cather's *Death Comes for the Archbishop*), the nearby Loretto Chapel, the San Miguel Mission. Sights she had profoundly wished to see but likely never would because of her dire situation.

Compared to the courthouses in Lower Manhattan, the Santa Fe County Courthouse looked astonishingly contemporary, with its square lines, adobe and white exterior, rectangular columns, and state and federal flags flapping in the wind. Such thoughts provided a welcome distraction for Marin, but as soon as she was ushered into the courtroom, her anxiety skyrocketed.

Seated with her attorney Elaine at a table across the aisle from D.A. Cordero, Marin kept her hands in her lap so as not to reveal her nervous wringing. All three participants rose as Judge Madison swept into the room, up the stairs, and into her chair. Spying the judge's austere expression, Marin lost all hope.

"We are seeking bail for my client, Your Honor," Elaine said. "She has no record and is an important member of the artistic community, both in Santa Fe and in her home city of New York. She should be released on her own recognizance."

"Your Honor, we beg to differ," the D.A. countered. "The defendant's fingerprints were found on the murder weapon."

Elaine shook her head. "That's not illogical, given the circumstances. It was not unnatural for her to pick up the knife. She was in shock."

"She may be performing in Santa Fe at the moment," Henry continued. "But her home is two thousand miles away. She is an obvious flight risk."

The judge deliberated only briefly. Marin took that as a bad sign. Her heart sank.

"I agree the defendant is a flight risk," "said the judge. "She will be remanded and remain in custody until the trial."

"But the New Mexico Constitution guarantees that people charged with a crime have a right to be released pretrial, Your Honor," Elaine protested. "Since passage of the 2016 constitutional amendment to reform New Mexico's pretrial release and detention system—"

Henry interrupted Elaine. "Revisions that went into effect in July of 2017 state that district court judges can lawfully hold felony defendants in jail before trial if they are shown to be too dangerous for release, Your Honor. Defendants charged with a felony are subject to pretrial detention, and Ms. Crane is charged with murder," he said. "She could be extradited to New York, where she resides. Aggravated Murder and Murder in the 1st and 2nd Degrees are Class A-1 Felonies in New York. NY Penal Law § 125.27 provides life imprisonment without parole for first-degree murder."

Marin felt like her legs were about to give way under her.

"I agree with Mr. Cordero," said the judge. "My decision stands, Counselor. We are adjourned."

The judge pounded her gavel, rose, and disappeared through the door from which she entered.

Elaine was furious. "Life imprisonment without parole? Are you kidding me, Henry?"

"Hardly," he replied. "In any case, she'll need a super-aggressive defense lawyer."

"She's got one." Elaine exchanged defiant looks with Henry. "This isn't over," she said.

Chapter Sixteen

Fuggi, regal fantasima...Via, spaventosa imagine!
Away, royal phantom!...Away, frightening vision!
—Verdi, *Macbeth*, Act 3

T he rumor mill was working overtime at the opera house. When Julia heard that Marin had been denied bail, she was grief-stricken but found herself agreeing with Larry's plan for a brief respite from the theatre. The name of the hotel he had chosen, La Posada de Santa Fe, translated from the Spanish as "place of rest." She needed that. Desperately.

Julia admitted this to Larry as they sat over lattes amidst the lunch crowd at the company cantina. Glancing around, it looked to her as if every member involved in the current production was frenetically trying to seize the opportunity to gobble down a few bites during their fleeting moments of hiatus from work.

"So maybe it's not such a bad idea. La Posada, I mean." Julia waved to Magda at the cash register with Sándor and motioned to her to come over. Magda waved back. Taking Sándor by the arm, she maneuvered him to Julia and Larry's table.

"Júlia, this is my brother, Sándor."

Sándor took Julia's hand and kissed it delicately. "*Örvendek*, Júlia. Nice to meet you."

"Nice to meet you, too, Sándor. How did you know I spoke Hungarian?"

"Magda shares everything with me. She told me about you. About your beauty."

Larry cleared his throat. Julia eyed him, uncomfortable. "Magda and Sándor, this is my significant other, Larry Somers. He's a detective with the New York Police Department."

Sándor turned red. "Oh, I am so sorry. I should not have—"

"Don't worry about it, pal," Larry said. "I'm used to it. Price to pay for associating with loveliness."

"How are you doing, Julia? I mean, with all that has happened?" Sándor asked.

"Honestly? Not very well," Julia replied. "Marin and I were—are—close friends."

"I am very sorry to hear about that," Magda said.

"I'm taking Julia away from it all for a night of respite," Larry said. "To La Posada."

"A good idea. She deserves it," Magda said. "It is one of most beautiful places in Santa Fe."

"Only under protest," Julia said. "I can't afford to take a night off when I'm still trying to prove myself worthy of my position."

"I'm sure it will revive you, to bring new energy to your work, Júlia."

"Now there's a voice of reason," Larry said. "If you won't listen to me, listen to Magda. She's very wise."

"And old." Magda smiled. "Thank you, Larry. Now, if you will excuse us..."

Taking Sándor's arm, Magda guided him through the tangle of tables and toward the exit. Larry looked intently at Julia.

"You're full of surprises. Hungarian?"

Julia smiled cunningly. "There's still so much you don't know about me, Larry."

"Magda was right about La Posada, you know. The grounds there are some of the loveliest in the city. Just looking at them will reenergize you," Larry told her.

"Since when do you use the word 'lovely?' Have you got something up your sleeve?"

"Have I ever steered you wrong?"

She not only was annoyed at his nerve to answer a question with a question, but she also wasn't in the mood for loveliness; not yet, anyway. And she knew Larry was well aware of it.

"Okay. But I'm bringing my violin to practice."

"Can't you be without it for one night?"

Her withering look gave him his answer.

* * *

In exchange for going along with his plan for a night at La Posada, Julia had made Larry promise her a tour around Santa Fe. Guidebooks in hand, they poked around the adobe art galleries and shops on Canyon Road, replete with tribal pottery, bronze sculptures, and characteristic Southwest-style landscape paintings. They dropped in on San Miguel Mission and visited the Palace of the Governors, with its block-long row of Native American artisans hawking their wares under the front portico. They gazed at the monument in the middle of Santa Fe Plaza, the city's hub, honoring combatants who had died in battles with Indians over the New Mexico Territory, and at the plaque marking the original portal to the Manhattan Project.

As enthralled as Julia was by their touristic sojourn, she still fretted about the events of the previous night.

"I shouldn't be sightseeing, Larry. I should be thinking of ways to support Marin."

"You can do that after you've had a chance to chill first," Larry said. "Learning about the historical and cultural background of Santa Fe will clear your mind."

Julia sighed. "I hope so."

Often, when she was stressed out, Julia toyed with her locket, twisting the chain in one direction and then the other. She tried to be subtle about it since she knew Larry would recognize this sign of her tension or worry and give her grief about it.

Fortunately, at that moment, Larry was focusing on the youthful musicians, playing guitars and drums and serenading onlookers in Spanish, in the shadow of the monument and brought it to Julia's attention. She was glad of the distraction.

"They're so different from the street performers in New York City, who are classically oriented or hip in a contemporary vein," Julia told Larry. "These are more historic and folk-like. You can feel the Native American and Spanish influence."

"And they're so much more laid back. You should take a cue from them."

Larry also insisted on visiting some of the city's architectural wonders. Of these, the Romanesque Cathedral Basilica of St. Francis of Assisi and Loretto Chapel impressed Julia the most. Despite having grown up Jewish, her best friend at the High School of Music and Art had been Catholic. Because of this, Julia felt an affinity for Catholicism and for the music and art inspired by it. Thus, the religious Spanish name of the city at the time of its founding in 1610, *La Villa Real de la Santa Fé de San Francisco de Asís—The Royal Town of the Holy Faith of Saint Francis of Assisi*—held great significance for her.

Larry studied his guidebook. "Too bad the Roswell UFO Festival is over. I would have loved to check out the night SkyWatch and hear some of those UFOlogists's theories."

The thought of revisiting the subject of the paranormal made Julia flinch, but she tried to hide her discomfort. "Just as well. I have no interest in the paranormal."

Larry could tell by her expression that there was something secretive behind her protest, but he wisely did not pursue it. "How about we check out some of these southwest-themed boutiques instead?"

At this point, Julia was feeling weary but couldn't resist Larry's invitation to visit the enticing shops that lined the streets forming the Plaza Square. In one trade post on East Francisco Street, a pair of cowboy boots in the window caught her eye: mushroom-colored leather, yellow embroidery bordering the pointed toe and V-shaped top, and a purple and white flower stitched at the apex of the V.

"Ooh. Can you see me in those?" she asked Larry.

"As long as you're not wearing anything else." Off Julia's raised eyebrows, Larry pointed to a nearby display of intricately engraved daggers with jeweled hilts. "How about I get you the boots, and you get me one of those turquoise-encrusted William Henry knives?"

"There's nothing under a thousand dollars, Larry."

He chuckled. "The one set with banded agate and black onyx cabochons is priced at only sixteen hundred dollars."

Julia cringed as images of Marin's blood-stained hands holding a knife invaded her senses. "What's so special about them, anyway?"

"A knife is the most basic human tool, Julia. These particular ones elevate that function to the most exceptional high art. Gentleman's knives that become heirlooms."

"Or murder weapons."

Larry eyed Julia's disturbed expression. "Sorry, point taken. How about visiting La Fonda Hotel. They say it's populated with former 'guests' who, well, never checked out."

Julia still felt uncomfortable being reminded of her unnerving encounter with the ghost in their hotel room.

"Since when are you so interested in the paranormal?"

"I've been studying Santa Fe history on the sly while you've been practicing *Lulu.*"

Larry's comment made Julia feel even more distressed at the thought that she should have been practicing rather than tooling around Santa Fe. Fortunately, he didn't seem to notice.

"Did you know the city was built over an abandoned Tanoan Indian village? Their burial grounds might be just below us. Isn't that fascinating?"

"Not."

When is he going to stop bringing up the subject of apparitions and specters and the departed?

Julia's frustration was bringing her to the point of tears. "Can we just get off the subject of spirits and related phenomena? Please?"

"You're right. Forgive me." Larry put an arm around her and held her tightly. "'*Dolce signora, che mai v'accora...Darei la vita per asciugar quel pianto...* Oh gracious lady, what grieves you? ...I would give my life to wipe away those tears."

Julia looked at him, incredulous. "Since when are you quoting *Tosca*? In Italian, no less."

"Only when Puccini and his librettist said it better than I could," Larry replied. "But it's clear you need to relax. Let's go to the hotel."

"Finally, you're making sense," Julia said.

"But promise we'll get to some haunted places before too long. I'm itching to see a ghost or two, aren't you?"

Julia groaned her response, after which Larry kept quiet—at least for a short while.

Chapter Seventeen

Certo moto d'ignoto tormento dentro l'alma girare mi sento, che mi dice...
cento cose che intender non sa
I feel some strange suspicion stirring in my breast which tells me...
a hundred things I don't understand
—Mozart, *Don Giovanni*, Act 1

"**D**idn't I say it was perfect?" Larry said when they entered the property of La Posada, located steps from Santa Fe Plaza.

Julia nodded, impressed. La Posada was indeed magnificent. Lush gardens with multicolored flowers and elegant fountains nestled between charming pueblo-style adobe *casitas*, all of which surrounded Staab House, the original nineteenth-century Victorian mansion that was the hotel's centerpiece.

Violin case strapped to her shoulder, Julia stood gazing at the façade while Larry started to recount the hotel's sad history of Julia Staab, the mistress of the house, her untimely demise and her spirit's ostensible sporadic appearances to the hotel guests. Hearing this, Julia's uneasiness came hurtling back with a vengeance.

"It's haunted? By a ghost named Julia?"

"Everything is haunted in Santa Fe. It's one of the most haunted cities in America. That's how this town has preserved its rich past. All those Spanish, Mexicans, pioneers, and Crypto Jews have stuck around," Larry said. "Evidently the ghost in La Posada was not pleased with the modern additions to her house."

"I don't like ghosts. Especially ones with my name."

"When was the last time you saw one?"

Julia did not reply. It had been several days since her ghostly encounter at the Pueblo Inn, but she still felt uncomfortable at the thought of sharing the experience with Larry. That La Posada, the largest private residence in New Mexico, was one of the few hotels in the U.S. with an art curator on staff was no antidote for Julia's overall feeling of disquiet. She wondered how such a beautiful place could be haunted. Then she remembered: it was in Santa Fe.

The concierge, Peter, offered them a mini-tour of the historic section of the house. "Our porter, Eldred, has been here longer than any of our employees. His great-great-grandfather worked on the architect's plans for the original Staab House, constructed by nineteenth-century merchant Abraham Staab for his wife, Julia, after they emigrated from Germany."

Julia's anxiety began to escalate. She suppressed a shudder.

A ghost named Julia? From Germany? This is getting too close to home.

"Sounds fascinating," said Larry. "Let's do it."

Peter led them inside. "By the way, Larry, be sure to take a photo of the mirror above the mantel in the room with the marble fireplace. The one with the marble cross positioned on top of it," he said. "When you look at the picture afterwards you'll see a blue light reflected in the mirror that's not visible when you look at the mirror itself."

Larry extracted his cell phone from his pocket. "Why isn't it visible?"

"Because the blue light is Julia's ghost, which only appears in photographic images."

Larry seemed unfazed, but Julia's disquiet continued unabated. She hovered in front of the flagstone entrance to the older portion of the hotel, hesitant to enter, as Larry snapped photos.

Peter sensed Julia's apprehension. "Don't be anxious about our ghost. She's totally non-threatening. Even the musicians who perform here on weekends have had all sorts of 'supernatural' experiences here, without any untoward consequences. Mysterious disembodied voices harmonized with them, sound systems going out suddenly and then coming back on. All in all, it's not harmful. It just adds to the atmosphere."

"Julia's got an advanced level of intuition. If there are any spirits around, they'll glom onto her," Larry said. "Remember that psychic on the Upper West Side of Manhattan who said you were a medium, Julia?"

"Really? We could use one of those in 'ghostly' Santa Fe," Peter said.

His observation did little to quell Julia's discomfort. But when she gazed at the dark wood entrance, with the initials "A.S." mounted on the mahogany frame above the entryway, something came over her. Perhaps it was the darkened corridor with its steep wooden staircase, lit only by ancient-looking chandeliers suspended from the ceiling, or the feeling of going back in time.

Whatever the reason, Julia's artist's imagination took over. She was able to envision the gas-lit chandeliers in their former glory, bearing witness to Victorian women's floor-length taffeta dresses sweeping up the steps. The idea left her completely entranced.

Also timeworn was the look of the wizened elderly gentleman who approached Julia and Larry. The old man's chalk-white hair encircled his face in tufts, his overstrained eyes blinking in the dim light. He reminded Julia of Frantz, the servant character from the "Antonia" act of *The Tales of Hoffmann*.

"This is Eldred," said Peter. "Eldred, these guests will be staying in Room One Hundred."

The old man regarded Julia, open-mouthed, scrutinizing her face with a combination of tenderness and incredulity.

"Julia!" he cried. "You've come back."

* * *

"Excuse me?" Julia said.

Peter leaned over and whispered to Julia. "Eldred has dementia, though it's mild considering his advanced age. Don't let it bother you." He spoke more loudly to the old man. "Take good care of our guests, will you?"

Peter exchanged bemused glances with Larry and walked off. Julia, unnerved, avoided Eldred's gaze.

"I always knew you would come back, Julia," the old man continued. "Great-great-grandfather said so. You're just as beautiful as he told me you were."

Julia remained confused. "But—"

"Go along with the old gent," Larry murmured. "I'll back you up."

Waving away her concern, Eldred gently took her arm. "Come, Julia, let me show you what remains of your house's former glory."

Larry followed, continuing to snap photos, as Eldred guided Julia through the portal into the hallway by the stairs. "Here," he said, pointing to two gold-framed black and white vintage photos. "Remember when the house had three stories, the way your husband Abraham first built it before the fire?"

Not waiting for her reply, he led her into another room. Its walls were lined with mahogany bookcases, between which stood a marble fireplace topped by an enormous wood-framed mirror alongside two matching red-upholstered Victorian-era sofas that faced each other.

An elegant mahogany bar dominated the adjoining room. Above the bar, five wood-framed glass cabinets displayed panoplies of colorful liquor bottles.

"It was you who insisted Abraham build the bar to such massive proportions."

Julia was speechless.

"But nothing can equal the magnificence of this mantel," he said, steering her to the next room, where another large gilt-framed mirror hung above a marble fireplace, and an additional antique chandelier adorned the ceiling.

Julia stared at the marble cross entwined with elaborate carvings positioned on top of the mantel. She couldn't argue with the old man; the entire effect was awe-inspiring.

As per Peter's suggestion, Larry took multiple photographs of the mirror behind the cross. "You see, Julia, there's no blue light. Nothing to worry about."

"I have never understood the presence of the cross on top of the mantel,"

Eldred said, "Considering that you and Abraham are Jewish."

"Jewish?" Julia echoed. She flashed a look of disbelief at Larry, who, at this point, was beginning to look spooked. He nonetheless persevered with his photography.

"Come, Julia, I'll take you to your room," Eldred said.

Julia trailed Eldred up the staircase in a fog, followed by Larry. Reaching the top, Julia gazed downward to the bottom of the stairs. Then, looking to the left, she saw a windowed alcove with two leather chairs, which served as a sitting room. In front of her, an open door led to a room labeled "Julia Staab Suite."

Julia whispered to Larry. "Did you know the ghost's name was Julia? And she was *Jewish?*"

"That was part of the surprise. I thought you'd be pleased or at least intrigued."

"That's not a surprise. It's sabotage," she said through her teeth.

Julia inwardly admitted that the room's past-era furnishings were exquisitely tasteful: the four-poster bed with its pristine white linen coverlet, sheets, and pillowcases; the vintage-tint gilded-frame photos hanging above the bed; the two matching tables and lamps on either side. The shiny mahogany desk and Louis XVI chair positioned in front of a lace-curtained window and jacquard rose pattern-upholstered "courting" settee in one corner completed the picture.

"You always had a discerning taste, Julia," Eldred said.

But Julia was entirely unprepared for what she saw above the mantelpiece: a portrait of a beautiful woman with wavy brunette hair, ebony eyes gazing into the distance, dark, finely arched brows, lips the color of a fine claret pursed together in an all-knowing yet unknowable smile of a strong-willed woman. A smile as enigmatic as the Mona Lisa.

It was as if she was looking at herself.

Chapter Eighteen

Sola, sola, in buio loco, palpitar il cor mi sento
All alone in this dark spot I feel my heart is throbbing
—Mozart, *Don Giovanni*, Act 2

"I'm not spending the night in this room," Julia told Larry when they were alone.

"If I were you, I'd be flattered. Julia Staab was a stunning woman," Larry said. "Surely you're not going to let a few coincidences spook you?"

"Coincidences? Seriously, Larry." Julia opened the brochure she found on the desk blotter. "Listen to this. 'It is said that Julia, a classical pianist, went into a deep depression after the loss of her last child, shortly after its birth, and thereafter, Julia took to her room and spent most of her time there. Unhappy with her home becoming a hotel, her ghost has been seen at the top of the stairs on countless occasions, and her footsteps are heard. People report the sensation of being watched, feeling cold streams of air even though windows are closed. Outside doors to the inner courtyard are violently opened. Lights unexplainably being turned on or off. A piano is mysteriously being played. Julia's ghost blows past employees and guests. Trays fall over; drinks are spilled. A vintage non-connected telephone rings. A voice answers...speaking Yiddish!'"

"It's all urban legend," Larry said. "You don't believe in that stuff, do you?"

Julia was still staring at the brochure. "You have to admit, it seems more than coincidental. The same name as mine. She was Jewish, came from Germany, and spoke Yiddish like my ancestors did. And she was a musician.

It's creepy," she said. "For all we know, she may have burned down the place herself."

"I think it's fascinating." Larry deliberated for a moment as to the wisdom of showing Julia the photos of the mirror behind the marble mantel. He decided against it. The bizarre blue light that appeared in all of them likely would unnerve Julia even further. "How about we go for a drink at 'Julia's—A Spirited Restaurant and Bar.'"

Julia flung the brochure at him.

* * *

That night, Julia was restless. She was miffed at Larry for springing the surprise on her and spooked that the ghost of a woman with the same name and religious-cultural background, who came to a violent end, was trolling the halls—perhaps even watching as they slept—in the "place of rest" Larry had chosen for Julia's supposed R&R away from her recent traumas at the opera.

Julia remembered being curious about Judaism's views on ghosts when she was little, but her father, Sol, died before she could put her thoughts into coherent questions. She did recall overhearing a conversation between Sol and her aunt Zsófia about two different schools of thought on the subject. Both systems believed in the Afterlife, but according to one, souls are purely spiritual beings and cannot appear physically. The other view was that angels can appear physically if they so choose. But there were conflicting opinions as to whether spirits are from the dream world—or a sign of mental illness.

Sol and Zsófia also debated whether ghosts can be real but agreed that one should avoid calling them. It came down to whether the deceased takes physical form or exists merely in the spiritual realm. Julia did not understand most of what Sol and Zsófia had said. But after Sol died, Julia liked to think that he was in heaven with her mom, even though Zsófia had tried to persuade the young girl that her father's spirit lived on as a cherished memory.

But Julia's encounter in her room the night before had felt so real, so palpable, she was convinced that whoever had visited her was an example of a dead person appearing in physical form. Whether dream or mental illness, she was not entirely sure.

Ghosts notwithstanding, there also was the creepy old man who had insisted Julia was the regeneration of the former mistress of Staab House one-hundred-fifty years previous.

In any case, Julia made sure to close the bedroom door as tightly as possible. Eventually, she fell into an exhausted sleep, but dreams haunted her: of Marin, her hands stained with blood; of prisons and prison guards, lawyers and prosecuting attorneys.

Around four a.m. Julia awakened to the sounds of the door opening and closing and footsteps in the hallway. She tried to attribute the noises to her overall state of anxiety, but when she felt a sensation of being watched and a sudden feeling of cold overcame her, she cautiously opened her eyes.

Did I leave the window open?

Squinting to adjust to the darkness, she glanced across the room and saw the window was still closed, but her violin case was open on a chair. Despite her fear, she started to peel herself off the bed to secure the case when a familiar sound filtered into her ears: her violin strings being plucked. G, D, A, E, individually; then a G major chord.

Am I dreaming?

But it was no dream. She could hear the plucked strings' vibrations resonating. Terrified, she roused Larry, who, as usual, was sleeping soundly.

"Larry, wake up."

He stirred. "What's going on, Julia?"

"Somebody is playing my violin."

Now, she had his attention. He opened his eyes halfway. "That's crazy talk."

"No, it isn't. Listen."

"I don't hear anything."

By now, the strumming had stopped. "I don't care if you believe me," Julia insisted. "I heard strings being plucked."

"Your fatigue and stress are making you hallucinate. Go back to sleep."

"I can't."

"I suppose you think it's Julia's ghost?" Larry said. "Or it could be a poltergeist. They're the mischievous ones. They move things."

"Right. Thanks a lot; that makes me feel much better. Not," Julia said. "It's the troubled souls who stay around, Larry. And she was a musician, after all."

"My grandmother had a saying, Julia. 'The dead can't hurt you. Only the living can.'"

Julia rose and approached the violin. There was no evidence the strings had been vibrating. But she was sure she had left it wrapped in its maroon silk drawstring pouch. She plucked the strings, making sure the climate—or anything else—had not unduly damaged the instrument. Then she lovingly rewrapped it and clicked the case shut.

Maybe I am crazy, after all. 'Meshuggeneh,' like Aunt Zsófia used to say.

Seeing that Larry was fully awake, Julia kept talking, if only to keep her nerves from fraying further. "Okay, maybe I imagined the violin. But I can't stop thinking about Marin in that horrible place. What if they send her to the penitentiary? One of the most violent prison riots in the history of the American correctional system occurred at the New Mexico State Penitentiary in 1980. Thirty-three inmates died."

"Marin's not in the State Penitentiary, Julia. She's in county jail. The Northwest New Mexico Correctional Center. Or maybe the New Mexico Women's Correctional Facility or Western Women's Correctional Facility. They've renamed it a few times."

"Whatever, I'm sure it's unspeakable. And she has no one else here but me. What if they transfer her to a maximum-security prison? No, no, I have to get in to see her somehow."

"But the county jail's way far away."

"I don't care. If I don't do something, I will go out of my mind."

"Okay, okay, only for you." Larry forced himself awake, rose, and sat at the desk in front of his iPad. He opened the browser, Googled the "New Mexico Corrections Department" website and scrolled down until he found

"SPECIAL VISIT REQUEST APPLICATION."

For the first time since they had checked into La Posada, Julia felt relieved. At least she was doing something to allay her anxiety. Checking out of the hotel would be the next step.

Chapter Nineteen

Il carcere mi ha dunque assai mutate
Prison, then, has it wrought such a great change in me
—Puccini, *Tosca*, Act 1

Since Marin had no immediate family members close by, Julia's application was fast-tracked and approved by the Assistant Warden sooner than she and Larry had expected. The day after the two had checked out of La Posada and returned to their original abode, a tech rehearsal was scheduled for the opera and the orchestra was off, leaving Julia free to visit Marin in prison.

The visiting directive Julia had received via the hotel desk specified a lengthy list of restrictions that Julia found daunting. No physical contact was allowed, nor controlled substances of any kind. The Dress Code for Visitors was strictly adhered to: no short skirts, shorts, or sweat clothes; undergarments required; and no tank tops or see-through clothing. Julia was more than willing to comply with any requirements that would result in her being able to show her support for Marin, whom Julia sensed was receiving no other moral encouragement from the outside.

Julia and Larry drove south from their hotel, through barren desert landscapes, crossing over from one Indian reservation to another, until they found themselves in an isolated area with low hills and little in the way of vegetation but scrub brush and chaparral. It was even more desolate an environment than Julia had imagined.

"To think she's in that overcrowded place, with drug addicts and violent criminals with tattooed heads who barely passed their GEDs," Julia said as they pulled up in front. "It's the pits. It got one star on Yelp. They said it's totally run down. And the food is inedible. It's been called the 'Santa Fe weight loss center.'"

She peered at the foreboding entrance with its flat-roofed adobe-looking buildings and fences and restrained herself from shivering.

"Only one visitor allowed," the Shift Supervisor at the reception desk told them. "You'll have to wait here during the visit, sir."

"No problem," Larry said. "I'm just her escort."

Larry observed as the Shift Supervisor had Julia sign the Visitor Statement of Understanding, in which she acknowledged she might be searched. She filled out a questionnaire and surrendered her driver's license, which the Shift Supervisor scrutinized closely.

"I need to be sure you're over eighteen. Under eighteen have to take a drug test," he said.

"Does she look underage?" Larry asked.

The supervisor ignored his question. "I also need your cell phone and whatever cash you have on you over twenty dollars. Do you have any other electronic devices, Ms. Kogan?"

Julia shook her head.

"The metal detector is over there," the supervisor said. "Are you afraid of dogs?"

Julia glanced at a large German shepherd hovering nearby. "Not generally, but this one doesn't look too friendly."

"He's there to sniff for drugs."

Julia suppressed her impatience. "I don't take them, but if I did, I certainly wouldn't bring any with me."

"You'd be surprised what people try to smuggle in here."

Julia flashed a look of stupefaction to Larry. He smiled his encouragement as she stepped through the metal detector.

* * *

The prison was less dank than Julia had expected. Bright fluorescent ceiling lights illuminated the cavernous rooms. The walls, rather than battleship grey, were a much lighter cream color. The inmates wore blue shirts and black pants instead of orange jumpsuits.

Still, Julia felt the heaviness of the somber atmosphere weigh on her. The gloomy appearance of the security guard who led her into the visiting room emphasized the graveness of the situation.

When Marin trudged in, Julia had to restrain her shock. The singer looked diminished. Her figure, usually on the ample side, was a mere shadow of its former state. Her normally round face was drawn, her complexion sallow. She attempted to smile without success as she sat down opposite Julia.

"I didn't think they'd let you come."

"I admit it wasn't easy getting here. But more importantly, Marin, are you all right?"

"Do I look all right?"

Julia hesitated.

"It's okay to be honest, Julia," Marin said.

"No. You don't."

"That's what I thought."

"Marin, I'll do anything I can to get you out of here. Anything."

"Is that true?"

"Of course it is. I know you didn't do this. The question is, who did?"

Marin leaned in closely toward Julia. "Talk to Deborah."

"Who's Deborah?"

"She's one of the apprentices. Emilia's understudy," Marin said.

Julia had heard much about Santa Fe Opera's famed apprentice program, which was run by Rob Cheever, a former Met Opera tenor who now lived in Santa Fe full-time. More than fifteen hundred singers had been through the program under Rob's direction. She was anxious to learn more, but the present circumstances weren't exactly favorable ones.

"Wait," Julia said, "I know that an apprentice can get their big break here, but...murder?"

"Talk to her. She desperately wanted a chance to sing Lulu. She looked overjoyed when Emilia walked out during rehearsal. And she was practically throwing herself at Salman." Marin lowered her voice. "Which is weird, considering she also was sleeping with Emilia."

Julia gasped. "You're kidding. That sounds like a twisted 'Three Faces of Eve' scenario."

"Some people would throw a singer off a cliff to get a crack at a role," Marin said. "Or 'accidentally' shove someone in the pool and give them a cold so they'd have to cancel. Or make sure they get the most belligerent horse."

Julia was puzzled. "What?"

"Riding is a popular leisure pursuit here. One singer had to cancel...after being thrown." Marin lowered her voice. "If you get my drift."

"I can understand that kind of competition," Julia said. "Still...killing someone?"

In her experience so far with *Lulu*, Julia had had some bleak moments when she felt like killing herself, but she didn't think it wise to share that with Marin in her current fragile state.

"Talk to Deborah about her rivalry with Emilia. And to Rob, too. He knows more about the apprentices than anyone," said Marin. "Will you do that for me?"

"Of course."

Marin paused, reflecting. "It's so ironic, Julia. This role took such a long time to prepare, and now—"

"How in the world can you sing twelve-tone music, Marin? I barely can find those pitches on the violin," Julia said.

"I admit, at first, I hated the music. I came from a *bel canto* background, and *Lulu* is not exactly *Lucia*. I thought, this is impossible. I can never do anything with that score. And there was so much going on with the staging. It was downright scary."

Julia knew and loved the irresistible nineteenth-century *bel canto* "beautiful singing" style represented by such composers as Rossini, Bellini, and, coincidentally Donizetti, the composer of *Lucia di Lammermoor*.

"But all that *bel canto* helped me tackle the role of Countess Geschwitz,"

Marin continued. "I was determined to conquer that beast of a role. And I did. Now, someone else is taking it over, through no fault of mine. It's just not fair."

The more Julia studied Marin's tortured face, the more worried she became. "Marin…is there…something else you should be telling me?"

"I…"Marin hesitated. "…I was sleeping with Deborah, too. Until Emilia lured her away," she murmured softly.

"Oh, my God. Does anyone know?"

"My attorney. And, unfortunately, Detective Peregrine and…" Marin bit her lip. "The DA. He's charging me with premeditated murder."

Julia was stunned.

The security guard appeared at the door. "Time's up."

Marin rose with great effort. She held Julia's gaze, her expression grave. "If I'm found guilty of premeditated murder, I could get life in prison, possibly without parole. Even non-premeditated, I could get eighteen years. *Eighteen years.*"

"Oh, my God. Seriously?"

"Believe it. If that happens, I'm toast."

"It won't happen," Julia said. "I won't let it."

"Thank you, Julia. You're a true friend."

Julia watched with trepidation as the guard led Marin away. She was at a loss as to how to obtain justice for Marin. She wasn't sure if she was worthy of being called a true friend, but at this moment, she suspected, to her chagrin, that she was Marin's only friend.

I'll find a way for her. I have to. She deserves that. At the very least.

Chapter Twenty

Eine Frage: Kannst Du die Wahrheit sagen? - Ich weiss es nicht
A question: Can you tell the truth? - I don't know
—Berg, *Lulu*, Act 1

With two major roles suddenly vacant because of Emilia's demise and Marin's incarceration, an emergency "cover dress," or rehearsal specifically for understudies accompanied only by piano, was called for all the apprentices involved in *Lulu*.

As the rehearsal was to take place in one of the small outdoor studios, Julia thought it a perfect opportunity to corner Deborah surreptitiously and question her as Marin had advised. When Julia asked Stewart if she could sit in on the rehearsal, which was not required of her, to her surprise, he didn't inquire as to her motives. She figured he was too preoccupied with such game-changing cast modifications to argue with her. He even introduced her to Rob Cheever.

"Rob has been in charge of the apprentice program for over three decades," Stewart said. "He performed in the chorus for the U.S. premiere of that crazy Hindemith opera *Cardillac* the night before the theatre burned down in 1967."

Julia was curious. "I've never heard of that opera. What makes it so crazy?"

"Oh, nothing, just a bunch of mysterious murders, secrets and lies, a lynching, and other mayhem tied to a lot of gold jewelry. In other words, your average operatic confusion, but the dark side."

To Julia, Rob seemed young and energetic. "Considering your long history with the company, you don't look old enough to have performed that long ago."

"Thank you, Julia. I'll be sure to tell my wife you said so," Rob said, laughing. "I've been listening to your solos in *Lulu*, by the way. Absolutely gorgeous."

"Thank you." Julia felt vindicated, especially with Stewart standing right next to Rob, but she suppressed a desire to say anything to that effect. She smiled graciously.

It was Rob who flashed a meaningful glance at Stewart. "Recognition where it's due."

"If you were here in '67, you must have known Crosby, Rob. What was he really like?" Julia asked.

"He was a force. Brilliant. Hypercritical. Sometimes aggravating—though you didn't hear that from me. But because of his dream, the world of opera will never be the same. He made opera a tourist attraction. We're all the better for it."

"Indeed, we are." Stewart excused himself and walked over to a small podium facing the stage, opened his score, and began studying it.

"Whatever his shortcomings, Julia, you can't fault Stewart for not being thorough," Rob said. "Is this your first time hearing the apprentices?"

"Yes."

"Well, you're in for a treat. They're always looking for chances to sing real roles." He leaned close to Julia. "Some of them sing better than the people they're covering. But you didn't hear that from me."

"Of course not. I think your faith in them is inspiring."

"They also love to do outside events, like the ones we've held in Whole Foods. I usually wheel in an electric keyboard. The apprentices sing a forty-minute program. I always tell people it's going to happen in Bread," he said, laughing. "But seriously, when you're an apprentice, all eyes are on you. And you quickly learn that solo singers are *not* prima donnas. That's an important lesson, because the so-called 'real' opera world is not so friendly."

Julia thought of Marin's comment about the opera business being nasty. "I've noticed that." She peered at the stage and noticed a young, extremely attractive female singer to whom Salman had directed his attention. "Who's the singer Salman is talking to?"

"That's Lorelei Forman," he said. "Marin's understudy."

It had never occurred to Julia that she not only might want to talk to Deborah, who had a vested interest in usurping Emilia's role, but also to the singer, who might have wanted to get Marin out of the way.

"Come sit. I have to stay close by Andrew, but you can park yourself right behind me."

Julia had heard of Andrew Stillman, one of New York's most influential, high-profile impresarios. Over the previous four decades, Andrew's go-getting organization had represented the world's most celebrated opera singers. Up until a couple of years ago, he had been called "The Harvey Weinstein of Opera" until the infamous ongoing controversies surrounding the film producer sparked a spate of revelations in the industry. Given that and the recent severe sentence laid on top of Weinstein's previous harsh verdict, Andrew had tried to divest himself of any association with the former Hollywood legend.

On the small stage, Salman was giving directions to an attractive young female singer, whom Julia assumed to be Deborah, while a group of young apprentices stood by and observed.

"...Stanislavski and the importance of theatrics for singers," the director asserted. "Every word you sing must reach the audience. Your body must be liberated from all tension, not integral to the drama. You are communicating music to the audience straight from the heart."

Where have I heard that before?

Julia sat down and, trying not to be too obvious, took a quick glimpse at Andrew. Pale blue eyes twinkled behind wire-rimmed glasses that framed his wide face, with its neatly trimmed, sand-colored beard and mustache. His stout body and large frame were almost too ample for the undersized folding chair in which he positioned himself. To her eyes, he was unquestionably an authority figure.

Glancing around her, Julia saw several other company members in attendance.

"Who are all these non-singing people?" she asked Rob. "I met Magda in the costume shop on my first day. I don't know the others."

"They're all here to get a jump on what might be needed for the actual performance," Rob told her. "Magda always comes to rehearsals, even the extra ones scheduled for the understudies, to analyze a person's movements so she can dress them most efficiently. She's an expert at knowing how best to build a costume that allows the singer to move the way the director wants them to. Next to her is Daniel, the wig and makeup person. It saves him time to watch the singers in action so he can fabricate the best possible wig for each one of them."

Stewart checked his watch impatiently, then signaled the pianist. "It's time we began," he said. "Act Three, Scene Two."

Julia gave an involuntary shiver as the familiar dissonances of the opera's brutal, final murder scene filtered into her consciousness. She was taken aback to see Andrew flapping his hands, making conducting gestures along with Stewart, waving at Deborah, and leaning over to comment to Rob while Deborah was singing.

"Fabulous, right, Rob?" Andrew said. "No problem, eh? Who needs Emilia?"

Rob simply nodded and kept watching. Julia couldn't see Andrew's expression, but she was appalled at his callous chattering about the deceased diva, whose body had scarcely had time to grow cold. Even detestable people deserved a modicum of respect after their demise.

"Yes indeed," Andrew said. "Deborah's going to make a magnificent Lucia, too."

Lucia, too? Marin was right. I need to talk to this gal.

* * *

As the rehearsal broke and the singers came offstage, Julia quietly rose and approached Deborah. The young singer's build reminded Julia of many other sopranos she had seen perform onstage: what the Germans called *zaftig*—lush, to put it politely, or juicy in more contemporary terms; not the typical look for the role of a *femme fatale* such as Lulu. But Deborah's olive-skinned face and coal-black eyes framed by thick black hair cascading to her shoulders showed remarkable beauty and intensity. Her air of confidence reflected her awareness of it.

"Hi, Deborah. I'm Julia, concertmaster of the orchestra. You sound great."

"Thanks. I'm impressed that you would come to a dress rehearsal with only piano. Since there's no orchestra, technically, you're not required to be here."

"I like to know as much as possible about the operas and the people involved, especially since this is my first time working here in Santa Fe," Julia said. "Is this your first year as an apprentice?"

"Yes. It's like a dream come true to be here with the apprentice program. There's so much competition to get in," Deborah said.

"A plum assignment for your first time, singing the part of Lulu, under such problematic circumstances."

"Yes...." Deborah hesitated. "It is."

"It must be difficult for you to fill Emilia's shoes with so little notice."

Deborah shrugged. "We're trained for that. Though she did have a rather large shoe size if you get my drift."

Deborah's cavalier attitude gave Julia pause. "Sounds like you had some issues with her."

"Everybody did. She was notorious."

"So I've gathered. Was there a specific rivalry between you two divas?"

"I don't consider myself a diva," Deborah said. "I haven't reached that status yet."

"I'm curious. As a musician and not a singer. How would you define that status? Does it have to do with what they call the applause meter?"

"According to the late, great Christa Ludwig, it's not so much about how much applause a diva gets but more about how she receives it. No names were mentioned, but one soprano would fall to her knees, arms raised, milk it for what seemed like hours, and then rise very slowly. People would think of her as a diva without question. They lapped it up."

Christa Ludwig's recordings had represented the benchmark when Julia had first started listening to opera. She was impressed that Deborah had used the famous mezzo as an example. "Did Ludwig have anything to say about the difference between 'diva-dom' and 'stardom'?"

"She did say that being a 'star' isn't something you think about. You become it. Though, in her case, she admitted to feeling lucky that her 'rivals' at the time were either too old or too young, I think she was much too modest."

"I agree," Julia paused. "Were you backstage the night of the *Lulu* opening?"

"We always have to be in the house when we're covering a role," Deborah said. "But space is limited backstage. They don't like anyone hanging about who doesn't belong. We usually wait around in the dressing room area."

"Did you notice anything or anyone unusual there?"

Deborah's expression suddenly turned dark and unfriendly. She shifted uncomfortably. "I'm afraid I have to go warm up now. Enjoy the rest of the rehearsal, Julia."

Julia watched as Deborah hastened away, scurried over to Salman, and began to speak to him, her arm placed in an intimate gesture around his shoulder.

No question that he's totally flattered at getting attention from a young, pretty singer. Whatever her sexual persuasion.

Julia shook off her feelings of disquiet. She watched with interest as Magda took Deborah aside and adjusted the shoulder pads on her filmy black blouse and the pleats on her gauze skirt. Magda acknowledged Julia's wave with a nod, then went back to fussing over Deborah.

Julia spied Rob chatting with Lorelei and moved toward them.

"Julia, have you met Lorelei Forman?" Rob said. "Lorelei, this is Julia Kogan, our new orchestra concertmaster. She came here all the way from the Met."

Lorelei gasped. "Oh, I love that orchestra! They're the greatest opera orchestra on the planet. It must have been so exciting to perform with them."

"Thank you," Julia said. "It was, absolutely. And you must be so excited to be playing Geschwitz. Have you sung the role before?"

"Are you kidding?" Lorelei said. "Who gets to do that? Unless you're, like, Jennifer Larmore or something."

"Or Marin Crane," said Julia.

Lorelei frowned. "Right."

"That's why you kids come to Santa Fe, to have a crack at those rarely done roles. Right, Lorelei?" Rob said.

"Um-hmm." Lorelei thought for a moment. "It's a real shame about Marin, though."

Julia couldn't tell whether Lorelei was trying to be sincere or polite. But when the assistant conductor called an end to the break, she realized her window of opportunity had closed.

"I guess you'd better run," Julia said. "By the way, were you in the theatre opening night?"

Lorelei flushed. "Well, I—"

Rob interrupted. "The apprentices generally are required to attend every possible event, especially if they're understudies. They're here to learn, after all."

"Of course," Julia said. "I can't wait to hear you nail that last scene, Lorelei. Break a leg."

Lorelei mumbled her flustered thanks, and rushed off. Julia resumed her spot behind Rob and Andrew. She felt gratified to have been able to ask at least a few questions of the young singers.

But she didn't notice Stella positioned at the back corner of the studio.

Chapter Twenty-One

Cielo! Sempre novel sospetto
Heavens! Always some new suspicion
—Verdi, *Rigoletto*, Act 1

Once the understudies' dress rehearsal had ended, regularly scheduled rehearsals started in earnest for the next production in the repertoire: Gounod's *Roméo et Juliette*, which the company had added to their repertoire for the first time in 2016. Julia had performed the opera in her first Met season and, as was her habit, had studied the libretto to enhance her understanding of the work. She found all of the music inspiring, but the Act Two fight scene, resulting in Romeo's heart-wrenching exile, always gave her goosebumps.

Still bent on helping Marin, however, Julia made a point of picking the brains of her orchestra colleagues about the night of Emilia's demise. Before one rehearsal, she hovered outside the pit door among a group of gossiping musicians.

"Wish I'd been here for that *Lulu*," said one harpist. "I missed all the excitement."

"How come you weren't there?" Julia asked.

"There's only one harp in *Lulu*," the harpist said. "Second harp misses the good stuff."

"Well, I was here, and believe me, it wasn't pretty," said an oboist.

"Did you see anything suspicious?" asked Julia. "Anyone lurking around you'd never seen before?"

"I wasn't exactly looking," the oboist replied. "But I don't think that mezzo-soprano, Marin, did it."

Julia's ears perked up. "Oh?" she said. "Why?"

"I don't know exactly. She doesn't seem the type."

"Maybe the ghost of John Crosby did it," the harpist said, winking. "He did have some issues with divas, didn't he?"

Several musicians laughed, but Julia felt supremely uncomfortable at the memory of the mysterious apparition she thought she'd seen bustling among the scrub bush behind the theatre.

"I've actually seen his ghost," said Paul, a flutist. "And I'm not the only one who has."

"What are you, Paul, some sort of medium?" the harpist asked.

"Some say they can still feel his presence," Julia said. "Are you one of those company members who visit Crosby's grave every summer?"

Paul did not respond but held her gaze. Suddenly uncomfortable, Julia was relieved to hear the orchestra call over the P.A.

"Five minutes. Orchestra to the pit for *Roméo et Juliette*, Act Two."

As the musicians shuffled into the pit, Julia felt someone grab her arm from behind. She whipped around to see Stella and immediately sensed the detective was not happy.

"You seem on edge, Julia," Stella said.

"Who wouldn't be, given what's been going on?"

"Oh, I don't know. Maybe everyone else who isn't snooping around, interrogating company members."

Julia squirmed inwardly but tried not to show it. "Is there something on your mind, Detective?"

"Actually, yes. Word has gotten back to me that you've been asking people in the company all kinds of questions, none of them having to do with music, I might add. That's not acceptable. It's my job to investigate, not yours."

"I'm not investigating. I'm...naturally curious."

"Spin it however you like, Julia. You're interfering with my inquiry. And need I remind you what they say about curiosity?"

Julia did not respond.

"I thought as much." Stella turned to go, then faced Julia again. "Back off, Julia. I'm not going to tell you again."

Stella stomped off, muttering, her cowboy boots clicking on the concrete floor. "'O cursed spite, That ever I was born to set it right!'"

Julia heaved a large sigh and climbed the stairs into the pit. She lifted her violin from its case and pointed to the first oboist for the "A" to start tuning. She added her own tuning to the commotion, then sat in her chair and prepared herself psychically for the emotional roller coaster ride of Shakespeare's eternal tragedy.

Thank goodness for distractions.

* * *

After rehearsal, Julia returned to her room at the inn and placed her violin case on the floor next to her side of the bed. Larry, immersed in an online article titled "Alban Berg's *Lulu*: The Exterminating Angel," looked up at her.

"Did you know Berg was a symmetry freak?" he asked. "Act Three is a mirror image of Act One, only by contrast. Luxury vs. squalor, husbands played by the same singers as her johns. And there's this cool spot in the second act, basically the hinge for the entire opera, where Berg writes a three-minute sequence that's an exact musical palindrome. Halfway through, the solo piano pauses at the midpoint. From that point onward, every single pitch and rhythm is played in exact reverse for another ninety seconds. The music for the film interlude is an exact palindrome of itself, too…"

He turned to see Julia flop onto the bed. Her desultory expression was impossible to miss. "What happened? Blatchley again?"

"No. He's bad enough, but now Stella is on my case. And it's all your fault."

"Me? What did I do?"

"You know very well. It was you who pushed me into investigating the murder."

"In all fairness, Julia, I didn't push. You were the one who was so concerned about Marin. And I'm not allowed to do any meddling, remember?" Larry said.

"You're right. I'm not being very fair. I apologize."

"No biggie. What exactly did Stella say to you?"

"Oh, nothing. Just back off or else."

"Or else what?"

"She didn't say." Julia turned on her side, clutched a throw pillow to her chest, and looked askance at one of the Indian portraits on the wall. It seemed to be frowning its disapproval at her.

"Larry, I can't afford any more turmoil. First Blatchley, now Stella is giving me grief. Not to mention Leaping Lenny breathing down my neck. I'm going to have to toe the line."

Larry gazed at her scrunched-up form. "If Stella only knew what happened to you at the Met. How scary it was for you. How the pit was a crime scene. Losing Abel, your mentor, was incredibly hard on you. Devastating." He lay down next to Julia and stroked her hair. "Anything I can do to make it better?"

"Take over the questioning for me."

"Julia, you know I can't."

"If you do it discreetly, no one will even notice, at least hardly." She turned to face him, her expression softening. "Please. I'm slowly losing my mind. And Blatchley is pressuring me."

Julia knew Larry couldn't resist a pout that would put any Parisian *jeune fille* to shame.

"Audacious hussy. You know I turn to mush when you fret so engagingly."

"You wouldn't want me any other way."

"Damn straight," he said, pulling her to him and not letting go.

* * *

A little girl stood in front of a music stand lowered to her diminutive stature. The violin tucked under her chin, a gift to her cash-strapped family from a benevolent donor, was too big for her tiny, ten-year-old frame—so big that she had to stretch her left arm to the max to hold it.

Perched on the stand was a piece of music by a composer named Pietro Mascagni:

CHAPTER TWENTY-ONE

*"Intermezzo" from an opera called "*Cavalleria Rusticana.*"*

Next to the girl, a man with a shock of wavy grey hair, a violin under his chin, was regarding her critically. He tapped his bow on the music stand, nodding his head in rhythm.

The girl creased her forehead, trying to understand the music. Tears began to stream from her eyes. All she wanted to do was escape, to run from the room. But she knew she couldn't; her father would never forgive her.

Finally, she stopped playing. "I hate this music," she cried. "I can't do it."

Her father lowered his violin and looked at her tenderly. "Yes, you can, Julia. You must."

"But why, Daddy?"

"Because this is great music."

"I'll never play it the way you want me to. Why are you so hard on me?"

"I want you to be the best, my darling, as I know you can be."

"No, no, I'll never be as good as you think I should be. I'll never live up to your expectations."

"You will, Julia. I believe in you."

* * *

In the brief moments that night when Julia did manage to sink into oblivion, images she couldn't shake—of herself as a ten-year-old, practicing violin with her father, who was relentless in his insistence that she play the violin to perfection—dominated her slumber. She always had felt incapable of achieving the goals he set for her. Clearly, she still felt incomplete in that regard.

She sat up in bed and revisited the scene in her now-conscious mind. It wasn't until she had grown up, long after her father had been killed, caught in the crossfire of an attempted bank robbery on Broadway across from Lincoln Center, that she realized he not only had wanted her to be the best; he wanted only the best for her.

Not a day went by that she didn't miss him. He was her guiding light, a light that had been snuffed out the day he stood in the path of a streaking bullet to save her from being killed. The bittersweet memories still manifested themselves in her dreams.

"Larry, wake up."

Julia kept nudging Larry until he partially opened his eyes and peered at the digital clock on the night table. "Julia, it's four a.m."

"I know, but I couldn't sleep. I had that dream again."

"The one about your dad? We've been down this road before."

"Yes, but...I suddenly grasped something important. When I first met Blatchley, I sensed he would be far more demanding than he had let on. After working with him, I realize I was spot on."

"And?"

"*And*, now I understand why he's been so tough with me."

Now Larry was listening. "And why is that?"

"It's because he wants me to be the best. Like my dad did. He wouldn't be so demanding if he didn't think I had what it takes."

"Wow, that is eye-opening. You're making perfect sense. I'm proud of you."

"You are?"

"Would I exaggerate?"

"Yes, actually, you would. You do it all the time."

"Well, not this time. Any breakthrough of yours is one for our home team." He kissed her on the cheek. "Any more revelations? Or can we go back to sleep now?"

"We can." Julia looked at him affectionately. "Thanks for being there for me."

"To quote Verdi's Otello, '*per sempre*.' Not 'farewell, sainted memories,' but in the good sense. *Toujours*. Forever—"

"Okay, I get it. Back to sleep, sweet prince," she said, sealing her statement with a kiss.

Chapter Twenty-Two

Ma vegli'l sospetto sui perigli che fremono intorno,
ma protegga il magnanimo petto a chi nulla paventa per sé
But may suspicion of the lurking dangers awaken
to protect the magnanimous soul which fears not for itself
—Verdi, *A Masked Ball*, Act 1

There was no question in Julia's mind that *Roméo et Juliette* was grand opera at its most glorious. The music was sublime and, from what she had seen thus far, the production was sumptuous.

Julia had gotten permission for Larry to attend a stage rehearsal. "Love comes to Santa Fe," Julia told him as they drove to the theatre.

"I think we've proved it's already here," he said.

She ignored his provocative smile.

Julia was glad to see apprentices and former apprentices performing in secondary roles, including Lorelei as Juliette's nurse. Julia had extracted a promise from Larry to subtly question Lorelei about her ambitions regarding taking over Marin's role in the run of *Lulu* performances.

But as Julia approached the pit, she noticed Larry hovering in the background, chatting with a neatly bearded young man who was holding two swords in one hand. She approached the men and whispered in Larry's ear.

"I thought you were going to speak with Lorelei."

"I will later, no worries. This guy is much more interesting," he whispered back. "Julia, have you met Sam Chapman, the opera's fight director?" he said for them both to hear.

Sam extended his free hand. "I loved your solos in *Lulu*," he said. "Gorgeous sound."

She shook his hand, her eyes focused on his swords. "Thanks, I appreciate that. I'm not so sure Blatchley's happy, though."

"He'd be foolish not to recognize how awesomely you handled those solos of yours in far-out rhythms, with simultaneous multiple-note chords. That one where you and the solo cello are playing together, high in the register. I can only imagine the difficulty."

"It's true. You have to stretch your fingers to the max to reach up there," Julia said. "Sometimes it can be painful, especially if you have small hands."

"Then I commend you for suffering to create something beautiful. I'll make my opinion known to Blatchley, just to make sure," he said, smiling.

Julia warmed to him immediately. "You are a gentleman and a scholar."

She could tell Larry was feeling left out when he interrupted and said, "Sam says the swordplay in Act Two is so realistic; he was scared of some disastrous mishap in rehearsal."

"Not exactly," Sam said. "But since Shakespeare's time, audiences have expected lots of audacious swagger and adrenaline-charged swordplay, and that's what we want to deliver. We're fortunate to have a few members of the Wise Fool New Mexico troupe as supernumeraries. Those folks look like they've been sword fighting since they were kids."

"Maybe they have," Julia said.

Sam laughed. "You could be right, Julia. They love being a part of the opera and are more than happy to appear onstage in non-speaking roles. Plus, they're doing a great job helping the chorus members look as true-to-life as possible with their sparring."

"How do you make someone seem like they're stabbing somebody?" Larry asked.

"Aren't they afraid of someone swinging a sharpened steel blade in front of them, or having it pointed right at their face?" Julia added.

"Stage '*epées*'—rapiers—are never sharp. We make sure of that. They all have plastic tips covering the stabbing end. We've been especially careful since the incident with Emilia. Though, of course, that was a stage knife—or was supposed to be," Sam replied. "It's my job to generate the illusion of danger while keeping everyone as safe as possible. Ultimately, after much rehearsal, it should be about as safe as a dance. We even call it fight choreography." Sam pointed at the practice stage. "Even so, I admit having all twelve of those fencers the composer called for, with their foils simultaneously at play onstage, potentially could be dangerous. The trick is to keep sufficient distance between each of them so no one's in harm's way. It can be a fine line. It's also my job to help them conquer their fears.

"Together with Wise Fool, we've been rehearsing outdoors on the opera campus, working with the chorus and other supers, for several weeks on the grass. No weapons at first, slowly working up to speed. By now, they're all pretty much experts."

"I wouldn't mind being a super myself," Larry said. "Do you need any extras?"

Julia shot Larry a threatening glance. "Most people steer clear of fight directors," she said. "If they're smart, that is. I know I would."

"I'm not most people."

"Clearly. And evidently not that smart, either."

"We still have fifteen minutes till rehearsal starts," Sam said. "If you'd like, I can show you two a few stage combat moves."

"I appreciate the offer, but having said I steer clear of fight directors, I should stick to my words," Julia said. "Besides, I have to warm up."

"Oh, come on, Julia, it'll be fun," Larry said. "You don't have any solos in this opera to worry about. You're off the hook there."

This time, it was Julia who couldn't resist Larry's pout. Sighing, she followed him and Sam outside to a large, empty space near the white baffles.

"On the topic of handling a sword, have you visited La Fonda Hotel?" Sam asked.

"No," said Larry. "Why?"

"In 1940, when Errol Flynn was here for the premiere of *Santa Fe Trail*, he was staying at La Fonda. After the opening, he went back to the hotel and knocked back a few too many Margaritas. He started leaping between balconies, perching on balustrades, fencing with an imaginary adversary, and quoting lines from his movie, *Robin Hood*. Evidently, he thought he was back on his Hollywood set. The episode has become legend."

Larry whistled. "Not my style, but very cool."

Julia was fascinated. As a kid she had loved watching vintage action movies based on adventure novels, which evoked her inner Sir Walter Scott.

Sam handed a rapier each to Julia and Larry and showed them how to position their fingers on the narrow handle. "Keep a tight pincer grip. It should move freely in your hand. The cup hilt will protect your fingers. Especially important for you, Julia, as a violinist."

Julia weighed the handle in her hand. "Definitely heavier than a violin bow."

"You'll get used to it quickly enough," Sam said. "First thing you need to know is that it's natural to feel apprehensive holding the thing. You can get past it by thinking of this as a ballet rather than an adversarial battle."

"Oh, we're used to those. Adversarial battles, that is," Larry said with a wink.

Julia grimaced. "Suddenly, I'm feeling like I want to learn how to use this thing after all."

Sam smiled. "I can only imagine. Now, swords in front of you, turn so your sides face each other. That's the narrowest part of your body, so you present the smallest target. Extend your arms. This is called taking your measure; it's for safety. At this distance, you can see that you can't actually hurt each other. Larry, raise your weapon, thrust your foil as if you're going to skewer Julia. When you see that threat, Julia, raise the tip of your sword and deflect—sweep it over and around Larry's blade."

Sam demonstrated the movement he was describing. "Now step through, Julia, like this, and turn, so you're shoulder to shoulder with Larry. Nudge his shoulder with your sword arm. Remember, this is pretend, it's for show. And this is super important—be careful not to hit Larry's shoulder too hard. You can jar the nerve and make his arm go numb. With your other hand, slap your own thigh on the side the audience can't see—that makes a sound we call a 'knap'—and it will sound like you hit him pretty hard. Remember, just a nudge. Larry, sell the blow by acting like she walloped you. That's it. Lastly, Julia, use your thrust to deflect his sword, sweep his blade aside, right here, like this…knocking it out of his grasp."

When they had blocked out the fight, Julia, who had studied ballet before she had started playing the violin and was proficient at movement as well as following directions, executed Sam's instructions seamlessly. She parried Larry's thrust, quickly closed the space between them, turned, shouldered Larry. Then, sure enough, she smacked the sword smartly right out of Larry's hand. It clattered to the pavement.

Julia was amazed and pleased. She flashed a gratified smirk at Larry. "Wow, you were right, Larry. This is fun, after all."

"Beginner's luck," Larry muttered.

"I disagree, Larry. I think Julia's got a real gift. She's impressively light on her feet."

Julia could see Larry was trying his best to acknowledge her gratified smirk.

"Eight minutes," called the PA. "This is your eight-minute call, ladies and gentlemen."

Julia handed her sword to Sam. "I hate to leave you two warriors, but I actually have a real job," she said with a triumphant grin and strode toward the hall.

Sam turned to Larry. "I have to go, too. A few last-minute tweaks to the combatants' choreography before the music starts. Keep at it."

He walked off as Larry continued to practice his thrust and parry.

＊＊＊

Julia returned to the theatre in time to watch Sam make his last-minute adjustments. She was impressed with the way he put the choristers and supernumeraries through their paces, showing them how to make imitation kicks and punches look real. He clearly was a pro.

Sam showed a super how to simulate touching another person. "It's actually a 'para' punch, but we have to hear the knap—the sound of it. One way or another, the other guy has to end up on the floor. And the audience has to feel that the end result is going to be death."

The super in question followed Sam's instructions. Sam nodded his approval. "Well done. And I know you're having fun, but stop smiling," he said with a grin.

He turned to the two singers who were playing the dueling rivals, Tybalt and Mercutio.

"Remember, Mercutio, you're out for his blood. You can almost taste it. Make it look different from every other Mercutio-Tybalt fight you've ever seen on an opera stage," Sam said, as he watched them. "Side kick to the back of his thigh. Make that shoulder punch look real. No contact to his knee, okay? Here, let me demonstrate." Sam executed a quick movement and let the actors continue. "That's it! Fantastic. Your fencing is as dazzling as your singing."

After Julia had tuned the orchestra and taken her seat, she saw Larry wave to her from about midway back in the orchestra section. She mouthed the word "Lorelei" to him. He nodded and gestured a thumbs-up.

Stewart climbed up to the podium. "Act Two," he announced. "Fight scene."

Julia was trying not to watch the stage as she negotiated the aggressively difficult violin part. But between the slashing and stabbing on stage and the powerful, goose-bump-inducing music, both in the orchestra and from the singers, she was having a hard time concentrating.

Capulets, Capulets! Montaigus, Montaigus! Race immonde! Frémissez de terreur!

Que l'enfer seconde...Sa Haine et sa fureur!

[Capulets, Capulets! Montagues, Montagues! Vile clan! Shake with terror!...

May hell assist our hate and our fury!]

Unable to restrain herself despite risking Stewart's ire, Julia chanced a look up at the stage. At the very back, at the far limit of her sight line, a shadowy figure who was not in costume and clearly not part of the action crept in the background behind the players.

What...who...?

From the person's attire—Bermuda shorts and a straw hat—Julia could tell he or she was not a stagehand. When she blinked, the figure disappeared. Puzzled, she shook her head and turned her attention back to the action, wincing as she saw Mercutio throw Tybalt to the floor with all-too-convincing violence. Tybalt recovered his balance, jumped up, and, as Mercutio came to offer him a hand up, vengefully ran Mercutio through.

A grief-stricken Romeo confronted Tybalt.

Tybalt! Il n'est ici d'autre lâche que toi! À toi...!

[Tybalt, you're the only coward here now! To you...!]

Romeo drew his sword from his scabbard. He swung it once in a furious "*en garde.*" As he did, Julia was horrified to see the blade suddenly separate from the hilt. Even more terrifying, the blade was flying full force toward the pit.

And it was coming straight at her.

Chapter Twenty-Three

Mir sträubt sich schon das Haar...mir fällt kein Mittel ein!
My hair stands on end...I can see no way out!
—Beethoven, *Fidelio*, Act 1

A collective gasp emitted from both stage and pit as performers watched the blade hurtle through the air, graze the left side of Julia's rib cage, and crash onto the pit floor with a loud clang. Julia was more worried about the damage to her instrument than to herself. With only a split second to react, she instinctively clutched her violin to her chest and turned, presenting the narrowest part of her body.

Larry, watching from his seat in the hall, leapt up, tore down the aisle to the pit, and leaned over the rail. "Julia, what happened? Are you all right?" Seeing the gash in her torso, he drew in a deep breath. "Oh, my God, you're hurt!"

Not waiting for a reply, he rushed to the backstage area, climbed up to the pit door, threw it open, and pushed his way through the music stands and musicians to Julia's desk, where he could see she was immensely shaken.

Matt, hovering over her with concern, murmured to Larry. "She doesn't seem as agitated as I'd expect. I think she's in shock. In any case, they've called 911."

Julia, her arms still wrapped protectively around her violin, murmured through tight lips. "It's only a scratch. I'm fine."

"You definitely are not. You're bleeding," Larry said. He felt her hands and gazed at her ashen face. "You're pale. Your hands feel clammy. And you're definitely agitated."

She looked down at her left flank and frowned. "Doesn't matter, as long as the fiddle is okay. Good thing I wore red today."

"You're right; she is in shock," Larry murmured to Matt.

Two EMTs approached Larry. One of them took Julia's wrist. "Her pulse is racing."

"There's a stretcher waiting in the hallway," the other said. "No room for it in here. I'll have to carry her out."

"I don't need a stretcher," Julia said. "I'm fine."

"You're in shock," Larry said. "They're going to take you to the hospital."

"But...my violin—"

"Give it to me," Matt said. "I'll take good care of it."

He reached for the instrument, but Julia still gripped it tightly. Larry gently pried it away. "You always can trust Matt, Julia," Larry said. "You know that, don't you?"

"Yes, I do, but..." She started to swoon. "I feel a little...spacey."

The EMT caught her before she keeled over. Julia reluctantly let go of the violin, relinquishing it to Matt, as the EMT held her tightly and wrapped gauze around her torso.

Sam rushed to Julia's side, panicked. "Julia! I'm so sorry. I don't know how this happened. We've never seen anything like it. We'll find out who's to blame for this, I promise."

"It's...it's...not your fault, Sam," she said, trying to catch her breath. "It must have been John Crosby. I saw him lurking around the back of the stage during the fight scene."

Sam frowned at Larry, who raised his eyebrows at Matt. "Shock," Larry whispered.

"But...didn't you say that the...the blades weren't sharp, Sam?" Julia asked.

Sam picked the blade up from the floor and inspected it. "They shouldn't be."

Stella and Constantin arrived on the scene a moment later. Stella caught sight of Julia's wrapped torso. "Whoa, what's going on? Are you all right, Julia?"

"Does she look all right?" Larry said.

"No, poor thing, she doesn't. How did this happen?" Stella looked at Sam and the fragmented blade in his hand. "Who are you? What's the deal with that sword?"

"I'm the fight director," Sam said. "The rapier came apart when one of the singers pulled it from his scabbard. It flew off the stage—and into Julia."

"Holy crap. Has that ever happened?" Stella asked.

"Never," Sam said. "In fact, this one doesn't look like one of ours. First thing, it's too sharp. And the plastic tip is missing. Someone has tinkered with it."

Constantin didn't wait for Stella to react. He pulled two evidence bags from his pocket, placed them at either end of the sword, and held it firmly.

Meanwhile, one of the EMTs carefully lifted Julia up. "We'd better get her in the ambulance pronto." Acting swiftly, he carried her out of the pit, making sure to avoid bumping into any music stands, and placed her on the waiting stretcher outside the door.

Larry turned to the other EMT. "I'm riding in the ambulance," he said.

They both hurried out of the pit. Matt stayed behind, Julia's violin in his grasp.

Stella held Sam's gaze. "Don't go anywhere."

* * *

At the hospital ER, Larry watched as the resident cleaned and dressed Julia's laceration. "She was very lucky. A blade that penetrates the rib cage can do a bunch of damage. Collapse a lung, lacerate the liver. This was a superficial flesh wound, no stitches required," the resident said. "But she'll have to be careful about keeping it clean." He handed Larry a sheet of discharge instructions. "She should follow up with her PCP," he said.

"No can do," Larry said. "We're from out of state, here for the summer."

"Then be extra careful about changing the dressing. Watch for fever above a hundred-and-one, swelling, or excessive draining. And bring her back here in two days for a follow-up."

"That we can do."

Julia began to moan softly. Then she murmured, "'The Royal Town of the Holy Faith of St. Francis of Assisi.' That's so beautiful. Can we go to Assisi in Italy, Larry? It would make my Inner Catholic happy."

"You are a strange creature." Larry turned to the resident. "Could she be hallucinating?"

"It's possible," the resident said. "She's been through a trauma. You should take her home."

"Are you okay to go?" Larry asked Julia.

"Of course," she said, but without her usual conviction. "I need to get back to rehearsal."

The resident shook his head. "I'm afraid no violin playing for you till after your follow-up. At least for the next couple of days."

"But…they're expecting me to work."

"Not after what you've been through." Larry addressed the resident. "Thanks for your help, Doc."

With his arm held firmly around her waist, Larry led the incoherent Julia out of the ER and toward the hospital entrance.

"I'm going to find out who's responsible for this," Julia said, with as much self-reliance as she could muster in her weakened state.

"Are you delirious? You asked me a while ago to take over questioning for you. Now you want to start investigating again?"

"How can I not?"

"Easy," said Larry. "Let the SFPD handle it."

"They've already got their hands full," Julia said. But her resolve was flagging.

"And so do you. Healing your wound." Larry helped Julia into the Lyft car, awaiting them in front of the hospital. "No arguments."

"I do appreciate your trying to take such good care of me, Larry, but—"

"But nothing. Taking care of you, not to mention keeping you from getting into yet another heap of trouble, is a tough job. But I'm happy to do it."

Julia brooded for a moment as she stared out the car window. She wasn't ready to give up yet. "And what about Marin? She's still in trouble. I promised her to do everything I could to help her cause. I can't give up now."

"You're injured," Larry said. "She'll understand."

The car sped through the streets. Julia didn't even try to hide her discontent.

* * *

Marin was worried. She had not heard from Julia since Julia had visited the prison the first time. Other than a brief note from Blatchley, no one else from the company had contacted her. She had been allowed to send an email to her vocal coach at the Met Opera, asking for help in finding a lawyer who might get her released from prison. The response was not what Marin had hoped for. No New York attorney would be allowed jurisdiction in the state of New Mexico.

"I'm doomed to rot in this prison," Marin thought. "What the hell has happened to Julia?"

Alone, forsaken, despairing, Marin found she had nothing but time. Time stretching before her in alarming quantities. Time to contemplate one of her favorite quotes from one of her most admired writers from hundreds of years before, which now terrified her.

Abandon hope, all ye who enter here.

Chapter Twenty-Four

Dalla sua pace la mia dipende...È mia quell'ira, quel pianto è mio
**On her peace of mind my own depends...her anger and her sorrow
are mine**
—Mozart, *Don Giovanni*, Act 1

Julia was still moping when the car dropped her and Larry in front of the inn. But her expression turned to surprise when she saw Sándor standing by the fireplace in the lobby.

He rose and approached the couple, his brow knit with worry. "Julia, I was so distressed when I heard what happened. Is there anything I can do?"

"Sándor, you didn't have to come all the way here to check on me. I'm fine."

"It's no trouble. I needed to know you were not in danger. Maestro also wanted me to let you know not to be concerned about work. He said to take your time and heal."

"That's very big of him," Julia said, surprised and a bit wary.

Sándor indicated a large, comfy leather sofa. "Might you have a moment to talk?"

Larry frowned. "She's supposed to rest. Doctor's orders."

"I have two days to do that, Larry. I want to hear what he has to say," Julia said. "It's not every day Blatchley shows signs of sympathy. Hell has frozen over."

Julia wearily sank into the sofa. Larry gave her a worried look but made no attempt to argue. When all three were seated, Sándor took Julia's hand

and looked into her eyes.

"You've had a difficult time since being here, and I feel terrible about it. I wanted to offer suggestion to help you cope."

"After what I've been through, I'm open to anything."

"I've been living here long time and am familiar with stresses of performing in our company," Sándor said. "We are all family, tribe if you will, devoted to our way of life and to one objective. Highest possible standard in every undertaking. That was Crosby's ideal."

"I'm certainly aware of it by now." Julia's interest was piqued. "And?"

"We've followed that principle at Santa Fe Opera ever since Crosby first guided modest but daring troupe of freethinking artists in tiny open-air theater first season. He kept on that pathway in all his efforts, leading from podium or planting flowers and bushes in gardens. He didn't care if some critics called contemporary operas unsingable or decadent, as was case with *Lulu*. If Maestro Blatchley is tough with you, it is only because he is committed to maintaining paradigm."

"What's your point?" Larry asked.

"Creating art is gift that comes from greater being. As artists, we have 'divine afflatus,' spiritual element we are attuned to that helps us access highest selves, feeds us and propels us into creative realms we could not conceive of ourselves. I think we have ability to be in touch with, to reflect it upon those around us." Sándor paused. "I remember when preparing to sing tough role of Apollo in *Daphne*. It felt fine working on, but when I got out there and started to struggle I thought, 'What is going to happen here?' Then something came over me and suddenly I was in total control. I surprised myself how well I sang. Moments like that…for performer they happen without necessarily knowing how they happen."

"Creative people are not always the nicest to be around, though." Given her recent experiences, Julia was well aware of that fact. "Beethoven, cranky. Brahms, blustery. Mahler, grumpy. Not to mention conductors, who are in a class by themselves."

"True. But when we get out of our own way, afflatus makes us respond to its own spiritual harmonies and wonderful things happen, especially in extraordinary atmosphere of Santa Fe," Sándor said. "I strongly believe in spiritual energy of early Indigenous people here. It gives us beauty, mystery, and feeds our art. I have friend, Miles, Navajo shaman and spiritualist, leads one-day vision quests up in mountains. I think he can help you heal, physically and spiritually."

"What makes you think she needs spiritual healing?" Larry said.

"Most of us need our sprits fed. With high, dry climate, azure skies, mountains and canyons, here we live in one of most restorative environments in world," Sándor said. "Julia has been through much difficulty in short time. She might benefit from resetting her spiritual compass, to help overcome traumas, to live fully in present. It might help you, too, Larry."

"Me? It's not in my DNA to be spiritual."

"If you have questions, Larry, I am happy to answer them," Sándor said. "Let me give you my cell number. You can send me text whenever you like."

"If you insist."

"Thank you." Sándor tapped his number into Larry's phone.

"Sandor's right, Larry. I have been dealing with a ton of stuff since I've been here. I need to sort things out, in a different atmosphere from here. And I have two days to do it." Julia turned to Sandor. "I'm in."

"Julia, you can't be serious," Larry said. "The doc said you need to rest."

"Unburdening my stress will benefit me more."

"If that's what you want, I'm all for it," said Larry. "But count me out."

Julia's challenging gaze countered Larry's skeptical one. "I don't think so," she said.

Chapter Twenty-Five

Cosi accasciata? Via, mia bella signora, sedete qui...e favelliamo
So downhearted? Come, my fair lady, sit down here...and we'll talk
—Puccini, *Tosca*, Act 2

J ulia and Larry met Miles on a high desert mesa in the Sangre de Cristo Mountains, ninety miles northeast of Santa Fe. To the east lay the western border of the Great Plains. To the west, the eastern edge of the Taos Plateau. Ponderosa pine forests, rocky ridges, valleys, and meadows were visible in all directions. The setting was exquisite.

Miles's rugged, weather-worn face, waist-length ebony-colored hair, and broad shoulders made him seem older and taller than he was: serene and otherworldly, despite his work shirt and frayed jeans. The dreamcatcher hanging from the rearview mirror of his van, a drum encircled by eagle feathers, was a clue to his mystical nature.

The first thing he did was hug Julia and Larry. He took note of Julia's surprise and Larry's discomfort. "It's normal for some men to feel awkward at a stranger's hug," Miles said, smiling.

"That's not the only thing that makes me feel uncomfortable here," Larry said.

"I understand, Larry. Some people are reluctant to connect with their higher selves and to believe in the concept of becoming one with the Spirit."

He pulled a photo from his shirt pocket, which showed a handsome Native American man in army uniform. "This is my dad. When he came back from Vietnam, his PTSD was so severe that he lost his way in a haze of alcohol.

He found himself again by doing vision quests. He never drank again." A faint smile crossed his lips. "Then one of our Navajo brothers taught Dad to make traditional pottery. Now, his work is considered some of the most authentic, being sold at the Native American market in Santa Fe Plaza. The Opera also has commissioned this year's poster art from him."

Julia's eyes shone. "What an inspiring story."

Miles gently clasped Larry's hand. "Our ancestors called this land *Dancing Ground of the Sun*. New Mexico's most magnificent mountains surround us, mountains whose crystalline rock core is five-hundred-seventy-million years old. The ley lines, the invisible straight lines that connect important and sacred sites the world over, crisscross Santa Fe to create a special electromagnetic energy vortex, heightening the spiritual and psychic energy of our terrain. As the day evolves, you will comprehend the worth of our journey."

The shaman reached inside his van and pulled out three highly ornamented drums and three colorful pueblo-style blankets. He offered Julia and Larry each a blanket and a drum.

"Sándor tells me you've come from New York to perform with the Santa Fe Opera here, Julia," Miles said. "As a kid growing up, I watched dress rehearsals from their Pueblo Opera Program, where they bused us to the theatre from the reservations. I was skeptical at first, but then I became hooked on opera. Now, I am eternally grateful for that opportunity."

Miles seated himself cross-legged on the ground, wrapped a blanket around his shoulders, and gestured to Julia and Larry to do the same. "Julia, Sándor told me about your recent traumas. Would you like to know more about what the Great Spirit has in mind for you?"

Julia, sitting on the ground beside Miles, was beginning to feel drawn to his fervor and to the dynamism of his personality. She nodded. Larry took a seat beside her and stayed close.

"The desert is a place of revelation, where we retreat in order to meditate, to return to civilization with wisdom and clarity. In our wilderness ceremony, we learn unifying lessons of love that have eluded us since leaving childhood by forming a meaningful relationship with human nature and

Mother Earth and removing the masks we wear that distort our normal ego consciousness. This broadens our limitations and deepens our connection to Nature, beckoning us to reconnect with our ancient tribal roots. It is a deeply transformative journey of self-discovery that is woven into our Indigenous culture. The wisdom and experience of our Native American ancestors, especially the Anasazi cliff dwellers, will help us on our path."

"How do I know if it will help *me*?" Julia asked.

"Mother Earth does not exclude anyone," Miles said. "Thus, all are invited to experience our native transformative ceremony to discover their own power, as we are surrounded by the geologic wonders of our lands. That is why we use these ancient shamanistic tools. A vision quest will guide you to physical and spiritual healing."

Larry stared down at his drum, frowning.

"I'm sure you're wondering about the rationale behind our drumming, Larry," Miles said. "Rhythm has been a part of our makeup since we were conceived. We are created from it. Drumming connects us with larger, cosmic rhythms—of the seasons, the planets, the galaxy— and most importantly, with the mountain ranges and diverse cultures of the Pueblos around us," Miles said. "The Tiwa people of the Taos Pueblo pray the sun up daily. Look around you, and you will see petroglyphs of the Pueblo peoples etched into many boulders."

Julia turned her head and spied a rock escarpment with symbols engraved on it. She motioned to Larry, who raised his eyebrows in acknowledgment.

"As you drum, close your eyes and think of yourself as unbound from your mental turmoil." Miles demonstrated a slow, gentle rhythmic tapping. "Clear your body and mind, that you can contemplate who you are and who you have always wanted to be. Remove the toxins from your soul. All things around you—rocks, trees, air, birds, even your blankets—are alive, mindful, and voicing their being to you."

Miles continued to drum. He nodded to Larry.

"You try, Julia," Larry said. "You're the musician."

"We are all musicians of the spirit," Miles said. "Mother Earth responds most generously to collective communication from all of us."

Julia, eyes closed, imitated Miles's example. After a moment, Larry tentatively joined them. Soon, the sounds of their beating punctuated the mountain air.

"A mind preoccupied with thoughts and worries will hinder your understanding of the Spirit. Divest yourself of the debris that litters your mind, Julia. Think about your traumas. Not only recent ones but those from times past. What hunger at your soul level needs to be satisfied?"

As Julia further immersed herself in the hypnotizing rhythm of her drumming, she became cognizant of her obsession with her work responsibilities. Visions played in her mind: she with her violin, Abel, her father, and Sidney, all hovering over her, love and caring in their regard. An unexpected emptiness began to ache inside of her. She was grieving for the loss of her father, of Abel, of Sidney. She was worried about losing Marin. She felt broken. Then, a desire overcame her to connect more deeply with Larry, to know him, and to better understand their relationship. Profound sobs that seemed as if they would never end surged up from her core.

"Be in touch with your pain, Julia," Miles said. Give it back to Mother Earth."

Larry stopped drumming and glared at Miles. "This is not helping," he said. "I don't like seeing her so upset."

"On the contrary, Larry. It is all part of the process. By healing herself, she is healing the Earth, returning the Earth's gifts to the living creatures around us."

Julia was too engrossed in her personal experiences to be aware of the conversation. In her mind, she could see the approval in her father's and Abel's expressions that soothed her soul.

We're always with you.

Then, the specter of a man in a tuxedo holding a baton entered the image and gave her a penetrating stare. At first, she was confused, but when she recognized him from the photos she had seen of John Crosby in his conductor's attire, she gasped.

Is he trying to tell me something? Is he distraught over all the violence in his company?

The true identity of the mysterious figure she had seen lurking in the shadows behind the opera house still eluded Julia, but whether or not it actually had been the ghost of Crosby seemed less important than the message that came to her over the divide:

Find the killer.

∗ ∗ ∗

After what seemed like hours, Julia's visions started to fade. She felt a profound sadness, but ultimately, she was filled with a tranquility deeper than any she had ever known. The wound in her side no longer hurt. Her fears and feelings of emptiness inside were replaced with what could only be the Spirit that Miles had described. She knew she was on her way to healing, ready for anything life was going to hand her from that point onward. Then she opened her eyes to the most exquisite sunset she had ever seen, a golden orb that seemed to melt into the horizon.

"When the Native Pueblo Indians briefly overcame the Spanish in the Revolt of 1680," Miles said, "A dying Spanish priest prayed to heaven for a sign. The radiance of the sky as it turned crimson was what he had yearned for. He died with the words, '*Sangre de Cristo,*' 'The Blood of Christ,' on his lips. That's how these mountains got their name." He gave Julia a penetrating gaze, focusing on her half-heart locket at her throat and the tiny gold Star of David visible behind it. "But perhaps your ancestors date back much further than that? From the Spanish Jewry who persisted in practicing their religion in secret despite persecution and danger, somewhere between the tenth and eighteenth centuries?"

"I...I'm ashamed to say I know very little about the Crypto-Jews, though I am aware of their success culturally in New Mexico," Julia said. "But you're right. They undoubtedly are a part of my heritage."

"An important part. Inquisition trial records clearly show that they not only could be found among the New Mexico colonists in the mid-1600s, but with few exceptions, their presence did not attract attention from the authorities. They made huge efforts to keep alive their achievements in science, philosophy, and the arts after they were expelled from Spain and Portugal and managed to gain a foothold in North America, coming from across the continent."

"So much of the culture here seems dominated by Spanish, Mexican, Native American, and Jewish influences," Julia said. "Can you imagine what it's like to grow up in such a multicultural atmosphere?"

"Actually, yes," Larry said. "It's called New York City. This is like a small slice of it, but much more laid back."

"You're right, Larry. And when it comes to the Crypto-Jews, symbols of their struggle for aesthetic identity appear even today, all over our lands," Miles said. "You might find a menorah engraved on a tombstone in a Catholic burial ground or evidence of the oral histories of the Jews' roots in the Hispanic villages where hereditary groupings speak to Jewish ancestry. Knowledge of a Jewish past has been handed down through the generations to the present time. Even if you don't have the opportunity to explore this on your own in person, Julia, it's worth contemplating to keep your personal vision quest, your individual struggle alive, and ask Mother Earth for enlightenment about it."

Miles allowed Julia several minutes of deep reflection. Then he stood up. "Let's join hands and thank Mother Earth for her endowments."

He hummed softly for a long moment. Then he let go of Julia and Larry's hands and handed them each a small red stone. "This is a gift of your retreat. Keep it as a reminder of the love and constant presence of the Spirit."

He gave them each another hug. Julia wasn't sure, but she thought that the hug she received from Miles was longer and more intense than the one he gave Larry.

In any case, she was now ready to tackle the job at hand: to pour her heart and soul into performing opera. To exonerate Marin and obtain her release. And to find out who was behind the brutal murder of a recalcitrant soprano.

Chapter Twenty-Six

Ich glaube, es ist schon lange her, dass er gefangen ist?
Er muss ein grosser Verbrecher sein!...
oder er muss grosse Feinde haben
I believe he has been imprisoned for a long time?
He must have committed a huge crime!...
Or he must have great enemies
—Beethoven, *Fidelio*, Act 1

D.A. Cordero sat at the table in the county jail interrogation room opposite Marin and her defense attorney, Elaine. Marin had lost so much weight that her prison jumpsuit hung off her body. Elaine had informed Marin that Henry had fast-tracked the trial date in order to secure swift sentencing. What Marin didn't know was that the D.A. had been coordinating with Stella Peregrine, who had been frequenting the forensics lab at the New Mexico Department of Public Safety, making note of their results and consulting with them about providing their expert testimony in Marin's trial. Stella also had questioned Deborah, who had confirmed Marin's deep-seated resentment about Deborah's transferring her affections to Emilia.

Elaine had been conferring with the DPS lab and with the lab's assigned analyst to keep track of the case's status and to arm herself with as much information as possible, anything that might mitigate Marin's situation.

Unfortunately, there was little evidence to favor Marin. Subsequent testing confirmed the initial findings, and no other evidence was available.

The Latent Print Unit had processed the knife and the crime scene for the presence of invisible prints. Elaine knew they used the latest scientific chemical and illumination techniques in their search efforts and, when relevant, also used AFIS, aka the Automated Fingerprint Identification System, to compare prints with other records in their database. They also would offer testimony if needed.

The Biology Unit had analyzed the weapon and the scene for DNA and compared it with Marin's. The fact that none of Marin's DNA was evident on Emilia's body was the only factor in Marin's favor. Other than that, there was nothing to help plead Marin's case, aside from her being a first-time offender. With so little to go on, Elaine was at a loss when Henry made his plea offer.

"Twenty-five years to life," he said.

"You've got to be kidding, Henry. Marin has never so much as killed a cockroach. Five years and a fifteen thousand dollar fine."

"What you're proposing is a sentence for a first-degree felony. A fine is not part of the picture when it comes to murder. She's committed a capital crime."

"You'll have to prove it first. The jury will side with her for sure."

"What makes you think so? She bumped off a famous opera singer, with whom she had a known dispute that resulted in witnessed heated discussions on more than one occasion."

"Marin's famous, too. Or have you forgotten?"

"Then there's her jealousy over the stolen lover," Henry added hastily. "Whose identity, by the way, we've confirmed."

Marin tried to suppress her tremors of fear. "Excuse me," she said. "I'm right here."

"No judge is going to sentence a woman as severely as you're proposing," Elaine said.

"I disagree. Women's incarceration rates have exploded over the last few years," Henry said. "If she takes the plea, at least she'll have the possibility of parole."

Elaine flashed an inquiring look in Marin's direction.

Marin shook her head. "I'm innocent," she said through her teeth.

"I know you are," said Elaine. "We're done here, Henry."

"Suit yourself. But don't wait too long. The offer will get cold before you know it."

* * *

Sex. Violence. To Julia, at times, that seemed to be all that opera was about. It certainly was true in the current Santa Fe Opera season.

By the time Julia had returned to work, she already had missed two days of rehearsal for the next opera, *Lucia di Lammermoor*. One of the most famous of the so-called *"bel canto"* operas, with a legendary mad scene for the coloratura soprano, *Lucia* was about jealousy and sexual manipulation and featured one of the most brutal murders in the opera repertoire, albeit one that thankfully took place offstage.

Larry, who had gotten permission to attend the rehearsal, accompanied Julia to the pit to make sure she was psychologically ready to handle being back at work after her recent traumas and the intense vision quest experience. He could tell from her general mien that she was apprehensive.

"Are you positive you're up for this?" he asked her.

"Oh, sure. Blatchley's been on my case since day one. Between him and 'Lurching Lenny' behind me, I've got enemy eyes and ears waiting for me to screw up," Julia said. "Other than that, I'm golden."

"It won't be long before you develop a thick enough skin to be resistant to Blatchley's criticisms and reproaches and to Lenny's nonsense," Larry said. "At least you're done with *Lulu* and all its butchery."

"*Lucia* may be in Italian, which sounds less violent than German. But even if the murder happens offstage, the opera's almost as bloody as *Lulu*."

"Point taken."

Having determined Julia was in possession of her faculties enough to perform, Larry ensconced himself in the second row of the theatre: at a respectful distance from the conductor but close enough to keep a watchful eye on her.

Julia received warm greetings from her orchestra colleagues, with the exception of Lenny who, predictably, looked none too thrilled to see her. Matt was especially attentive with smiles and sympathetic gestures.

As the musicians entered the pit, Paul, the flutist who had hinted at having seen John Crosby's ghost, whispered to Julia. "I'm surprised to see you back so soon. How did you manage such a speedy healing from your injury?"

Julia wasn't sure she knew Paul well enough to confide in him. But he did seem more open to so-called "spiritual" phenomena than other orchestra members.

"I went on a vision quest," she said softly.

"Wise choice. I applaud you. A vision quest is the best way to neutralize negativity."

"You've done it?"

"Many times. Most of us musicians have outside interests to handle performance stress. The second clarinetist studies astronomy and archaeology. The timpanist solves math problems in his extra time. The first trombone likes to fish. And then there are our softball matches," said Paul. "For me, it's vision quests. They can help you cope. Especially if you're sensitive to the spirits haunting this part of the world. And there are too many to count around here."

Julia winced, remembering her unsettling encounters, both in her room at the inn and in La Posada's "Julia Staab Suite," not to mention her sightings of what looked like Crosby's ghost.

"I've…seen a presence," Julia whispered.

"I see," Paul said. "Do you want to talk about it?" Seeing her hesitation, he said, "Most ghosts are easy, benevolent. Nothing to be afraid of. If you'd like to share any of your experiences, I'm happy to listen."

"Some other time. But thanks for asking."

Luckily there were no violin solos in *Lucia*, so Blatchley did not seem annoyed at Julia's absence from work. In fact, he was surprisingly solicitous to her.

"Are you all right, Julia? Not in too much pain, I hope?" he asked after she had tuned the orchestra.

"I'm fine, Stewart, thank you for asking. Two days off were all I needed."

"Good, good."

Well, that is an unexpected relief.

Julia suppressed a sigh. The conductor's effort at being concerned suddenly reminded her of the real difficulties that lay ahead. Somehow, despite the trials she had been through so far, she still would have to reestablish her abilities to handle the stresses of being the number one violinist and leader of the orchestra. In order to cope, she summoned up the spirit of her beloved mentor at the Met.

Please give me strength and courage, Abel. I could really use your help right now. I'm not sure I can do this.

To her surprise, in her psychic mind, she received a response.

I'm always with you, but you can do this on your own. Coraggio.

Hearing in her mind the Italian word for courage, perhaps the most oft-heard phrase in all of opera, Julia steeled herself. Abel was right. She was determined to prove herself up to the task at hand.

Stewart turned to the assembled musicians. "Act Two Sextet, please."

Lucia was not Julia's favorite Donizetti opera. She much preferred the composer's comedies, especially the captivating *Don Pasquale*, which, she had been told, was one of the great diva Beverly Sills's much-loved roles at the Met.

However, Julia had been a huge fan of Sir Walter Scott's evocative novels when she was growing up. Scotland's flamboyant—and bloody—history fascinated her. She had heard that the greatest operatic legend to sing the role of Sir Walter's Lucy of Lammermoor was Dame Joan Sutherland. Julia wished she had been around to see Sutherland and Sills perform.

Alejandro Fernandez, the production's South American director, made his wishes known to the ranks. "Places, please. Harold, collect everyone if you can."

The stage manager shepherded chorus and ballet members who had been peppering the stage. Alejandro then arranged the players in formation for the wedding reception scene.

"Chorus, make this a celebration to remember. The contrast between it and the tragedy to come must be startling."

Julia was surprised to look up at the stage and see Deborah take her place as lead soprano and protagonist Lucia.

"Deborah, again?" Julia said to Matt. "Isn't that unusual for an apprentice?"

He nodded. "She's been understudying everything. Her success story as apprentice-suddenly-turned-diva will go down in the annals of the company."

That seemed a bit over the top to Julia. "I wonder what Rob has to say about that."

"Ask him. I'm sure he'll fill your ear, as always. In her defense, she did jump in at the eleventh hour last season as Norina in *Don Pasquale* and did a fantastic job. They appreciate that sort of thing here."

"So I've learned." Julia watched a male singer move close to Deborah. "Who's that?"

"Adam Conrad, the *comprimario* tenor who plays Lucia's arranged husband, Arturo," Matt said. "Strangely enough, he's not an apprentice."

Julia lowered her voice to a confidential whisper. "He's terribly cute. I can't imagine this 'Bride of Lammermoor' could object to being married to him, whether it's diplomatically advantageous or not."

Alejandro steered Adam and Deborah toward the apron of the stage, where Julia was close enough to catch the drift of the two singers' conversation.

"SFeO's catchphrase for *Lucia* is 'a wedding to die for,'" said Adam.

"Well, that's what the lead tenor Edgardo gets for going off to France to flirt with French girls and leaving me in the lurch," Deborah said with a tinge of haughtiness. "Although a guy as hot as you could do worse, all things considered."

"And yet you reward me by stabbing me to death?"

Deborah chortled. "How else would I have an excuse to lose my mind in front of two thousand people?"

Chapter Twenty-Seven

Der Irrsinn hat sich meiner Vernunft schon bemächtigt
Madness has conquered my reason already
—Berg, *Lulu*, Act 2

The other four singers gathered around Deborah and Adam for the Sextet.

"Remember, Deborah, you are a woman on the verge of total emotional collapse who cannot bear your present reality," Alejandro said. "You're torn between forbidden love and family duty. This scene foreshadows your impending withdrawal into complete insanity."

Stewart tapped his baton on the podium. Julia followed his downbeat, leading the stream of plucking in the opening phrases by the strings. She listened as the principal tenor expressed his fury.

Chi mi frena in tal momento, chi troncò dell'ira il corso?

[Who restrains me at such a moment, who stemmed the flood of my anger?]

As the *pizzicati* transformed into a soaring melody, Julia had to admit the melody of the sextet was pleasurable, both to play and to hear. Donizetti certainly could write tunes on par with the best. Plus, he was astonishingly prolific: no less than sixty-five operas. The sweeping melodies of the Sextet brought to mind a caricature she had seen of the composer with a pen in each hand, writing simultaneously with both.

"Very good, everyone," Stewart called out. "Act Three, Mad Scene, please."

Julia watched Alejandro reposition the players onstage, shuffling them about like a deck of cards and moving Deborah, Adam, and the other soloists off.

The chorus sang of their exultation over the grand celebratory wedding reception.

D'immenso giubilo s'innalzi un grido, e avverta i perfidi nostri nemici
che a noi sorridono le stelle ancor.

[Let us raise our voices in wild jubilation and warn our perfidious enemies that fortune smiles on us still.]

Alejandro wove through the hordes of choristers and approached the apron of the stage. "Maestro, may we take a break now? I'd like to give the chorus some notes before we proceed to the Mad Scene."

"Absolutely." Stewart placed his baton on top of the podium. "Fifteen minutes, please."

Adam tapped Alejandro's shoulder. "Will you be needing me after the break? I could use a coffee. I'm dying up here."

"Not literally, I hope." Alejandro and Adam shared a laugh. "We may be doing the Sextet again after the Mad Scene, Adam. Don't go too far."

"Whatever you say, *Capitano*."

Matt leaned over to Julia. "I can't wait for the Mad Scene. That glass harmonica makes the atmosphere positively eerie."

Julia shuddered. Notwithstanding her fascinations with Sir Walter Scott, she didn't like being reminded of her ghostly encounters, either past or present.

* * *

Adam stretched out on the chaise in his dressing room with his latte, eyes closed, lights dimmed, feeling totally relaxed.

His role was a small one, but playing it in Santa Fe was like performing in paradise. The physical beauty surrounding him enriched his creativity. Cute bunnies cavorted around the lawns while birds chirped agreeably in the background; glorious melodies resounded from every corner; children's laughter emanated from the swimming pool. And stunning, multi-hued sunsets brought the idyllic days to a close. It was almost like something out of Disney, except more real.

Life was good.

Adam heard the door open, but he was too blissed out to acknowledge the person entering. He assumed it must be one of the dressers bringing some accessory for his costume.

"Felipe, is that you?"

Opening his eyes, Adam could see someone approach him in the semi-darkness, carrying what looked like a small object. "Is that the missing pommel from my sword?"

There was no response. He had no time to put down his latte. The ceramic cup fell from his hand and shattered on the floor as the sharp point entered his torso and tore his flesh. He uttered a brief cry—of surprise, of pain—before collapsing back onto the chaise in a glossy, wet patch of crimson.

* * *

The unending parade of dramatic *agita* onstage never ceased to amaze Julia, who knew from studying the libretto that Lucia's troublemaking brother orders the crowd to stop their merrymaking. Having heard terrifying moans emitting from the bridal chamber, he has discovered Lucia clutching the dagger with which she has stabbed her bridegroom to death.

From exultation to murder. That's opera.

Right on cue, Deborah staggered in, clenching the weapon, her expression crazed, her pristine white wedding gown soaked with scarlet. She stretched the melodic line through the rising melody with crystal clear coloratura soprano tones.

Il dolce suono mi colpì di sua voce!... Ah, Edgardo, io ti son resa.

[The sweet sound of his voice hits me! Ah, Edgardo, I return to you.]

Then Alejandro, his face as pale as Deborah's gossamer gown, appeared behind Stewart and whispered into Stewart's ear.

Stewart grimaced. "But we just had a break."

Alejandro whispered something else and rushed off. Stewart stopped conducting. Confused whispers circulated among the musicians.

Julia looked at Matt, puzzled. He mouthed the words, "I have no idea."

Rising to her feet, Julia stood on her tiptoes, trying to get a better look at the stage. In the wings, she could spy chaos: Harold, Alejandro, Deborah and several stagehands were involved in a heated discussion. It was all but inaudible to Julia, but clearly, they were highly distressed.

Stewart placed his baton inside his orchestra score and turned to Julia. "I'm afraid I have to go backstage to try and help control the calamitous situation."

"Calamitous situation?"

"Yes. Harold found Adam in his dressing room. He's been stabbed to death."

Chapter Twenty-Eight

Egli è là...morto!
He's there...dead!
—Verdi, *Rigoletto*, Act 3

For the first time in her SFPD career, Stella felt overwhelmed. A second operatic murder. Stacks of witnesses waiting to be interviewed. Constantin likely was experiencing a similar state of mind. Something had to give. It was time to search further afield for some backup aid.

On the plus side, she sensed she would not have to look far. There was another detective, practically on her doorstep, to whom she likely could turn for help.

She was right. When she reached out to Detective Somers, he was more than willing to offer his assistance.

* * *

Reports of Adam's demise quickly circulated among company members. Some were sanguine: accounts of senseless violence were all too frequent in the U.S., and many people had become inured to such tragedies. Others panicked. Julia was among the latter.

"How is this possible? How can it be happening again?" Julia said to Katie as they sat together on sofas in the orchestra lounge.

"Rhetorical question, right, Jul?"

Julia nodded gloomily. "I suppose we'll have to wait till they interrogate us, like last time. Once they're done, I'm out of here."

"Me, too."

"No," Julia said. "I mean truly out of here. I want to go home. To New York."

"What? But...you can't."

"Oh yes, I can. Face it, Katie. The vibes in this place are unreal."

"They're not worse than the Met, if you remember," said Katie.

"Is that supposed to make me feel better?"

"I think that was the general idea. At least Katie's trying."

Larry had appeared by Julia's side. He sat next to her, placed his arm around her shoulder, and smiled ironically. "If there's anything we found out at the Met, it's that opera can kill you."

"That's not funny. And it definitely doesn't make me feel better."

"On the bright side, you rose to meet adversity," Larry said. "Have you forgotten your investigative efforts at the Met were responsible for finding the real killer?"

"Thanks for reminding me that once being the target of a killer is enough. I'm still going home. To New York."

"Are you sure? After I finally convinced Stella that you're the person she needs to consult with to get to the bottom of these murders?"

"You *what?*" Julia was appalled. "Why would you do that?"

"Because I could use your expertise."

Julia looked up to see Stella hovering nearby. "I'm afraid you're laboring under a misconception, Stella."

"On the contrary. Once Larry filled me in on the details of your tireless work in uncovering the truth behind the Met murders, I realized you could be a valuable asset here."

"I'm done with investigating." Julia lifted the hem of her T-shirt to reveal her bandaged torso. "I think I've already sustained enough damage in the line of duty here."

"That was an accident," said Katie.

"Or not," Julia said.

"You think someone had it in for you?" Larry asked.

"'Sigh no more, ladies, sigh no more,'" Stella said. "I know I've been hard on you, Julia."

Julia frowned. "You think?"

"And I apologize. But we really could use your skills. I'd like you to team up with us."

"Which means you're not going anywhere, Jul," Katie said.

"Think about it, Julia. Grabowski is backstage interviewing cast and crew, an enormous task. This opera has huge numbers of performers. I have yet to get started on the orchestra." Stella sat down next to Julia and held her gaze. "You know how musicians think, what makes an opera company tick. I respect that. And it could be very useful."

Julia looked over at Larry and Katie, whose expressions were upbeat and hopeful. Then she turned to Stella. "Why are you being so nice to me all of a sudden?"

"'Patience, I say; your mind perhaps may change.' Now that I know more about you, your experience, I realize how much you could contribute to our investigation."

"I'll consider it. If you rethink Marin as a suspect." Julia saw Stella's eyebrows raise, but she went on. "After all, she was in jail when Adam was murdered, so clearly she didn't kill him. Plus, I've found out Deborah, Emilia's understudy, had a vested interest in commandeering Emilia's role. Given that, do you still think Marin had a motive for eliminating Emilia? Even if they had their disagreements?"

Stella thought for a moment. "You have a point. I'll think about it. And if I agree, I'll talk to the judge and see if she will consider bail."

"Thank you, Stella. There is a murderer on the loose. No question. But it's not Marin."

"We'll see about that," said Stella. "So, where were you when the fun began?"

* * *

148

Constantin heaved a sigh as he entered Stieren Hall and spied the throngs of stagehands, choristers, and soloists waiting to be interviewed, Harold, Alejandro, and Stewart among them.

The detective decided to begin with Harold, who looked noticeably agitated.

"You found the victim?"

"I...I went to his dressing room to tell him that Alejandro—the director—was calling him back for notes after the scene was finished. He...he was all...bloodied. And when he didn't move...." Harold shuddered. "Oh, God."

"Did you see anyone in the hallway outside the dressing room?"

"The usual people. Stagehands, the costume director, and wig person."

"Was there any sign of a weapon anywhere?"

"No, there was nothing there except...Adam's...body." Harold broke down and sobbed.

"Okay, that's all for now. Don't go anywhere."

Constantin moved on to Stewart and Alejandro, who were huddled together in a corner.

"It's beginning to feel like *déjà vu*, isn't it, Mr. Grabowski?" Stewart said.

"At least this time it happened in rehearsal instead of a performance, Maestro."

"I suppose we have to count our blessings, such as they are," Stewart said.

"Another opera with a stabbing as part of the action. Is that normal?"

"Aside from comedies, most operas contain some element of violence," said Stewart. "But in this case, clearly some psychopath has infiltrated our ranks and is using our venue—and our particularly...violent slate of repertoire—to perpetrate his or her malicious agenda."

Constantin turned to Alejandro. "Would you say that's accurate?"

"Yes. This opera season, we have an especially, shall we say, bloody program."

"Any particular reason?"

"No," Alejandro said. "Our general director chooses repertoire based on what he thinks the audience will most enjoy."

"And buy tickets for," added Stewart.

"As director, do you decide whether those bloody scenes take place on or offstage?"

"In *Lucia*, it's specified in the libretto that the murder takes place offstage."

"But not, as I understand it, in *Lulu*."

"That was an artistic choice," Stewart said. "Emilia's wishes notwithstanding."

"I see."

Constantin glanced at his watch. Too many other interviewees waiting in the wings. He thanked Stewart and Alejandro. Next would be Magda and Daniel. He was all too familiar with them. From the last murder.

* * *

Having satisfied a modicum of her quota of orchestra members and found out little of what she had hoped to discover, Stella entered Stieren Hall with Julia in tow and brought her over to Constantin. Julia immediately noticed his quizzical look.

"It turns out Julia here helped solve some murders at the Met Opera, Grabowski," Stella said. "I've asked her to tag along. Given the massive scale of this case, another pair of eyes and ears couldn't hurt."

"Whatever you say, boss."

"Meanwhile, did you find out anything significant?"

"That depends on what you think is significant. I did find out from the director…" Constantin pointed out Alejandro. "…That this opera has yet another stabbing scene."

"Oh, great." Stella grimaced. "You tell him that until further notice, I myself will inspect all weapons, whether onstage or off, before they're used."

"You got it, boss."

"And make sure to talk to that singer, Deborah, the one with the bloodstains on her dress. Maybe she had it in for the tenor. She was offstage when he was killed, so she had opportunity."

"But not motive."

"We don't know that yet. See what you can find out. And have the bloodstains on that dress tested. We need to assess whether they're imitation—or the real thing."

"I'm on it. Oh, and speaking of bloodstains, you and Julia might want to talk to the properties director. I'm told he's an expert on blood. At least the fake kind."

Julia recalled an uncomfortable *Salome* moment backstage at the Met when she collided with an all-too-real disembodied head of Saint John the Baptist staring at her from a pedestal.

"Those guys know how to make those props look gruesomely real," she said.

"No doubt." With a deferential nod to Julia, Constantin walked off.

"I'd be willing to bet the bloodstains on Deborah's dress aren't real, Stella," Julia said. "They use fake blood, like in the movies."

"We don't know for sure. Sounds like a good idea to get input from the props guy. I'd also like you to talk to the costume lady."

Julia frowned. "Magda? What about?"

"She's always behind the scenes. I've heard she's been here longer than anyone else, so she might know more than anybody. See if you can get any information out of her."

Julia was flattered but uncomfortable at the responsibility entrusted to her.

What was I thinking, signing up for this?

As she pondered Stella's assignment, Julia glimpsed Stewart coming toward them. Worried he might interpret her presence in some negative way, she tried to prepare herself.

"I've heard you might wish to leave us, Julia."

Julia was taken aback. "How...did you...?"

"Nothing passes me by when it comes to this company. Not even orchestra scuttlebutt." Noticing her appalled expression, he gave her a conciliatory smile. "But please, Julia, don't worry. I completely understand how you feel. And I do realize how demanding I've been of you in your work. But it's only because I believe in your abilities. I do hope you will stay on with us. It would mean a great deal to me personally, and to the company."

Julia wasn't sure whether to be flattered or suspicious. "I…I don't know what to say."

"Don't feel obligated to say anything. Whatever you decide, I will be totally on board."

"Thank you, Stewart."

After he had walked away, Julia turned to Stella. "Wow, that was totally uncharacteristic of him. I'm in shock."

"It's in his interest to make sure important talent stays with the company. He has to do everything he can, explore all possibilities to get to the bottom of these acts of violence," Stella said. "We'll be needing your help, more than ever. Not to worry, I'll coach you in some of my time-tested interrogation techniques."

"Really? I'm intrigued."

"Good. Any further thoughts?"

"Not at the moment, but I'm sure I'll think of something."

Julia wanted to visit Rob and gain some insights from him, especially about the apprentices, but she didn't want to mention that to Stella yet. She had other priorities.

Chapter Twenty-Nine

Du kannst mich nicht dem Gericht ausliefern!
You cannot deliver me to the Law!
—Berg, *Lulu*, Act 1

Julia was ecstatic. True to her word, Stella had appealed to the judge about having Marin released from the county jail, and it worked. When Stewart gave Julia permission to take off the next morning's *Lucia* rehearsal to deliver Marin from her captors, Julia was further elated.

Marin was waiting by the front entrance when Julia and Larry drove up in front of the prison. Julia tried not to reveal her shock at Marin's haggard look as she ushered the battle-weary singer into the back seat. "I've made a reservation at Clafoutis, Marin. A local favorite."

"You look like you could use a decent meal," Larry said.

Julia frowned at him. "You could try to be a little subtler."

"That's okay, he's right," Marin said. "But right now, I'm feeling like I don't want to be around people. Could you take me back to my hotel?"

Larry revved the engine. "You got it."

Julia slid into the front seat next to him and turned to Marin. "What are your plans? Are you going back to New York?"

"Not a chance," Marin said. "I'm sticking around here till they find out who set me up."

"Wise choice," Larry said and took off, leaving a cloud of Santa Fe dust in his wake.

* * *

Julia made sure to text Rob before invading the Apprentice Program office. She was pleased when he invited her to pay a visit, though she didn't reveal her reasons for doing so.

She was surprised to see how small and cramped his quarters were. The outer office was barely big enough for his desk, with his assistant's equally tiny space located in an adjacent room. Through an opening behind his desk, Julia could see another small area filled with shelves.

"Those are the opera archives," Rob said. "Shall we take a look?"

Julia followed Rob through the doorway and into what struck her as an embarrassment of musical riches. Every inch of the floor-to-ceiling steel racks was packed with opera scores and chorus materials, some standing upright, others arranged alphabetically in file boxes: from Bellini to Bizet, Massenet to Mozart, Donizetti to Puccini to Verdi and Wagner. Materials that didn't fit on the shelves were stacked on the floor in cardboard boxes.

Julia had never seen such a sanctuary. It was an operatic nirvana. "Wow, how do you keep track of all of these?" she asked.

"Believe me, I know every sheet of music and where it can be found," Rob said. "It's my haven when I don't want anyone to find me," he added, laughing.

"It definitely is very private back here." She explored the crammed room, trying not to bump into anything. There was barely enough space for her to step between the shelves.

"Perfect for, like…a romantic tryst or two?"

"It hasn't been part of my experience." He smiled. "But I can only speak for myself."

"Mind if I take a closer look?"

"Have at it. I'll be in the next room."

Rob went back to his desk, leaving Julia at liberty to examine the materials more closely. A box labeled "Berg" caught her attention. She carefully pulled it from the shelf and scanned its contents. Wedged next to a vocal score of *Wozzeck* was one marked *Lulu*.

Julia extracted the *Lulu* score and flipped through the pages, shuddering when she came to the passage where Jack murders Lulu. It looked as frightening on the page as it did onstage.

Terrifying associations came hurtling back, and she quickly closed the manuscript. As she did so, she noticed two pages stuck together. She debated as to whether she should attempt to separate them; perhaps that was best left for Rob.

But Julia's natural inquisitiveness overcame her better judgment. As she gently pried the pages apart, a minuscule slip of paper dropped out and fluttered to the floor. There was such a scarcity of space in the room that when she stooped down to retrieve the paper, one of the shelves started to teeter, threatening to collapse on top of her.

She barely managed to stop it in time. *"Merde!"*

"Everything okay in there?" Rob called out from the next room.

"No worries."

Julia examined the paper, and the few words scribbled on it. It took her a moment to recognize the language in which they were written.

Hungarian.

She pocketed the scrap, returned the box to its rightful place, and headed out the door.

* * *

In order to drop Julia in front of the theatre before the opening performance of *Roméo et Juliette*, Larry had to drive through throngs of tailgaters in the opera parking lot with their overflowing wicker baskets. They were enjoying pre-performance repasts on tables bedecked with linens, candelabras, colorful dinnerware, and champagne flutes.

Julia, watching wide-eyed through the window, was struck by the revelers' creativity in attire. Some wore denim and cargo pants, but many of the women wore formal gowns, their escorts decked out in black-tie tux and red cummerbund regalia, and most sported elaborate feathered masks. Julia felt as if she had happened upon a New Orleans Mardi Gras celebration.

Glancing up toward the terraces, Julia spied numbers of operagoers taking in breathtaking mountain and desert and turquoise sky views. The entire scene was an affirmation of the best of all possible operatic worlds, true to the most idealistic descriptions of life at Santa Fe Opera.

"When Santa Fe Opera was starting out," Julia told Larry, "it was called 'One of the country's most beloved venues...A miracle in the desert...A shining white cloud in the red hills.'"

"With a sky as clear as this one, I'd be surprised to see even one white cloud," Larry said.

"Wait a minute or two. That flawless sky can change without warning."

"Like it did on opening night?"

"Yes. Unfortunately." Julia grimaced. "And it did not bode well."

Once in the pit, Julia was reluctant to play full-out because of her wound and gingerly held back in the opera's first act. But when she discovered that even with aggressive playing, she felt not a twinge from the gash in her left flank—a testament, she thought, to her mountaintop experience with Miles—she gradually resumed her usual leadership mode until the scene in Act Two where the sword incident and its resultant injury had occurred during rehearsal. At that point, she began to tremble, her bow shaking as she drew it across the strings.

Blatchley noticed Julia's look of trepidation and smiled his encouragement, but the memory of that moment of terror took control of her rational mind, and she feared she would have to stop playing. As she was about to lower her violin and bow, a voice entered her head.

Divest yourself of the debris that litters your mind...Give your pain to Mother Earth.

She tried mentally to return to her vision quest, making a supreme effort to clear her mind as Miles had instructed her and to visualize the scene in which she had felt at peace. As suddenly as her fear had overcome her, an immense calm pervaded her being, her bow ceased to quiver, and her strokes once again became strong and steady.

I'm fine. I can do this. Abel would want me to.

Finally, in the last scene, as Julia watched the young lovers' tragic self-sacrifice, she imagined their souls ascending to heaven. The music was heartbreaking, but she suppressed the fountain of tears that were threatening to gush forth. If she were to loosen her emotions from their restraints, it was best done away from the curious stares of her orchestra colleagues.

As Blatchley motioned to the orchestra to rise and acknowledge the audience's applause, Julia heard a soft buzz from her cell phone. She discreetly reached for it and stole a surreptitious look at the screen.

Stella: Tomorrow, Café Pasqual's, 8 am. Breakfast and interrogation instruction.

When she had investigated Abel's murder at the Met, Julia was operating totally on instinct. This time she had an opportunity to hone her skills under the tutelage of a professional. Whatever Julia could learn from Stella would make her probing more sophisticated and efficient.

There was no time to waste expressing opera-induced emotions. She had work to do.

Chapter Thirty

Warum denn nicht? Ich habe Mut und Kraft!
Why not then? I have courage and strength!
—Beethoven, *Fidelio*, Act 1

S queezed into a corner table at the always packed Café Pasqual's off Santa Fe Plaza, Stella and Julia chatted over lattes and bowls of red quinoa with berries, toasted almonds and grilled figs topped with coconut milk.

Julia thought the dish pricey but worth every penny. "I've never tasted anything so yummy," she told Stella.

"Now you know why this place is perpetually jammed," Stella said. "Although I almost expected you to go for Julia's Wild Salmon Gravlax."

"Seems my name is ubiquitous in this town, given her presence here and at La Posada. But Cognac-cured Salmon is a bit much at eight o'clock in the morning. Plus, I'm allergic to dairy and potatoes and vinegar. So, no *Gruyère*, Potato Cake, *crème fraîche* or lemon vinaigrette."

"Aren't you the hothouse flower? For me, it's all good. If 'Music be the food of love,' then food is music." Stella chuckled and scarfed down a large mouthful of quinoa. "Okay, here's your crash course. How to get the whole truth from victims, witnesses, and hopefully perps."

Julia reluctantly put down her spoon. Still chewing, she extracted her phone from her bag and brought up her Notes app.

"Number one," Stella said. "They'll have a 'tell,' like in a poker game. They'll fidget—touch their nose, pull an ear. Two, and this is tough if you aren't familiar with how any of them normally act. If they don't look you in the eye, they're probably lying. Or at least couching the truth."

Julia banged out the information as quickly as she could. Luckily, as a millennial she was practiced in tapping rapidly with two thumbs. But she also knew she had to be careful about overuse: trigger thumbs and fingers, often a consequence of too much playing, especially for string players, were to be avoided at all costs.

"Three. They'll talk so fast you can barely understand what they're saying. They do this on purpose to avoid being heard."

Julia was puzzled. "They don't want you to hear what they've said?"

"They might have something to hide. And sometimes, they'll repeat the question to stall you while they think of a lie that sounds believable. They'll say something like, 'Hold on, is this for real? Let me make sure I heard you right.'"

Julia's touch screen had never seen so much action. "Wow, I never knew."

"Most people don't," Stella said. "One more thing. They'll try to sidetrack you by switching the topic. Or make you think you're the one who's crazy. Don't fall for it. Got it?"

"I think so." Julia put down her phone and swallowed another mouthful of berries. She wasn't sure if the food tasted so good because it was organic or because her body was still healing from her injury and needed the extra nutrients. Whatever the reason, she was almost tempted to order another bowl.

Evidently, Stella was on a similar wavelength. "I'm still hungry. Think I'll try some of Julia's Gravlax. You?"

"No thanks, I'm good."

Julia was astonished. Either Stella's large frame required a great deal of nourishment, or detective work made one especially hungry. In any case, she was looking forward to putting Stella's valuable recommendations to good use.

Holding up her menu, Stella motioned to a nearby waiter, who hurried over. "Yes?"

Stella pointed to Julia's namesake dish on the menu. "I'd like one of these.

And another latte. Oh, and a chile cheeseburger." She looked up at Julia. "They put chiles in everything here. There are, like, two dozen different kinds of peppers."

"Red or green?" said the waiter.

"How about both? I'm feeling adventurous today."

The waiter moved off. Stella turned to Julia. "So, what have you got so far?"

"Not much, I'm afraid. Just this." Julia pulled out the scrap of paper she had found in the archives and handed it to Stella. "I found it in the archives in Rob's office."

"Rob?"

"The head of the Apprentice Program."

"Oh. How have I not met him yet?" The detective scrawled a note in her phone. Then she stared at the words on the paper. "What the hell language is that, anyway?"

"Hungarian."

"I should have known. What does it say?"

"It says..." Since the words were unfamiliar, Julia hesitated a bit as she read them. "*Hívja...azonmmal...a...rendörséget!*"

"And it means...?"

"I have no idea. But I know someone who does."

"Great. Meanwhile, let's go see what the props director has to say about creating blood and gore."

The mention of such an unsavory subject made Julia feel queasy. "Ugh, I just ate."

Chapter Thirty-One

No mysl reviinaya, chto yeyu drugomu obladat tomit menya
But the jealous thought that she might be another's, tortures me
—Tchaikovsky, *The Queen of Spades*, Act 1

Head stagehand Steve, who had found out Stella and Julia wanted to visit the properties department, offered to show them the way. Stella asked Constantin to tag along. When they had reached the bottom of several sets of stairs, Steve said, "Here we are in Hades. Kidding, it's actually the sub-sub-basement."

"Like 'C-Level' at the Met," said Julia.

"If that's the Met's underbelly, then yeah. This barn over here is the properties shop."

Steve walked them to the entrance of a dimly lit room as cavernous as an airplane hangar, with sky-high ceilings and catwalks that evoked nervous memories of Julia's childhood when she nearly fell off the top deck of the Staten Island Ferry.

Julia peeked in, squinting. "How can they work when the lighting is so...shadowy?"

"Oh, they're used to it," said Steve. "It's all about creating art. They love what they do."

Overcoming her fear of high places, Julia asked, "Can we go in?"

Steve motioned them inside the vast room, where Julia could see the space was jam-packed with construction materials and gargantuan machines. Overstuffed period furniture shared space with breastplates and chain mail, masks and tiaras, swords, rapiers and daggers. Julia gaped at the beehive of activity, with craftsmen hammering, carving, gluing, and fashioning statues and other objects out of faux substances of everything from Styrofoam to stainless steel.

The properties director, Manuel, was more than forthcoming in granting Stella's request for a demonstration, as he was painting blood on the head of St. John the Baptist in preparation for the upcoming production of Richard Strauss's grisly opera, *Salome*.

Julia was not as eager as Stella to see how the head of Saint John was created. The image of her former confrontation with a similarly realistic-looking replica at the Met invaded her memory, and the reminder was not a pleasant one.

While she had been looking into the murder of her mentor, Abel Trudeau, Julia hadn't realized she herself had become a target of the killer, who had tried to frighten her away from the investigation by placing a very real-looking replica of a severed head in her path. The unexpected encounter had shaken her already-stressed psyche, and henceforth, she had felt acute discomfort at the thought of colliding with another disembodied head.

But now Julia knew she had to repress such feelings in order to provide Stella the help she needed. She realized the prop was a mere imitation but still found it disturbing. Nonetheless, she tried to show a keen interest in Manuel's process.

"That looks incredibly real," she told him. "Positively gruesome, in fact."

"Thank you. That's precisely what I was going for. It has to be, to make people believe it's actually the head. If it doesn't look hideous, I'm out of a job," he said, grinning. "You can 'ruin the moment' if you don't actually believe it's the character's real head. Or at least the head of the person who's singing him."

"That makes sense," Stella said. "How is it done?"

"We make a likeness of the singer in clay, then a mold, then a hollow fiberglass core with silicone. Inside the core, we put the blood, and it comes dripping out. Then we put on the hair." He held up the head by its hair and showed her the cut-off neck, "blood" oozing from it and dripping onto his hands. "You wouldn't believe how many hours it takes."

"Believe me, I do," Julia said, suppressing a wave of nausea.

"Do you use the same implements as the wig director does, Manuel?" Constantin asked.

"We only use a few of those," Manuel said. "Daniel and I combine the best of each of our own methods. He uses more of the dangerous tools."

Constantin grimaced. "Yes, I remember. The ones that can injure you, right?"

"Yep," Manuel said. "Generally, we in the prop department stay away from those sharp gadgets. I prefer fake blood to real blood."

"Don't we all," said Stella.

"And our heavy-duty workers would much rather risk banging their fingers with a hammer than get punctured with one of those pointy things that can get stuck in your leg or arm. If you know what I mean."

"I think I do," Constantin said and made a note: *Go back and talk to Daniel again.*

The discussion was unsettling for Julia. She was beginning to think she had no business signing up for the investigation. Blood was just not her thing.

"Are you okay, Julia? You look queasy," Steve said.

"I'm fine," Julia said and turned to Manuel. "Thank you for the demonstration."

"Anytime," Manuel said and went back to his work in progress.

Next was the scene shop, a vast space with workers noisily sawing and hammering. One, his head encased in what looked like a black Japanese Kendo mask with blue mesh covering his nose and mouth area, noisily soldered two large metal frames together. Julia thought he looked like a character from a Samurai movie.

"Like the costume shop, the scene shop is newly expanded," Steve said. "Our production staff here is as expert and committed as they come. Not that the orchestra isn't more so," he added, catching Julia's eye.

"Is it my imagination, or does this work look even more hazardous than the wig-making?" Constantin said.

"In some ways, yes, it is," Steve said. "But any enterprise involved with the backstage workings of a theatre has its risks."

"Generally, those risks don't involve murder, though, do they?" Constantin asked.

"No, at least not in this opera company. No offense, Julia."

At this reminder of her grueling experiences at the Met, Julia felt a wrenching in her gut, but she didn't want to reveal it. "None taken," she lied.

"I think we've got a pretty good idea of the most important departments, Steve," Constantin said. "It's time I reported back to my partner. Thanks for all your help."

"Anytime," Steve said. "Would you two like to see the 'Ranch'—the cantina, the pool, the gardens, the mountain views?"

"I think we have some murders to solve before we can avail ourselves of that," Constantin said. "But at some point, I'm sure we would."

"Gotcha. Come and find me when you're ready," Steve said. "You, too, Julia."

Julia noticed Steve's admiring glance and thanked her lucky stars that Larry wasn't there to see it.

Chapter Thirty-Two

Ora facciam la recita!
Now let's do the show!
—Leoncavallo, *Pagliacci*

Getting through the opening night of *Roméo et Juliette* had been a huge relief for Julia. The enchantment of the surroundings—the mountains glowing in the distance, the iridescent sunset, and the crescent moon floating among the stars when the sky turned inky black—fueled her motivation to give the music its best possible rendering.

The entire performance had gone off so smoothly, Julia began to wonder if she had been hallucinating, especially when Stewart uttered some generous words of praise to her afterward.

"That's the first time he's said anything positive to me about my work, Katie. It's unreal."

"Take it and run," Katie said in her usual nonchalant manner. "Gift horse and all that."

"I guess you're right," Julia said. "Do I dare hope that all this opera-induced adversity is now in the past?"

"Believe it, Jul. I certainly will."

Julia accepted Katie's wisdom and began to feel like she could handle resuming *Lucia*.

At her first rehearsal, Julia was surprised to see Sándor onstage in Adam's place. His vocal range and timbre were well suited for the role, but she still felt bewildered as to why Sándor would be performing so frequently.

At the break, she and Katie set off to the cantina, where company members hovered together at tables, deep in discussion, hashing out details about the productions in which they were involved. It seemed to Julia that their passion for discourse over their art was boundless, whether lunching on the terrace, hanging by the pool, or pausing on the lawn to gaze at Donna Quasthoff's distinctive *Orpheus and Eurydice* sculpture.

Julia and Katie found Sándor in line at the cash register, paying for a green tea. "You sound great, Sándor," Julia said.

"Thank you, Julia."

Katie took note of Sándor's admiring glance directed at Julia. "I second that," Katie said. "I think you're perfect in the role of…what is he called?"

"Arturo," Sándor said.

"I knew that," said Katie. "Hey, want to join us?"

The three of them found a table in a far corner of the crowded outdoor space.

"Miles told me your vision quest was great revelation for you. Is true?"

"Yes, it was amazing," Julia said. "Thank you for arranging that for me."

Sándor's eyes glowed. "My pleasure. Always."

"I didn't know you were understudying Adam's role," Julia said, sipping her latte.

"Oh…" Sándor cautiously tasted his tea so as not to burn his tongue. "Actually, I wasn't. But apprentice understudy did not feel prepared, so they ask me to step in."

Julia thought Sándor seemed caught off guard by her comment. "Magda must be happy about that."

"No one is happy, after what happen to Adam. But Magda is always pleased to see me onstage."

"Of course she is," Katie said. "Her kid brother being so talented."

"Magda is talented, too. When we grow up in Hungary, our father encourage both of us to follow our dreams of being opera singers. But Magda always put my career ambitions first. She said she inherited mother's sewing abilities but I inherited father's musical ones."

"Well, I've never heard her sing," Julia said, "But judging from what I've heard of you, she may have been right on track."

"She is much too selfless. There is nothing she would not do for me. I never feel I am worthy, or I can repay her properly." Julia watched as Sándor wrapped the string around his spoon, strangling the life out of his tea bag. "Julia, have you seen Magda recently? You should stop by costume department, say hi to her. I'm sure she would be delighted to see you."

"You're right. I've hardly talked to her since the day we first met." Julia paused. "I'm curious, though…what range was Magda's voice?"

"It was…" Sándor hesitated. "High dramatic soprano."

"Like in *Lulu*?"

"Yes."

"That's amazing. What a talented family you have." She paused. "How well did you know Adam?"

"Not very."

Julia held Sándor's gaze as he idly stroked his nose. After an awkward moment, he said, "I had better get back. They will be wondering what happen to me."

"Of course. I did have a favor to ask you, though." Julia reached into her purse and extracted the paper with the Hungarian words written on it. "I was looking through the scores in the archives and found this inside one of *Lulu*. Can you translate it?"

Sándor quickly scanned the words, frowning. "Handwriting is difficult to read. Do you mind if I get back to you?"

"Not at all. Thanks, Sándor."

"*Szívesen*." He pocketed the paper and rushed away, clutching his teacup.

Julia murmured under her breath. "Not looking me in the eye. Changing the subject. Fidgeting. Even opera singers have 'tells.'"

"What did you say, Jul?"

"Oh, nothing." Julia realized she had to be more careful about thinking out loud. Much as she loved Katie, she grasped the importance of keeping her collaboration with Stella under wraps, even when it came to her best friend.

"Did you see how Sándor was looking at you? He has a thing for you."

Julia was glad Katie had switched topics. "Don't be silly."

"Mark my words," Katie said. "I know a major crush when I see one."

"I'm sure you do, but you know I'm spoken for."

Katie grinned over her cup of coffee. "Right. Poor Julia. So many men, so little time."

* * *

Sándor panted as he scurried along the path from the cantina to the theatre. What he had read on the piece of paper troubled him. He couldn't fathom what Julia was doing with a piece of paper that said, "Call the police!" in Hungarian.

But he knew it did not bode well.

Chapter Thirty-Three

Komm nur herein, mein Schatz! Komm!
Come in, my love! Come in!
—Berg, *Lulu*, Act 2

Notwithstanding Stella's assignment, Julia found herself looking forward to talking to Magda again. At their first encounter Julia had found the woman fascinating; even more so, now that Sándor had revealed some of the Kertész family background.

When she arrived at the costume shop, Julia peeked inside to see Magda, alone, poised in front of a mannequin. She quietly entered and approached Magda from behind. As she drew closer, Julia could see that Magda was adjusting a costume on the figure. She recognized it as the white wedding dress and veil from the Mad Scene in *Lucia*.

Julia softly cleared her throat. Magda turned around abruptly. "Who is there?"

From Magda's irritated tone, Julia realized she had interrupted Magda's concentration.

"I'm so sorry to disturb you, Magda."

"Oh, it's you, Júlia. I apologize if I sound impolite. I am focus so hard on my work."

"I completely understand. You must forgive me. I didn't mean to interrupt. I saw Sándor at rehearsal, and he reminded me that I've hardly seen you since my first day. I dropped by to say hello." Julia smiled. "But I see you're busy. I can come back tomorrow."

"No, no, it's kind of you to visit. I can take brief respite."

Magda repositioned a straight pin on the dress and turned back to Julia. "I heard you were injured in *Roméo* rehearsal. Are you all right?"

"Oh, it was nothing, a superficial wound. I'm fine now. Thank you for asking." Julia jockeyed position to get a better glimpse of the garment. "Is that the wedding dress from *Lucia*?"

"Yes. But it is replacement. Police took possession of original for investigation. It is my responsibility to build new one, exact duplication."

"That must be difficult. And time-consuming. So much extra work for you."

"It is true. With much beading and lace detail on dress, and especially delicate veil, it necessitates exceptional care. I must handle it personally."

"I'm not surprised. But I'm sure you will manage it very adeptly. You are so meticulous."

"Thank you for saying so."

"Is *Lucia* one of your favorite operas?"

"Yes. It is. Lucia character is vulnerable, complex. Her grief at losing mother, her longing for forbidden lover, her madness when she thinks he has betrayed her. Her entire world crashes down around her. World with no benevolence. As is ours."

Julia was amazed at Magda's astute, perceptive analysis of Sir Walter Scott's tragic heroine, an operatic character she herself did not consider particularly deep. "I never thought of Lucia that way. You are very insightful."

"I try to think of every opera character in this way. It helps in my work. I am closely linked with opera my entire life. In Hungary and in States," Magda said. "Of course, Sándor's talent far surpasses mine. All that matters for me is his success. I truly believe in him."

"With good reason. He sounded fantastic today."

"You are kind to say, Júlia."

"He told me you came from a musical family."

"Our father studied piano with great Béla Bartók at Liszt Academy."

Julia was dumbfounded at the thought of someone actually rubbing shoulders with one of the musical geniuses of the twentieth century. "No!

Seriously?"

Magda nodded. "Father told us it was frightening experience at first, in class with living genius. But Maestro never raised his voice, always spoke softly and slowly. He had unforgettable big, piercing eyes. You have played his opera *Bluebeard's Castle*?"

Julia studied the nostalgia in Magda's eyes and decided it was a good idea to probe the costume director's emotions. She knew the opera, with its multiple murders, torture chambers, and walls dripping with blood, was number one on any number of "bloodiest opera" lists. She didn't want to mention it.

"Not yet, Magda. I've read the libretto but have never played it."

"Is extraordinary. Rich and expressive. Colorful and strange. One of greatest pieces of music I know," Magda said, her expression faraway. "Librettist Balázs, friend of Bartók, influenced by Freud and Strindberg, based story on French folk tale. Deep psychological meaning. Begins with only one person onstage, speaking Hungarian. Then comes music."

Julia thought the piece sounded downright sinister and unsettling.

Magda came back to reality. "But what is your musical background, Julia?" she asked.

"My father was my first violin teacher."

"He spoke Hungarian?"

"No. My mother did. He was Russian, so he didn't speak Hungarian. But he and my mother often spoke Yiddish at home."

"Your father is still alive?"

"No. He was killed in a..." Julia's expression darkened. "An accident. When I was ten."

"I am so sorry. I know how difficult is to be without father."

Julia was touched by Magda's sincere look of concern. "Thank you."

"It must be getting late," Magda said, "*Hány óra van?*"

Julia checked her Fitbit. "Three o'clock."

"I'm sorry, I must go back to work."

"Of course. I've taken too much of your time, Magda. But I look forward to next time."

Once outside the door, Julia lingered for a moment, deep in thought. Magda's observations reminded her that opera was brimming with panicked heroines. *Lucia* represented one of them, a woman on the verge of a total breakdown, as did *Bluebeard's Castle*, the story of a wife in constant fear of her creepy, murderous husband. But history was also laden with terrified women, like Julia's namesake at La Posada, who suffered profound emotional torment.

However, there was something about Magda that brought to mind opera characters other than Lucia or Judith, Bluebeard's wife. Strong female protagonists with an intensity as deep and profound as Magda's. Carmen... Tosca...Turandot...

Lady Macbeth.

Chapter Thirty-Four

Cosi accasciata? Via, mia bella signora, sedete qui...e favelliamo
So downhearted? Come, my fair lady, sit down here...and we'll talk
—Puccini, Tosca, Act 2

S tella had never been in an opera star's dressing room, and Deborah's seemed as good a place as any to interview the singer, though the detective would have preferred to learn less about the role of Lucia and more about the activities on the night of Adam's murder.

"Lucia is my favorite *bel canto* role, the absolute benchmark for the highest level of coloratura singing. I can't tell you how gratifying it is performing those high notes. Those vocal pyrotechnics and fireworks," Deborah said. "The themes are universal. Forbidden love, family duty. The story could be set anywhere, any time. One of the bloodiest operas ever. Scotland did have a rather 'colorful' past. Look what happened to Braveheart, and Mary Queen of Scots."

"Bloody for sure," said Stella. "And the Mad Scene?"

"One of the most demanding in opera, technically speaking, a real showpiece. Dramatically challenging as well."

"I've heard that opera is like true life on steroids. 'All the world's a stage, And all the men and women merely Players,' as Jaques says in the famous pastoral comedy," Stella said.

"And 'what's done, cannot be undone,' as Lady Macbeth says in the play about the Scottish king whose name must not be mentioned," Deborah countered.

"Touché," Stella said. "How seriously do you take your part? Are you like Sarah Bernhardt, living the character? Do you ever get so into it that you lose touch with reality? Go a little mad like Lucia?"

"It is easy to get lost in the moment, especially in the Mad Scene, where Lucia is so deluded she retreats into insanity rather than face an actuality too horrible to contemplate. And yes, she's trying to escape. But if you're implying that I could possibly do what she does—"

"I'm not implying anything," Stella said. "I'm wondering how actors get into character. *Modus operandi*, if you will."

"As thrilling as it is to take chances onstage, you can't get too emotional. You have to know where to draw the line. Stay balanced, not go too far," Deborah said. "If I let myself get carried away, my throat could close up. That's the worst possible disaster for a singer."

"Of course." Stella took a different tack. "It must have been tough to adapt to *Lucia* when you just sang the title role in *Lulu*."

"It's true the roles are poles apart. The music in *Lulu* is wickedly difficult, so dissonant, no melodies to center you. The *bel canto* coloratura in *Lucia* is also hard, but for a different reason. In *bel canto*, you sing cascades of notes in a high register, in quick succession, all very exposed," Deborah said. "Those melodies are universally familiar. You can't miss one note, or everyone else will know. In any case, I was happy to make the transition. My voice was tailor-made for *bel canto*. It's what made me want to sing opera."

Stella reflected on the egos of opera singers. She was beginning to realize that everything she had heard about them and their heightened sense of self, both positive and negative, was true. Artists like Deborah were divas: great singers but arrogant and full of themselves. How the lower echelons of opera hierarchy were able to put up with singers' egotistical nonsense was eluding her as surely as Lucia's mind had become unhinged.

"And to sing such roles here, in Santa Fe, where even the weather has its own drama, is mind-boggling," Deborah said. "You could be dying of consumption onstage, and a storm rolls in, thundering your demise."

"Forgive me, but I have to ask. Where were you at the time of Adam's murder?"

"In my dressing room, changing into my bloodstained dress. I wasn't anywhere near Adam. You can ask my dresser, Felipe."

"I will." Stella tapped a note into her phone.

"Now if you'll excuse me," Deborah said, "I have to rehearse with Adam's replacement."

"So soon?"

"As the ringmaster says in the circus, 'The show must go on.' In this case, the director has to keep things going so the company won't panic. I'm merely a 'poor player.'"

"Of course," Stella said. "Thank you for your time."

"I'd like to say it was my pleasure, but unfortunately, it was anything but."

Deborah swept out of the room. As to Deborah's veracity with regard to Adam's demise, Stella had her reservations.

Chapter Thirty-Five

Ah, quelle est cette voix qui me trouble l'ésprit?
Est-ce l'enfer qui parle ou Dieu qui m'avertit?
Ah, what is this voice troubling my spirit?
Is it hell speaking or God who's warning me?
—Offenbach, *The Tales of Hoffman*, Act 3

Julia silently thanked Larry for his prescience in gifting her with a Fitbit. Though she wasn't using its technology to the max, she loved its sleek design and, especially, at the moment, its flashlight feature, which was more convenient to use than the one on her iPhone.

The last thing she had anticipated in coming to Santa Fe was exploring the isolated hallways and recesses of the opera house as she had done at the Met. Yet here she was, virtually breaking into the costume shop late at night, looking for clues. She had talked to Magda as Stella had delegated her to do but felt disappointed at not having uncovered any compelling information. Maybe if she had a closer look at the white dress, Magda had been working on...

She had tried all of the many doors providing access to the shop to see if any had been left unlocked. Her patience was rewarded when she found one side door handle that was unfastened. The light from Julia's Fitbit provided adequate but unobtrusive brightness. Guided by its illumination, she crept through the room in semi-darkness, dodging the corner edges of the huge worktables. But she wasn't familiar enough with the layout to avoid running into a metal table leg bolted to the floor.

"Ow!"

Julia rubbed her offended shin and looked around, anxious. But there was little likelihood that someone other than the night security guard could have heard her outburst. If he or she came to investigate the noise, she felt sure she could think of an excuse for her presence.

She found herself imagining for a moment what the previous shop must have been like: a small, dark hole, cramped and claustrophobic, with tiny windows and no air conditioning.

It must have made people working here irritated, to say the least.

Chastising herself for becoming distracted, she tried to determine the location of the dress. Even if she knew where it was, in the pitch blackness, it was difficult if not impossible to see anything, even aided by the light from the Fitbit.

Ah, maybe that's it.

Spying what looked like a mannequin, she shone her light in that direction and cautiously stepped toward it, carefully avoiding any further collisions with inanimate objects. Using her cell phone as a backup for the light from her Fitbit, she could see that the mannequin was indeed draped in the white dress from *Lucia*. She held both devices in front of the garment and moved the light from top to bottom, but to her chagrin, she couldn't see anything that looked unusual. The dress was pristine.

A useless, amateurish attempt, Julia.

"What are you doing here?"

Julia recognized the distinctive accent. Now it was time to come up with the excuse she had been so sure of inventing. But she felt too panicked to think clearly.

She turned to face Magda. "I'm sorry, Magda, I didn't mean to—"

"I think you had best leave. Allow me to provide you some light."

The sudden, glaring brightness from the ceiling's fluorescent lamps that Magda switched on made Julia squint with discomfort. There was nothing more she could do or say. She couldn't exactly ask Magda what she herself was doing there at this late hour. It was, after all, her territory; her ire was justified. And since Julia had been caught in an egregious transgression in what was clearly Magda's domain, retreat was her only option.

* * *

The Santa Fe DPS Forensics Lab was Stella's second home. She kept the number for the Office of the Medical Investigator on her speed dial.

Chief Medical Examiner Nick Pleasance never insisted on Stella's coming to the OMI at the University in Albuquerque; he was happy to meet her at the SFPD lab on Cerrillos Road in Santa Fe, unattractive though it was, to escape the UNM campus. In his opinion, forensics had less to do with academe and more to do with hands-on professional investigation closely linked to the on-site work of the SFPD. Despite the crime lab's daunting backlog, the high-profile goings-on at the city's venerated opera company were being given top priority.

The initial CSU findings had not been surprising. Much like the previous murder at the opera, the perpetrator had left a pristine crime scene: no prints, no DNA, no blood spatters. The sanguine fluid on the wedding dress had tested as stage blood. And since the murder weapon was not a firearm, there were no casings or traces of gunpowder to look for.

The autopsy data Pleasance had collected for Stella were similarly unspoiled. "This is some of the cleanest work I've seen," Nick told Stella as the two investigators hovered over the body of Adam, the deceased tenor. "This perp is meticulous. Picky, very hard to please. A real fussbudget. What's that thing they say about neat vs. sloppy psychopaths?"

"You think it's the same perp as last time?" Stella asked.

"Possibly," Nick said. "Though last time we had a weapon."

"It was obvious from the beginning that the knife caused the fatal trauma," Stella said. "You think it's only one culprit this time? No accomplice?"

"No, this perp knows too many cooks spoil the soup. He or she is too smart not to work alone. But this time, there's even less to go on. Though you might find this surprising." Nick pinpointed the wound site. "Unlike the other stabbing, this cut is jagged. The weapon we're looking for isn't a dagger or a sword, or even a knife, but something much smaller."

CHAPTER THIRTY-FIVE

"Still a sharp object, right?"

"Definitely. Like something you'd use to rip stitches from a piece of clothing, only much sharper, spikier, and jagged. Hooked, even. Sharp enough to rip your flesh."

Chapter Thirty-Six

Diesmal hast du zuviel dir aufgeladen...
This time you have taken too much upon yourself...
—Beethoven, *Fidelio*, Act 2

H aving failed in her mission to obtain evidence from the costume director, or from the costume shop, Julia was reluctant to share her glum feelings from Larry about her confrontation with Magda. But she also suspected Larry would recognize her dispirited demeanor when she trudged into their room at the inn, so she decided to confess what she had experienced.

"I blew it, Larry. Two for two," Julia said.

"Don't feel so bleak, Julia. I'm sure Stella's expectations were not as high as you think."

"I came away with no evidence, and I got caught. Some detective I am. I'm no better than a musical Nancy Drew."

"First of all, you're not a detective. You're trying to help out Stella, which in my opinion is above and beyond. You didn't have to do that," Larry said. "Second, you're too hard on yourself. Save it for your violin playing. And FYI, Nancy Drew rocked. Plus, she wasn't trying to be two things at once like you are."

Larry's efforts at consoling her didn't help Julia's disheartened mood. She set her violin case on the bed and flopped down next to it, crossing her legs Indian style on top of the duvet. "Is that supposed to make me feel better?"

"Yes, and I fully expect you to act appropriately grateful."

Julia couldn't resist a smile. "Exactly how do you mean?"

"Contrary to what you might think…" Larry eyed Julia's slim, muscular legs peeking out from under her peasant skirt. "Not everything about me has to do with sex."

Julia peered at him skeptically. "You brought it up, not me."

"However," he went on, "Since the next opera is *Salome*, I thought you might like to prepare for it by practicing the Dance of the Seven Veils for me. The orchestral part, not the actual dance. Though I wouldn't mind a little of both."

She gave a little laugh. "I'm sure you wouldn't."

"Give me some credit here. It's ten minutes long—or nine and a half, depending on the conductor—the only strictly orchestral piece in the opera. Knowing you, you'd want to practice the living daylights out of it, like a concerto. And I've seen you practice steadily each day, from early morning until late evening, till your fingers start to bleed."

"I'm willing to suffer for my art."

"No one knows that better than I do." Larry gently grasped Julia's left hand and eyed the painful-looking indentations the strings had made on the pads of her fingers. "Wasn't there an excerpt from *Salome* on your Met audition?"

"You remembered!" Julia was pleased by Larry's continued interest in the subtler details of her musical life.

Larry flashed a knowing smile. "I told you I wasn't all about sex, didn't I?"

"Granted. But since when are you so concerned with my musical practice habits?"

"I did my homework on this one."

"I'll bet you did."

"No. Really. It's a masterpiece. *Salome* was John Crosby's favorite Strauss opera, maybe his favorite opera, period. This is the eleventh time they've programmed it in the last fifty years. The 'Dance' is sheer orchestral brilliance from beginning to end."

Julia was impressed. "You *have* been doing your homework."

"You have no idea. I could give a whole lecture. Did you know there's a 'Dance of the Seven Veils Day'—an unofficial holiday, celebrated every

January to commemorate the execution of John the Baptist? The 'Dance' didn't occur in the Bible, though, only in the English translation of Oscar Wilde's French play, *Salomé*. A dozen years later, Strauss composed it into his opera."

"Given all your newfound knowledge, I'm sensing you've found out why Crosby loved Strauss so much?"

"Not quite. But I would like to hear you play the 'Dance.' Or at least one of the more sensuous passages. Would you do me the honor?"

"How could I say no to such a heartfelt plea?"

Julia unzipped the sheet music-sized pocket on the outside of her canvas violin case cover and extracted a sheaf of music from it. She opened the case and wedged the music on the inside so she could read from it as she played. Larry could see the title *Salome: Violin I Partitura* at the top of the first page. He rubbed his hands together in anticipation.

"The current production takes place in turn-of-the-century Vienna, the time of Freud and Richard Strauss," he said. "The conscious, preconscious and unconscious. Bible meets erotic decadence with blood and gore. Saint John warns everyone that the end is nigh."

"And, in the scene where Salome makes love to John the Baptist's head, Strauss wrote the most horrific chord in all of opera," Julia added. "But I'm still not sure why it was Crosby's favorite opera."

"Crosby got more pleasure conducting Strauss's operas than any other composer's. While he was general director, he produced thirteen of them, six of which were American premieres," Larry said. "Whether or not *Salome* was his favorite opera, his mind was similar to Strauss's music. Convoluted, intricate, and analytical."

Julia contemplated the apparitions of Crosby she had encountered since coming to Santa Fe. Her experiences during her vision quest had dispelled any doubts she had had about the realism of those specters. Now, with the prospect of rehearsing and performing Crosby's favorite Strauss opera looming before her, she was starting to feel concerned about the effects of his psychic presence. It was as if he wanted to bring attention to the abysmal state of affairs in his opera company the same way Jacob Marley's ghost had forewarned Scrooge.

Larry studied Julia's thoughtful frown. "What's on your mind, Julia? You look worried."

"After all that violence we've suffered through in the three operas so far, I'm afraid something horrible might occur again in this one."

"Another murder? I don't think anyone would dare. The SFeO campus is crawling with cops and plain clothes," Larry said. "You better believe that will help deter potential disasters."

Julia remained doubtful. "I hope you're right."

"Have I ever steered you wrong?"

"You've got to be kidding me. You want a response to that? Again?"

"Now that's more like it. I've missed your answering a question with a question."

"I'm getting ready for *Salome*. There are five Jews in the first scene."

Larry laughed. "Okay, you've outsmarted me as usual. But having done all this research, I'm curious to see how this opera ticks, violence and gruesomeness notwithstanding. After all, the audiences here are so sophisticated and knowledgeable, some people go to the same opera two or more times to learn as much as they can and compare casts. Surely, you could get me into one stage rehearsal."

"I'll see what I can do."

"Great. Now, how about that 'Dance'?"

Julia turned to a passage in the music marked *"ziemlich langsam"* ("as slow as before). She was ready to acknowledge that Larry deserved to hear a memorable rendering of the piece.

She only hoped it wouldn't prophesy that the end was nigh.

Chapter Thirty-Seven

Still, alles still, als wäre die Welt tot.
Still, all is still, as if the world died.
—Berg, *Wozzeck*, Act 1

With two murders in quick succession and such a plethora of company members to interrogate, Stella had found little time to compare notes with Constantin. After Julia's report of her failure to come up with evidence from the costume shop, Stella knew she would need to revisit Magda. But from the results of her consult with Nick, Stella also determined it was time to assess where things stood with her partner.

Stella met with Constantin over lattes at a large, round table in a secluded corner of the cantina. It was late in the day, and no one else was around. Only the sounds of children laughing and playing in the pool below them punctuated the hushed atmosphere.

Against the backdrop of the rosy New Mexico sky and what promised to be a spectacular sunset, Stella thought Constantin's pallid face looked washed-out and sallow. There were clear signs of battle weariness in his demeanor. His shoulders drooped, and his eyes held none of their usual inquisitiveness. He barely touched his beverage.

"You okay, buddy?"

"Dunno. These cases are making me crazy. So much killing. And so many people to question, we might as well put them all in a football field and point randomly."

"I hear ya. 'There is nothing either good or bad, but thinking makes it so.'"

Stella sensed Constantin was feeling too put-upon to react to her quote from *Hamlet*. Not waiting for his response, she opened a folder stuffed with files containing dossiers and photographs of opera singers, directors, conductors, and others who had participated in *Lulu* and *Lucia* and placed it in front of him.

"Have a big sip of joe. We need to go through and update our list of possible suspects."

Constantin took a huge hit from his cup. "What have we got?"

Marin's file lay at the top of the stack. Stella put it aside and opened another one. "Goran Řezníček, baritone."

"He had opportunity, but no motive," Constantin said. "He's the only one who didn't have a beef with Emilia. Aside from Sándor."

"Right." Stella placed Goran's file on top of Marin's. "Deborah Alley, Emilia's understudy. She was in the opera house that night."

"Plus, she stood to gain from Emilia's murder."

Stella found a separate space on the table for Deborah's file and opened another one. "Steve Cañon, head stagehand."

"He was hanging out by B-Lift with other stagehands while the murders were going down."

Stella placed Steve's file on top of Goran's. She and Constantin went through the rest, one by one, placing them in one pile or the other. When they were almost finished, the "active suspect" heap contained files of Deborah, Magda, Sándor, and Lorelei. There was one more.

Stella drained her cup. "Daniel Henderson. Wigs and makeup."

"I remember him describing those instruments of torture they use to make those wigs."

"Wait a minute. I don't remember your telling me about that."

"Didn't I? I thought I did," said Constantin. "Why? What's up with that?"

Stella revealed the results of Nick's autopsy of Adam.

Constantin suddenly perked up. "Jagged wound? Sounds like it could have been done by one of those implements Daniel uses."

He fired up his cell phone, swiped through his notes with virtuoso speed, and read from the screen. "*'If you drop one of those instruments and it goes into your leg or arm, you can really feel it when you have to rip it out. It definitely will* **rip your flesh**.'"

"Go on."

"*You have to be careful about pushing against it when pulling it out in order not to tear your leg or arm open.*'"

"I think we'd better pay Daniel another visit," Stella said. "'Lord, what fools these mortals be!'"

Chapter Thirty-Eight

Quanto fuoco! Par che abbiate paura di tradirvi
You protest too much! It seems you might be afraid of betraying yourself
—Puccini, *Tosca*, Act 2

W hen Julia found out from Stewart that he would not be conducting *Salome*, she thought it ironic. Now that she finally had proved her worth as a concertmaster to the music director, she would have to do it all over again with the new maestro, Giovanni Molinari.

On the plus side, she was well prepared. She had studied the music to *Salome*, along with its libretto, in detail—partly in preparation for her Met audition, but also because she found the opera enthralling. Its Freudian undercurrents fascinated her, and she found its protagonist as riveting as any in opera. She also adored the writings of Oscar Wilde, who had created the French play, *Salomé*, that the German author Hedwig Lachmann had translated into German, the basis for Strauss's own libretto for the opera.

More importantly, Julia found Strauss's score superb in its brilliance. The music was demanding in a way that made her want to keep examining and practicing every technically challenging passage and subtlety of phrasing. The violin solo where Salome declares her love for Jochanaan was as difficult as any concerto written for the instrument. Even the parts with both violin sections playing together were technically challenging to the extreme.

Which is probably why those sections were on my audition excerpt list.

Still, Julia felt puzzled over the concept of an Italian conductor for a Strauss opera in German. She knew that Toscanini was famous for his Wagner and for conducting Strauss's tone poems, those sweeping, monumental symphonic works that describe a poem, novel, or painting. But she was unsure if the iconic Italian maestro had conducted many of Strauss's operas.

Being Jewish, Julia was keenly aware that Toscanini was famously anti-Nazi, but Strauss's connections to the Third Reich were ambiguous. The great maestro once had said, "To Richard Strauss, the composer, I take off my hat. To Richard Strauss, the man, I put it on again."

But Julia also had learned that Strauss, whose daughter-in-law was Jewish, moved heaven and earth to send her out of the country to keep her away from danger. And she knew that Mahler, who also was Jewish, suffered great personal loss in his life. He, Strauss, and Wagner all lived in an atmosphere where antisemitism was the customary rule of the day. Julia's father never mentioned any of these details when she was growing up, but she sensed he would have talked to her more about antisemitism if he had lived longer.

Nonetheless, Julia was glad of the opportunity to practice her Italian with Molinari, who was known for his Verdi and Puccini, composers whose operatic works she worshiped unconditionally.

At the beginning of the first stage rehearsal, Sarah stood on the podium. "Please welcome, for the first time, directly from La Scala in Milan, Maestro Giovanni Molinari."

The players respectfully tapped their bows on their music stands. Giovanni took over Sarah's place on the podium and leaned over to shake Julia's hand.

"*Benvenuto, Maestro,*" she said.

"*Grazie.*" Smiling, Giovanni faced the orchestra and spoke articulately, albeit with a pronounced accent. "I am humble to follow the footsteps of the great John Crosby, whose interpretation of this opera was hailed by critics as conveying the feeling that *Salome* was 'one of Strauss's greatest tone poems.' I hope I can come close to replicate Maestro Crosby's achievement."

The director, a diminutive Frenchman named Achille Boivin, stood at the apron of the stage and gestured to Giovanni. "*Buongiorno, Maestro.*"

"*Buongiorno*, Achille."

Julia had no clue how the company kept track of their many different conductors, directors, and constantly revolving repertoire. She had observed plenty of these fluctuations at the Met, but their season was months longer than that of Santa Fe. She was filled with admiration for the efficiency of the administrative staff of SFeO and made a mental note to mention that to Alan the next time she ran into him.

Achille responded to Giovanni's query with an obsequious smile. "If I may, Maestro, I would first like to say a few words to my singers."

Giovanni returned Achille's smile, although with more sincerity. "Of course."

"*Merci*." Achille addressed "his" singers, not by their given names, but by their character names. "Jochanaan, I'd like to see perceptive singing with subtle gradation. Not the pompous barking so often seen in this character. Salome, dear..." He modulated his tone for the soprano. "Do not flaunt your high notes. Allow the music and its inherent drama to emanate naturally, from the depths of your soul. You are not only a sexually charged teenager but a complex personality. Now, Herod, Herodias, and the others—cut through the layers. Focus on the preconscious and unconscious thoughts below the surface that are too terrifying to contemplate."

Matt leaned over to Julia. "These French directors know how to lay it on thick, don't they? Notwithstanding their spotty reputations," he whispered.

Julia, silently practicing a difficult solo passage by tapping her left-hand fingers on the violin's fingerboard, nodded absently. "What do you mean?"

"They tend to come unprepared and keep changing their minds on staging," Matt said. "Opera singers have been known to walk out on them in protest. The last French director we had insisted that the baritone playing Papageno in *Magic Flute* sing the opening aria while running all over the stage. The poor guy had recently flown in and was adjusting to the altitude. He was so out of breath he had to take hits from the oxygen tank backstage in between arias."

"Maybe Boivin's the exception," Julia said optimistically. "After all, Jean Pierre Ponnelle was one of the all-time great directors."

"Don't get your hopes up. Boivin is no Ponnelle. According to what one opera singer told me, in France, they hire theater directors to direct operas, but too many of them have never even directed an opera—and never should," Matt said. "Boivin's great success as a theater director doesn't mean he has a clue on dealing with an opera with massive amounts of ensembles in it."

"Well, he certainly is well-versed in how to slather on the charm."

"But that's no guarantee he can figure out how to get singers situated on a stage. Just FYI, 'Achille' in French means 'He who embodies the grief of the people.'"

"I see your point. Where is Ponnelle when we need him?"

Julia also saw that, unlike Stewart, Giovanni didn't seem to mind faint chatter among the orchestra's ranks. He raised his baton. "Beginning, please."

Julia admired the sensitivity of his upbeat for the very delicate opening of the opera. She followed his lead, gesturing with her violin, to which he responded with a gratified smile.

Notwithstanding the French director, this might not be so bad after all.

A shimmering sound emitted from Narraboth, the tenor who sang the initial phrase.

Wie schön ist die Prinzessin Salome heute Nacht!

[How beautiful is Princess Salome tonight!]

Subtly glancing in the direction of the stage, Julia was astonished to see that Sándor was also playing this key character. She was happy for him, and he sounded wonderful, but seeing him cast in yet another role, and in such quick succession, left her wondering if this was a normal occurrence, even in this truly unique opera company.

It also occurred to her that Sándor's character Narraboth, like Alwa in *Lulu* and Arturo in *Lucia*, comes to a bad end. Such was the fate of *comprimario* tenors, those poor singers who play the minor solo roles like the supporting actors in Hollywood.

* * *

When Daniel looked up from setting the timer on the wig dryer to see Stella and Constantin coming toward him, he sensed trouble. He had never been involved in a crime investigation, but even the most mildly interested television police procedural aficionado knew that a second interview was not a good sign.

His efforts to hide his anxious demeanor proved fruitless. "What can I do for you, Detectives?" he asked shakily.

"Could you show us that instrument—the one you use to hook the hairs on the wigs?"

"Of course." Daniel walked to a table overflowing with plastic containers and trays holding makeup, hairbrushes, and other implements, lifted a small cylindrical object with a metal tip and a tiny fishhook at the end from one of the trays, and held it up. "This is what we use to tie the hair in. The little hook here grabs the hair. Is this the one you're referring to?"

"I think so," Constantin said. "I seem to remember you saying it was sharp."

"Yes, very. If you drop it and it goes into your arm or leg, it can be painful to get it out if you're not careful. But I've already told you that the last time you questioned me."

"Does anyone else have access to these tools?" Constantin asked.

"No. Except for my assistant, who only can use them under my direct supervision, I'm the sole person to work with them," Daniel said. "My assistant and I secure everything in a locked cabinet at the end of the day."

"Do you count them up then to see if any are missing?"

"No, I don't. We all know and trust each other here. We've been working together for years. It never has occurred to me to count them. What are you getting at, Detective?"

"According to the medical investigator's findings, the fatal wound on the body of that singer, Adam, was made by a weapon that's exactly the size and shape of that tool," Stella said. "Grabowski, call CSU. Have them come in to check all the tools in here for any traces of blood."

Constantin tapped a note into his phone, then asked Daniel, "Where were you when Adam was murdered?"

Perspiration formed on Daniel's forehead. "I was placing wigs in the dressing rooms."

"Was one of those in Adam's dressing room?" Stella said.

"Yes. It was."

"Did anybody see you?"

"No, I was alone back there."

Constantin exchanged glances with Stella. "I think we should continue this conversation down at the station."

"But I didn't do anything," Daniel said.

"Then you have nothing to worry about," Stella said. "You can tell us all about it."

Stella and Constantin led the protesting Daniel away, followed by the bewildered stares of dyers, seamstresses, and craftspeople.

"Whether or not we like him for this murder, we still haven't found a perp for the first one," Constantin whispered to Stella.

"He's the only thing we have to go on right now," she said. "We'll find out, to quote King Lear, if he's 'a man more sinn'd against than sinning.'"

Chapter Thirty-Nine

Non tel diss'io, che con questa tua pazza gelosia ti ridurresti a qualche brutto passo?

Didn't I tell you that your insane jealousy would get you in trouble?
—Mozart, *Don Giovanni*, Act 2

When the orchestra break was called, Matt stayed seated, practicing a passage from the Dance of the Seven Veils. Julia stood up to watch the stage as the director showed the soprano the large, ornate rectangular platter on which the severed head would be placed.

"You have the most difficult job of all," Achille was saying. "You dance savagely for ten whole minutes. Then you end by singing the most arduous music in the entire opera."

Julia felt a strangely ambivalent fascination for the entire concept: on the one hand, she found the idea of a bloodied head gruesome. But she had learned some enticing details from her study of the history of the opera, especially about Olive Fremstad, the soprano who sang the ill-fated debut of the role at the Met in 1907.

Evidently, the prim matrons of New York society found the subject matter disgusting and insisted on the show closing. But Fremstad, who ostensibly lived for the stage, had visited the Manhattan morgue to try carrying around a few decapitated human heads in order to determine how to look when she was holding that of St. John. Julia, who held immense respect for such a passionate commitment to one's art, tried to imagine what it must have been like to watch Fremstad perform.

"That soprano is attractive."

Julia came out of her musing to see Larry leaning over the pit rail.

"She's got to sing, too, you know, Larry," Julia said. "Strauss said she has to look like a sixteen-year-old princess but has to have the voice of an Isolde."

"I can't wait to see her shed those veils," Larry said. "I hope you're not jealous."

"Not a bit. According to what everyone is saying, she's one of the few who can cut it both vocally and dance-wise. A double threat. I admire that," Julia said. "But I hate to disappoint you; no veils will be shed today. Rumor has it the director and the choreographer haven't been able to agree on the moves yet."

"Bummer. Guess I'll have to come to another rehearsal."

"You were lucky to get into this one," Julia said. "I might be able to score you a ticket for the opening, though."

"Good. As long as I can see the important parts. Meaning the 'Dance' and John the Baptist's head."

"You saw both of those at the Met, remember?"

"I can't get enough," Larry said. "I feel sorry for the tenor, though, incessantly running around the stage and singing at the same time. What is that director thinking?"

"He's French," Julia said.

"That explains everything. Do you have enough break time for coffee?"

Julia checked her Fitbit. "I think so. I'll meet you at the cantina in a few. I got a text from Molinari. He wants to go over a few notes with me backstage."

Larry raised his eyebrows. "Hmm. A one-on-one with a hot Italian guy? I'm jealous."

"What's up with the jealousy thing?"

"It must be this mountain air," Larry said and headed toward the back of the theatre.

Matt stopped practicing and stood up next to Julia. "I could put your violin in the case backstage to save you some time."

"Thanks, Matt. You're the best."

Julia handed Matt her violin, wound her way through the music stands and out the pit door, and headed for the backstage wings. She was beginning to know her way around the theatre. The backstage area felt more crowded than the one at the Met, which was exponentially larger and had more space to accommodate props and scenery flats, but she did enjoy hanging around behind the scenes to watch the stagehands work their magic.

To reach the area where Molinari was waiting, Julia had to squeeze her way in between backdrops from four different operas that were in repertoire, which were being stored in between performances: *Lulu, Roméo et Juliette, Lucia,* and *Salome.*

Her mind was intensely preoccupied, divided between her determination to play her best and her bewilderment over the conflicting evidence in the two murders that had occurred. At the moment, however, she tried to focus on the matter at hand: whatever Molinari required of her.

Likely, Molinari wanted to go over the music for the very involved violin solo she was about to play in the rehearsal after the break. She never tired of the music, and of how brilliantly Strauss wove and dovetailed it in between Salome's vocal lines. But the passage also exemplified some of the composer's most difficult violin writing: five sharps in the key signature, terribly exposed in the upper register, some of it in *pianissimo*—the softest possible—dynamic, moving into the stratosphere of the instrument's range, then crescendo-ing to loud, or *forte*.

What am I thinking? I should be practicing. After I see Molinari I'll go back to the pit for the rest of the break and text Larry to forget about coffee. He'll understand.

Spying Giovanni at the rear of the wings, she hurried toward him while simultaneously initiating a text to Larry. Preoccupied with her screen, she paid little attention to where she was going—until she suddenly found herself face to face with a horrifying, bloody apparition: the severed head of St. John the Baptist, positioned on a table at her eye level, leaking blood onto a silver platter.

Julia was so caught off guard, the blood and gory features so lifelike, it took her a moment to realize that the countenance was a mere, if brilliant, imitation of a real human head. But her frightened shriek caused alarm among those nearest to her, one of whom was Sándor.

"Julia, what happened?"

Julia tried to take a few deep breaths to control her hyperventilating, but her sentences still came in short gasps. "I wasn't expecting to see…it looked so…real!"

"You must still be tense, with recent goings-on. It is perfectly understandable."

"That's kind of you to say, Sándor," Julia said breathlessly. "But I'm…I'm so embarrassed. I should have known better."

Giovanni heard the commotion and hurried over to Julia and Sándor. "What happened?"

"N-nothing, Maestro," Julia frowned apologetically. "After I got your text, I came over to find out why you wanted to see me. I got a little freaked out by this…this…head."

"But I did not send you a text."

Hearing this, Julia became more unnerved. "You didn't? Then who—"

"Perhaps it was a joke," Giovanni said.

Sándor tightened his grip around Julia's shoulder. "With all respect, Maestro, considering the strain Julia has been under lately, I can't imagine who would consider this funny."

Larry, who had gone searching for Julia when she hadn't shown up at the cantina, became deeply concerned when he found her backstage in an agitated state. "Julia, what's wrong?"

"Nothing, nothing, I…" Julia's voice quivered. "I…came backstage to see what the maestro wanted to discuss. It turns out he never texted me at all."

"What?" Now Larry was truly alarmed. "Then who did?"

Julia shook her head. "No one seems to know."

"You look totally freaked out," Larry said. "Are you going to be okay?"

Sándor put his arm around Julia's shoulder. "She'll be fine. She had little run-in with very life-like prop."

Larry took one look at the gruesome object in question and grunted. "The same thing happened to her at the Met. You backstage people shouldn't leave these things lying around."

"It's not their fault," Julia said. "There's limited space back here. They have to put things wherever they can. You'd think I'd know better by now."

"You are too hard on yourself, Julia." Sándor attempted a smile. "I think Daniel will be flattered to know you found his work so realistic."

But Daniel was otherwise occupied.

* * *

Daniel drummed his fingers on the table in the interrogation room at police headquarters, where he was seated opposite Stella. "Do I need a lawyer?"

"That's up to you," Stella said. "If you cooperate with us, the DA will bear that in mind—should it come to that."

"Need I repeat that I haven't done anything?"

"You tell me."

Daniel did not respond. Grimacing, Stella left the room and faced Constantin, who had been watching through the two-way mirror.

"He had opportunity and access to the type of weapon the CMI thinks caused the fatal trauma," she told Constantin. "But no motive."

"What do you mean, no motive?" Constantin said. "He already told us the first time we questioned him that he virtually wanted to suffocate Emilia."

"So did everyone else."

"Maybe Adam gave him grief, too. Some bad blood between them."

"There's no indication of that," Stella said. "I was hoping he would reveal some info that might lead to the killer. But we have no probable cause to keep him, and he could lawyer up. We'll have to let him go."

"Sonofabitch."

"There is a sonofabitch out there somewhere," said Stella. "But I don't think it's Daniel."

Constantin glowered. "Back to square one-and-a-half?"

"Not exactly. It's time we questioned the live guy who's been replacing the expired ones."

Constantin knew who she meant.

Chapter Forty

Recitar! Mentre preso dal delirio non so più quel che dico e quel che faccio!
Eppur...è duopo...sforzati!
Perform! While imprisoned by delirium I don't know what I'm
saying or doing!
Yet...it must be...force yourself!
—Leoncavallo, *Pagliacci*

L arry remained backstage with Julia while she tried to regain her composure. Despite Larry's protests, Julia insisted on continuing to rehearse, though she felt uneasy about what had happened and knew Larry did as well.

"Do you think this is a bad omen? A disaster in the making?"

"I don't believe in omens. But I would like to know who summoned you backstage," Larry said. "Someone clearly wanted you to run across the bloody head at the right time."

"You mean...they're trying to scare me on purpose?"

"Exactly. The question is, who—and why? At the moment, I'm more concerned about you trying to play in your condition. You still look shaken up."

"I'm fine now. Ready to get back to it."

"Are you sure? Even your solos?"

"Especially those. After what I encountered, a few solos will seem like nothing."

"Good. Because you're going to kick ass."

For the first time since her frightening backstage encounter, Julia smiled. "You've always had such a way with words."

* * *

When Stella and Constantin arrived at the theatre late in the rehearsal, Stella told her partner to wait backstage while she watched from the house.

Seeing Stella sit across the aisle from him, Larry discreetly rose from his seat, sat down next to her, and spoke in a stage whisper. "Something's happened to Julia."

Stella's ears perked up. "What was it? Is she okay?"

"A strategically placed prop spooked her backstage. Scared her out of her wits."

Stella stood up and motioned to Larry to follow her to the back of the theatre. She leaned in closely as Larry recounted Julia's alarming experience.

"Someone clearly found out she's been poking around," Stella said. "And is not liking it."

"I agree," Larry said. "Question is, what do we do?"

"First, we tell Julia to stop prying. It's too dangerous. Then you try and find out who wanted to send her a warning."

"Me? I thought you swore me off snooping."

"I changed my mind. I need all the help I can get. And you've got expertise."

"But I'm out of my jurisdiction."

"I'm aware of that. No one has to know."

"You're sure?"

Stella nodded. "You in or not?"

"I never say no to a gal in cowboy boots," Larry said.

* * *

Unlike Daniel, Sándor was anything but reticent when Stella sat with him in his dressing room, largely because Stella decided to angle her questioning to show interest in Sándor's personal history. He was voluble, and his responses were given freely—at least initially.

"I'm told you and your sister defected from Hungary."

"Yes. In years after 1956 Revolution, before fall of Communism in 1989, life in Hungary was harsh. Political repression, material deprivation, religious persecution and murder, all rampant. Our parents, suspected of being part of Resistance, were illegally deported to Soviet Ukraine, leaving us to fend for ourselves. We later found out they had died in work camps."

"I'm sorry to hear that. What happened then?"

"Magda and I were worried we might be next. We had to run for our lives. Magda found out where were most hidden alleys, so we could move about undetected. Under cover of night, we sneaked through streets to American Embassy at Szabadság tér, now called Liberty Square. They took pity on us, much as they did the passionately anti-communist Cardinal Mindszenty in 1956, took us in, protected us until they could find us home in U.S. Fortunately, because we both had musical talent, they were able to help arrange scholarships to Manhattan School of Music, and family to live with. So, we went to New York."

"What year was that?"

"1985."

"How old were you and Magda when you left?"

"I was fifteen. Magda was much older, thirty or so. Our parents had planned to have only one child."

"I see. And Magda has always been protective of you?"

"Always. Once we left school, money was tight. It was long struggle to find first professional singing engagements, many, many years. Magda gave up her own singing career and took job in costume department of Met Opera. There is nothing she would not do for me."

"You must be very grateful to her."

"I am. I will be forever. I owe her everything."

"How did you come to Santa Fe?"

"Magda heard about apprentice program here from people at Met. Through connections she was able to get me audition. When I was accepted, she applied for position in costume department. Eventually I started singing mainstage roles. We decided to live here all year."

"Is it unusual for you to replace three singers in quick succession?"

"Definitely. Has never happened before. Generally, I have one mainstage role per season and cover one or two more. But you must admit this season is anything but typical, yes?"

"Clearly. It must be exciting for you to step into a role at the last moment, though."

"It can be. But honestly, in case of Adam, it felt sad, very sad, to have to replace him under such heartbreaking circumstances."

Stella paused for a moment. "Tell me, Sándor, how important is it for you to be able to get up on that stage and perform?"

"There is nothing more important for me. Performing is my life."

"And you would move heaven and earth to make sure that happens?"

Sándor's expression suddenly darkened. "What are you implying?"

"Nothing," she said. "I was only wondering. 'One man in his time plays many parts.'"

"We are 'merely players.'" Sándor rose. "I must get back to rehearsal. Please excuse me."

"Of course. Thank you for your time. We'll be in touch."

"I am sure you will."

Stella ushered Sándor out of the room. Constantin was waiting outside.

"What do you think?" he asked. "Do you like him for Adam's murder?"

"As ambitious as he is, he strikes me as too sensitive a soul to be capable of violence."

"You never know. Hungarians can be pretty feisty. He did escape from the Communists."

"Seems his sister was mostly responsible for that," Stella said.

"Magda told me when I questioned her, his middle name is Béla," Constantin said. "She says 'Béla' means 'gutsy' in Hungarian. Maybe he's not as fragile as you think."

"I don't put much credence in those things. 'Men at some time are masters of their fates.' At least that's what Shakespeare attributed to Julius Caesar," Stella said. "What counts more is what his colleagues think about him. Have you heard any chitchat from the grapevine?"

"He seems to get along with everyone. His sister...that's another matter."

"By the way," Stella said, "Do you know how to tell when someone's fudging on the truth?"

"How?"

"When they use the word, 'honestly.'"

Chapter Forty-One

Il passo è periglioso, può nascer qualche imbroglio
The path is dangerous, some unwanted trouble may arise
—Mozart, *Don Giovanni*, Act 1

J ulia protested when Larry told her she was under orders not to do any more investigating.

"But I was just hitting my stride."

"We want to make sure nothing hits *you*," Larry said. "Remember what happened with that scenery at the Met?"

Larry's prickly question brought back an uncomfortable reminder of her investigation into her mentor's murder at the Met. As her probe had begun to heat up, both she and Larry could tell she was being threatened in critical ways. Not only had a weighty piece of scenery come loose from the proscenium high above the stage, crashing down on the stage and narrowly missing her, but ominous written notes had been attached to her sheet music on her music stand in the pit.

"And more recently, the incident with that prop sword," Larry added.

"Those are not likely to happen again," Julia said.

"Still, you must admit that staying on the sidelines would be much safer. You have to give full attention to *Salome*. Opening night is tomorrow. You have some very tricky solos."

Julia realized Larry was right. The solos in *Salome* were technically difficult, completely exposed, and attention-grabbing. Playing them with as much virtuosity as possible was her most important task—her *raison d'être* for being in Santa Fe.

But a piece of the puzzle was missing. And she was not about to leave the big picture unfinished.

* * *

Given Julia's umbrage at having to desist from sleuthing, Larry thought it best not to mention Stella's request that he take over Julia's role. Thus, he didn't tell her about his plan to invade Magda's space.

Since Stella had delegated him to poke around, Larry thought picking the costume director's brain would be a good start. Magda probably had been with the company longer than anyone currently on staff. As a veteran cop, he knew there was no substitute for experience.

Still, he needed a credible excuse to drop by casually. Borrowing some duds for the Santa Fe Opera Guild's *Salome* opening night post-performance costume party seemed the perfect pretext. Invites to swanky company *soirées* were among the perks Julia enjoyed as concertmaster, and Larry was happy to act as her squire.

"I hope I'm not intruding," he told Magda as he followed her from the costume shop into the costume storage area located in a far-off corner of the theatre. "I thought I'd get a head start on the costume search since Julia is busy practicing her head off for opening night."

Magda smiled her agreement. "It is completely understandable."

Larry stared, wide-eyed, at the high-ceilinged, warehouse-like space and the scores of racks holding padded hangers with a vast assortment of stage clothing draped on them.

"Julia would be blissed out at all this," Larry said. "But it's pretty intimidating for me. I have no idea where to begin."

"Do not worry." Magda gestured at the sea of racks. "Something romantic for a couple, yes? *Roméo et Juliette* would be ideal, but still being used at moment."

She led him through endless rows of female operatic couture—from Rosalinde in *Die Fledermaus* to Adina in *Elixir of Love* to Violetta in *La*

Traviata—flicking one hanger after another, until finally she stopped, pulled out a costume and held it up.

"Zerlina's wedding dress designed for beautiful new *Don Giovanni* production in 2015," she said. "Julia would look like vision in this."

Larry gazed at the confection fashioned of cream-colored silk with brocade bodice and delicate crimson roses cascading from the *décolleté* down to the skirt hem. Judging from the pride in Magda's expression, he could see she was inordinately fond of this particular garment.

"And she would flip over it, too," Larry said.

"However, costume for her fiancé Masetto is—how you say—generic by comparison."

"Not a problem. I'll be happy with it. Julia should be getting all the attention anyway."

"Excellent. You can both come by for fitting at your convenience."

"Thank you, Magda, I appreciate it." Larry turned to leave. "You know, I'm so glad Julia met you. She never told me about her Hungarian aunt. Thanks to you, I have another window into what made Julia the person she is."

"That is very kind of you to say."

"I've never been to Hungary. What is it like?"

Magda's eyes glistened. "Hungary is very proud country. When I live there, it is greatest place on earth. Sun is clear, air fresh and non-polluted. I don't like air here when I first come. I find fault with almost everything. I am used to it now. I realize I am not in Budapest anymore."

"It must have been tough for you at first, starting over."

"I had to give up much. I wanted to be opera singer. But I was blessed with other ability so I could get good job and help my brother."

"I'm sure Sándor is very grateful. They say Santa Fe Opera is a great place to work."

Magda nodded. "Yes. But at first, I could only find part-time work here. We needed to make ends meet. I had to work other places in Santa Fe. I was lucky they hire me at La Posada."

Larry's eyebrows shot up. He wasn't sure why, but hearing that Magda had worked at La Posada made him uneasy. Certainly, it would be better not to share that information with Julia. "La Posada? What did you do there?"

"I design room décor."

"How versatile you are. You must have gotten to know every inch of those buildings."

"Is true. You have been there?"

"Yes. Fascinating place. Lots of history." Larry decided not to reveal that he and Julia had spent a night there. "I'd better let you get back to work. So kind of you to spend time with me."

"Not at all. I will walk you out."

After Magda had pointed him in the right direction, Larry wandered around the backstage area, pondering his meeting with her. The revelation about Magda's role at La Posada was nagging at him. Undoubtedly, scores of people had passed through those portals en route to jobs in more important places of employment. Still, it was a remarkable coincidence.

Then he remembered: in life, there are no coincidences.

Chapter Forty-Two

Du siehst heute reizend aus
I find you so beautiful today
—Berg, *Lulu*, Act 1

L arry strolled along East Palace Avenue on his way to Radiance Gallery. He had read that the bricks in Santa Fe Plaza had been ripped out and swapped for new ones during a renovation in 1974. He wished he had been there to avail himself of a few when they were being given away. The quantity of history concealed within them must have been astonishing.

The gallery was easy for Larry to find. Located about one block west of Santa Fe Plaza, tucked on a street not far from the Georgia O'Keeffe Museum and the Museum of Contemporary Native Arts, Radiance looked small and unpretentious from the outside. But the interior space was expansive and airy, with hardwood floors polished to a gleam and glass cases of all sizes exhibiting one-of-a-kind pieces.

Spending time with Magda had reminded Larry that Julia had yet to visit the gallery to see the locket matching the one Julia's aunt had bequeathed her. Given the extraordinary difficulties, both personal and artistic, that Julia had suffered since coming to Santa Fe, Larry thought she deserved a nice gift, something refined and attractive, worthy of her sensitive nature. If it was for sale and he could afford it, he would show his appreciation and affection by presenting it to her.

Larry didn't consider himself a sentimental person; few people would say he was, least of all Julia. But since coming to Santa Fe, his feelings for her had burgeoned and intensified. Maybe it was the altitude, the romantic sunsets, the transcendent atmosphere of the mountain ranges surrounding them. Or, as Shakespeare had said in *The Merchant of Venice*, "…the sounds of music…creep in our ears."

Whatever the reasons, Larry lately had felt he wanted to take his relationship with Julia to the next level. He hoped that placing two halves of a heart together as one would symbolize that.

As soon as he entered, the gallery owner greeted Larry with a genial, though somewhat aloof, smile. "Welcome to Radiance. I'm Damian. Are you looking for something in particular?"

"I am. A locket. Or half of one. Half a heart, actually."

"Is it an antique, by any chance?"

"Yes. So I'm told."

"Ah. I think I know the piece you're referring to. Please follow me."

Damian led Larry past showcases of varied shapes and sizes to a wall at the rear of the store, where a brightly lit rectangular case held what looked like a few select vintage pieces. He unlocked the case, removed a small box, and carefully placed it on top of a glass countertop. Then he opened the box, revealing a delicate gold half-heart nestled in sapphire-blue velvet.

"We have only a small number of classic items. This one is the most unique, waiting for its companion."

"May I?" Larry asked.

Damian nodded, and Larry gently lifted the heart from its velvety cradle. To his untrained eye, it looked like the exact mirror image to Julia's half-heart, identical in every way.

"Exquisite, isn't it?" Damian said.

"It is. In fact, the other half belongs to my…significant other, Julia."

"Are you sure? Chances are very slim of it being the exact match. Is it a period piece?"

"Definitely. Julia inherited it from her late aunt, who brought it from Hungary," Larry said. "Did I mention Julia is the concertmaster of the Santa Fe Opera?"

"You didn't." Damian paused, his expression no longer standoffish. "We're very proud of our company here. Did you know they've even done an opera about a murderous jeweler?"

Larry, taking a long moment to examine the detail on the locket, looked up, intrigued.

"It was called *Cardillac*," Damian said. "Based on a story by E.T.A. Hoffmann about a goldsmith who is so in love with his creations he takes them back by murdering his customers. The work premiered in 1967, the night before the opera house burned down."

"Fascinating." Larry made a mental note to find out more about this murderous opera as he continued to study the locket's engravings. "That must have been some night."

"The air was even drier than usual, bristling with heat. Everyone partied till the wee hours. Then, around three-thirty a.m., people heard sounds like firecrackers. When they realized the theatre was on fire…well, Crosby had nightmares about those sounds for months afterward. You could see flames from miles away. Firefighters used every drop of water they could find. There was nothing anyone could do. It was like one big bonfire. They lost everything. Costumes, pianos, scenery. The only thing left of the theatre were two flights of stairs to nowhere. It was like the fire at the end of Twilight of the Gods from Wagner's *Ring* cycle, where Brünnhilde lights the funeral pyre and the flames consume Valhalla."

Larry was impressed by the analogy. "I heard everyone rallied to rebuild. That says something about the spirit of the company."

"Indeed," Damian said. "People sawed and hammered and sewed day and night. The community spirit was remarkable. Contributions came from around the world from people who cared deeply about opera."

Larry waited a moment out of respect. Then he held up the locket. "What do you know about the engraved inscription on the back?"

"I only know it's in Hungarian," Damian said. "Very difficult to decipher, even if one were familiar with the language."

"I see." Larry's police background kicked in as he inspected the letters etched into the piece. They were too tiny to discern, but a thought occurred to him. "Do you, by any chance, have any onion skin paper?"

"Yes, I do. Why?"

"If we do a rubbing of the inscription, we can blow it up and see what the letters are."

"I never thought of that."

"That's what twenty years of NYPD experience can do for you."

"Oh? You're...?"

"A detective with the New York Police Department." Larry waited for his response to sink in. "So, what do you think? About the onion skin?"

"It's worth a try."

Damian reached into a drawer at the back of the case and extracted a small sheet of wafer-thin, almost transparent paper. He rubbed a pencil lead over the letters on the back of the locket and handed the sheet to Larry. "Keep in mind, it's still in Hungarian."

"Not a problem. I can blow it up on the hotel printer, and I know someone who can translate it." Larry carefully pocketed the paper. "By the way, does the locket open?"

"Please allow me." Damian gently pried open the latch and handed the locket back to Larry. "Enough room for one cameo-sized portrait. To be paired with the other, of course."

"How much is it?"

Damian turned over the minuscule tag attached to the piece and put on his bifocals to read it. "Nine thousand three hundred thirty-five dollars, plus tax."

Larry let out a deep breath. "Whew."

"I admit it's a bit pricey, but it is a singular piece, an antique," Damian said. "If you own the matching half, I imagine it would be more than worth the price."

Larry was torn. He had no doubt that Julia would be thrilled. He also knew that such a purchase would stretch his resources to the max. But Julia's happiness was worth every dollar to him—and more.

"Do you gift wrap?" he said.

Chapter Forty-Three

Wenn ich einem Menschen auf dieser Welt angehöre, gehöre ich Ihnen
If I belong to any man in this world, I belong to you
—Berg, *Lulu*, Act 1

To Julia's great relief, the dress rehearsal for *Salome* went off without any incident: no stabbings, except those programmed into the action onstage; no anguished cries, except the ones specified by the libretto.

Julia had arrived at the pit well before the beginning of the rehearsal to do some last-minute polish on her solos. As she focused on her most difficult passage, out of the corner of her eye, she spied Stewart leaning on the pit wall above her, watching and listening.

She didn't allow his presence to make her nervous or to distract her. She kept playing and executed the music flawlessly. After she had stopped, she caught sight of Stewart's approving smile and felt gratified.

Now all I have to do is duplicate that on opening night for the other conductor.

Once the rehearsal started, Stewart made his presence known: seated in the first row beyond the pit wall, he peeked his head over the railing periodically to nod. Giovanni paid little attention to the music director; he had his hands full, keeping control of the massive Strauss orchestration and maintaining synchronicity between pit and stage.

Julia, who made an extra effort to play her solos more superbly than she had in her practice session, was rewarded with looks of approbation from Giovanni and Stewart. Having pleased the power duo, she allowed herself a peek at the stage as Salome lay atop a table, her virgin-white dress drenched in Jochanaan's blood, which, to Julia, still looked disturbingly real.

After an hour, Giovanni put down his baton. "Let's take fifteen minutes."

"Great job. Home run. Grand Slam, even."

Startled, Julia whirled around to see Larry standing behind her. She glared at him. "Are you trying to give me a heart attack?"

"How about, 'Gee, I'm so happy to see you, Larry,'" he said.

Julia turned to Giovanni. "*Mi dispiace, Maestro.*"

"No need to apologize, Julia," Giovanni said.

Julia turned back to Larry. "You're right. Sorry, I'm tense. Performance anxiety. Solos. You know what I mean."

"Of course I do. And I wasn't exaggerating. You knocked them over the right field wall."

"How did you get in, anyway? I heard rehearsal was closed."

"What a question. I managed to sneak past the security guard and watch the rehearsal from the back of the house. I can get around any barrier."

"Oh? How?"

"How? I'm a cop. Once a cop, always a cop. Isn't it so predictable by now?" he said.

"Not necessarily. Do enlighten me."

"As Shakespeare said—"

Julia groaned. "What, you, too? Are you trying to compete with Stella?"

"She's not the only detective who can quote Shakespeare. May I continue?"

"Please."

"As I was saying, 'Let me count the ways'—"

"That's Elizabeth Barrett Browning, not Shakespeare."

"Whatever. Do you want to hear this or not?"

"Of course."

"One, I'm intimately familiar with every nut job who lives in any given location. Two, I can name you every drunk and pross within a ten-mile radius of our Manhattan apartment."

Julia realized her limited familiarity with police procedurals would not be able to keep up with Larry's for much longer. "'Pross?'"

"Prostitute. How can you not know that? You watch *Blue Bloods* devotedly."

"Not lately. It's summer, they're on hiatus. Go on, this is fascinating."

"Three. When you introduce me to your friends, you always add, 'He's a cop.' Four, I look around a room and try to calculate how long it would take me to cuff the heftiest guy there."

"Okay, I get it." She peered at him. "You didn't come here to listen to my solos, did you?"

Larry smiled. Julia had that look about her, that certain radiance, like when she had completed playing a difficult piece to her own satisfaction. He remembered meeting her—how she wouldn't let anything or anyone touch her but her music—and thought about how far they'd come. "Busted. How did you know?"

"I may not be a cop, but I'm living with one. Plus, I've been dabbling in investigation. Some of your 'ways' have rubbed off."

"You're right, God help me. Actually, there's something I wanted to—"

"Julia." Sándor, still in costume, was leaning on the pit rail. "You sounded magnificent."

Julia looked up at him. "You did, too."

Sándor smiled. "Do you have time for coffee?"

Larry placed his hand over Sándor's. "Sorry, pal. I'm higher up on her dance card. Although, maybe you could do me a favor." Larry reached into his pocket and extracted the onion skin parchment with the engraving from the back of the locket rubbed onto it. "Could you take a look at this and translate it for me?"

"Of course, Larry."

"Thanks," Larry whispered, barely audibly, into Julia's ear. "As I was saying, there's something I wanted to…ah…share with you. Can we go somewhere more private?"

"I think I can find a place," she said. "Another time, Sándor?"

"*Természetesen*, Julia. Of course."

Sándor pocketed the paper and walked away. "I'm learning some new words from him, Larry," Julia said. "Isn't that cool?"

"*Természetesen*, Julia," he said, only slightly tripping over the syllables.

＊＊＊

All the musicians had departed the orchestra lounge when Julia and Larry entered. The atmosphere was quiet, peaceful. Appropriate for presenting Julia with his distinctive gift.

He sat her down on a chaise. "I got you something for good luck tomorrow night," he said. "I hope you'll like it."

"For a supposedly predictable cop, you can be full of surprises." Julia eyed the diminutive velvet box with its Radiance Gallery logo that Larry extracted from his pocket. "But you didn't have to get me anything."

He deposited the package in her lap. "Stop protesting and open it," he said lovingly.

It took her a moment to comprehend, but once Julia recognized what she was gazing at, she let out a cry of delight. "Is it…? Oh, Larry, it's…perfect."

Julia lifted the treasure from its velvet nest and stared at it in disbelief.

"Are you going to gape, or do you maybe want to put it on?" Larry said, grinning.

"Oh, yes. Please."

Larry unfastened the clasp on Julia's necklace and, cognizant of the miniature gold star placed behind the half-heart locket, carefully threaded the tiny bale attached to the newly acquired half-heart through the chain that held the other half and gently pressed the two heart halves together. They fit seamlessly as one.

Julia, at first speechless with joy, threw her arms around Larry's neck and squeezed tightly. "I love it," she said finally. "But it must have cost a fortune. You shouldn't have."

He returned her embrace. "You're worth it," he said.

And he meant every word.

Chapter Forty-Four

Et le péril, il est en bas, il est en haut, il est partout, qu'importe!
And peril lies below us, above us, everywhere, what does it matter!
—Bizet, *Carmen*, Act 3

Once the final dress rehearsal of *Salome* had finished, Julia hurried to the costume shop. Despite Larry's queries, she insisted on not divulging her plan to go for her fitting by herself, without him. She didn't want to tell him she thought it bad luck for him to see her in a wedding dress before the opening night extravaganza, even if it wasn't technically a wedding. She knew he would make fun of her superstition.

"I can't tell you where I'm going. I'm concocting a surprise for you. Trust me."

"Who am I to argue with the Queen of Hearts of Santa Fe Opera?" Larry quipped.

One thing Julia knew for certain: the now-complete heart locket and her costume would complement each other superbly. After instructing Larry to wait for her at the inn, she headed off alone to find Magda. She felt slightly guilt-ridden for not revealing to Larry where she was going, but she didn't want to worry him.

Despite Stella's orders not to investigate, Julia felt she needed one more chance to grill Magda. She knew Stella had been working single-mindedly to solve the murders, but no progress had been made in uncovering the identity of either Emilia's or Adam's killer. The investigation had reached an impasse. Something else had to be done. Julia believed if she could manage to slip in a few subtle questions during her fitting with Magda, she might find some clue, some evidence Stella had overlooked.

When she arrived at the costume shop, Julia was surprised to find Magda in a cordial mood. Perhaps the costume director was not one to cling stubbornly to resentments. Whatever the reason, Julia thought it best not to touch upon the subject of their recent disastrous encounter.

"You have come for your fitting, Júlia?" Magda said, smiling.

"Yes. Larry tells me you've found something special."

"Is true. I have set aside for you." Magda gazed at Julia's locket, now complete and perfectly positioned in the hollow of Julia's neck. "I see you have now other half of heart."

"Larry got it for me. To make up for all the troubles I've had lately."

"He is very generous. It will go perfectly with costume. Come. I show you."

Magda led Julia along the hallway toward the far-off costume storage area as she had done with Larry. The passageway seemed longer and darker than the others Julia had seen. Uncomfortable, she decided to add some small talk to the awkward silence.

"This season has been a bit tricky for you, hasn't it?" Julia said.

Magda quickened her pace. "Tricky?"

"I mean, keeping up with costumes, with so many, well, cast changes because of the..."

"Murders?"

"Well...yes."

"I am used to numerous changes, for many reasons," Magda said.

Sensing increased tension in Magda's disposition, Julia tried to lighten up the atmosphere.

"*Salome* is going well," Julia said. "Despite my little run-in with a severed head."

"Yes. I heard. Sándor said you were shaken. He was very worried."

"News travels fast," Julia said. "I was touched at his concern."

"He likes you very much."

"I gathered that. He's very sweet." Julia fingered her locket. "It's amazing, isn't it, that he's been able to sing so many roles in quick succession so early in the season? Such a coincidence that he has had an opportunity to step in for singers who have been…indisposed. I haven't been working here very long, but I know that at the Met, it's very unusual for one singer to fill in that much. Not that Sándor doesn't deserve—"

Magda lowered her voice. "He has more talent than all of them."

"Oh, I agree. His artistic and vocal skills are outstanding. He certainly demonstrated that at the *Salome* dress rehearsal. Were you there?"

"I always come to rehearsals. I must be available in case costumes need adjustment."

Julia detected some irritability in Magda's tone. "Oh. Of course. Sándor did a fantastic job singing Narraboth, didn't he?"

"Always he does."

"Yes." Julia paused, trying to get a handle on Magda's inscrutable expression. "You know, Magda, after all the…mishaps, it was such a relief that there were no other incidents in *Salome*. Like the one that happened to me during the *Roméo et Juliette* rehearsal. I wouldn't want to go through that again."

"Opera is sometimes dangerous."

"A little more for me than other people." Julia attempted a lighthearted laugh. Magda did not respond.

Sensing Magda's increasing annoyance, Julia was relieved finally to arrive at the enormous costume storage area. Silent, Magda guided Julia between a sea of hanging racks holding the vast collection of stage attire, until they reached the most remote corner of the room. There, on a padded silk hanger separated from the rest, hung the brocaded, rose-embroidered wedding dress Magda had shown Larry.

Julia gasped. "It's exquisite."

"I think it will fit perfectly. Last soprano to sing Zerlina was petite like you."

"May I try it on?"

"Of course. Screen is over there in corner." Magda removed the garment from the hanger and placed it in Julia's arms.

Julia stepped behind the screen, removed her clothing, and slipped the dress over her head. "You're right, Magda. It feels like it was made for me."

"There is mirror here," Magda said, as Julia emerged wearing the costume.

Julia positioned herself in front of a floor-length mirror, feeling as regal as a princess.

"Only thing missing is veil," said Magda. When I took out of storage, I notice lace needed repair. Do you have time to go back to costume shop and try it?"

Chapter Forty-Five

Tut chto -to ne ladnoe tvoritsya!
There's something suspicious about all this!
—Tchaikovsky, *The Queen of Spades*, Act 2

Julia followed Magda back to the costume shop, all the way to the rear wall by the exit door, to a worktable next to a bank of tall picture windows. Julia squinted at the late afternoon sun gleaming through the glass. It was bright: so bright it almost obliterated the view of the hillside behind the opera house; so bright that Julia couldn't see Magda bolting the exit door and locking the main entrance to the shop.

Magda lifted the costume veil from the work table and held it up for Julia. It was made of cream-colored organza trimmed at the bottom with white lace. The headpiece was a crown-shaped tiara edged with red rosettes that matched those embroidered on the costume.

Julia was enchanted, happy to see Magda's former irritable expression had softened.

"Try it on," Magda said. "Do not be afraid."

Slowly, gently, Julia raised the veil, careful not to damage the delicate fabric, and placed the rose-bedecked crown on her head. The veil reached to Julia's waist.

Magda adjusted the fit. "Now effect is complete," she said. "With locket, is perfect."

Again, Julia thought Magda's assessment spot on. The necklace was positioned at exactly the right place to set off the sweetheart neckline and

220

décolleté of the dress.

Julia looked around for a mirror. Finding none, she stood at a window and admired her reflection. She expected the costume director to voice her approval, but instead, Magda, her back turned away from Julia, was opening the door to an adjacent cabinet.

Julia watched as Magda rummaged through the cupboard. "What's in there?"

"Props."

"Aren't they usually kept in the prop room, or the dressing rooms?"

"Yes. But when opera is in repertoire, we keep extra props here in shop for singers to try, together with costume. I have access to all props. For instance, this one…"

As she watched Magda reach into the cabinet, Julia narrowed her eyes to get a better look at the contents. Hanging on a hook on the top shelf, she thought she saw something that looked like a straw hat and a pair of men's Bermuda shorts.

Is that…could it be…?

She blinked and looked again. This time, she was sure. The hat and shorts matched the clothing she had seen…worn by the ghost of John Crosby.

"Cuando llegue el momento, me conocerá a mí, y mi obra," Magda said under her breath.

Julia wasn't sure why, but the pronouncement made her strangely uncomfortable.

* * *

Larry was feeling a combination of impatience and disquiet. Anxious about what might be keeping Julia so long, he wished he had insisted on going with her, or at least knowing where she was going. Given the near calamities that had befallen her, he should have known better. Now, he was worried. He needed to go looking for her, but he had no idea where to start.

He tapped a text on his phone: *"Julia, where are you?"*

There was no response. He tried to think of who might know where Julia was. There was Sándor, but Larry hesitated. He had been feeling pangs of jealousy at the singer's all-too-obvious play for Julia's attentions. But he sensed that the tenor might have a clue as to Julia's whereabouts. Larry swallowed his pride, looked up Sándor's number, and tapped. To his relief, the singer picked up.

"Hey, Sándor. Where are you?"

"In Opera Shop. Maestro told me historical Leonie Rysanek *Salome* recording is in. I have now found it."

"Do you know where Julia is?"

"No. Is something wrong?"

"Hope not. Julia said to meet her here at the inn, but that was a while ago, and she still hasn't showed up. I'm concerned," Larry said. "When did you last see her?"

"Not since rehearsal. Where did she say she was going?"

"She wouldn't tell me. Any idea where she might be?"

Sándor thought for a moment. "Perhaps going over solos for *Salome* with the maestro?"

"Yes, of course. That makes perfect sense."

"Do you know where dressing room is?"

"I was there our first day here. I think I can find it. Thanks for the tip."

"Anytime. It is my pleasure. Good luck."

Larry raced out the door and through the hotel lobby, on a mission.

* * *

While he waited for the cashier to ring up the CD, Sándor pulled the onion skin parchment from his pocket and studied the writing.

"*Tól Magda, hoz Olga.*"

He hurriedly paid for his purchase, squeezed past the cash register and through the back door of the shop. He had his own notion as to where to look for the missing violinist.

Chapter Forty-Six

Ella mi fu rapita! E quando, o ciel?
Possente amor mi chiama, volar io deggio a lei
She was stolen from me! But when, o Heaven?
Powerful love calls me, and I to her must fly
—Verdi, *Rigoletto*, Act 2

Julia didn't understand Spanish, but she recognized the language and tried to determine the significance of Magda's quote. "You speak Spanish, too?"

"All cultures important in melting pot of Santa Fe. I try to be part of them. Like Native Americans who tried to accept differences, to get along with *los conquistadores*. But resentments remained, finally they fought back against Spanish tormentors," Magda said. "Since escaping cruelty of Hungarian regime, I, as you say, relate to oppressed people. I feel same bitterness toward anyone who torments me."

Julia was puzzled as to how or why Magda's animosity applied to her. But when Magda turned to Julia clutching a large sword, Julia was taken aback. She instinctively flinched. "Wow, that looks so real."

"That is because it *is* real."

Magda drew nearer, brandishing the sword. Julia began to sweat. "I think I'd better change out of this costume. I don't want my perspiration to ruin it," she said, moving back from Magda.

"Is not necessary." With her free hand, Magda extracted the hat and shorts from the cabinet and held them up. "I see you have recognized my costume.

I like to wear costumes, too."

Julia's eyes widened. "Your...costume?"

"Do you really think ghost of Crosby still hanging about?"

"That was you?" Julia tried to comprehend. "But I don't understand."

Magda dropped the hat and shorts on the floor and grasped Julia's arm so tightly that the imprint of her fingers was visible on Julia's flesh. Her mouth curled up in a sly smile.

"I want to spook you. To frighten you away. That is why I fix sword, too."

"You...what?"

Magda pulled on the top end of the sword. The hilt separated from the shaft, as it had done during the *Roméo et Juliette* rehearsal when the blade went flying through the air, striking Julia. "I calculate so that it would go just enough far to hit you."

Julia gasped. "You did that? But why?"

"You are smart, smarter than detective, Júlia. I could not allow you to solve murder," Magda said. "After I kill Emilia, I watch you snoop around, ask questions. This torments me."

The realization streaked through Julia's consciousness like a bolt of dry lightning in a Santa Fe electrical storm. She tried to remain calm. "But why would you kill Emilia?"

"Emilia was terrible to me."

"She was terrible to everyone."

"True. But to me, unspeakable. For years she mistreats me. First at Met, then here. Always she complains, makes my life miserable. World is better place without her," Magda said. "After Goran pretend to kill Emilia offstage and show fake knife onstage, I go backstage to stab Emilia with real knife. Silently, quickly. No one there to see me."

Julia struggled to comprehend. "And you would implicate Marin, an innocent woman?"

"That is unfortunate. I know she is your friend. But, yes."

Julia was horrified. "And...Adam?"

"Also unfortunate. But that role was supposed to be for my brother."

"For Sándor?"

"Of course. I have protected Sándor since he was child. I would do anything to promote his career. Management pass him over for younger singer whose voice does not compare. Sándor's is rich, beautiful. Perfect. He deserved to be onstage."

"Maybe he did. But...murder...Adam?" Julia reeled from the revelation. "How...how did you kill him?"

"Everyone was on stage for Mad Scene. When Daniel was placing wigs in dressing rooms, I went to wig shop to get sharp instrument, then to Adam's dressing room." Magda smiled. "It was very quick. He did not suffer. Unlike Emilia. She felt knife. I made sure of that."

"Oh, my God." The weight of Magda's reveal made Julia feel faint. "Does Sándor know?"

"No. And he must never know. Do you understand?"

Magda held Julia's gaze. Then her eyes fixed obsessively on Julia's locket. "Seeing your necklace reminds me of my home. My childhood."

Julia breathed slowly as she tried to ward off her alarm. "I understand. If it wasn't a family heirloom, I would give it to you."

"Why?"

"Because," Julia said, "I have great respect for you, Magda. And you remind me of my mother. I miss her so much."

"That is nice," Magda said. "But still, you will give me necklace. It belongs to me."

* * *

Once Larry passed through the security gate, he managed to find the conductor's dressing room on his own. Hearing strains of piano music coming from inside, he hesitated to disturb whichever maestro might be practicing within. But his mission was too urgent. He rapped loudly.

Giovanni opened the door and peered at Larry. "Sì?"

"I'm sorry to bother you, maestro. I'm Larry Somers. I'm here with Julia."

"What can I do for you, Larry?"

Larry peeked inside the room. "Have you seen Julia? I thought she might be here, working on her *Salome* solos with you."

"Ah, no, her solos were *perfezione* at the dress rehearsal. No further work needed," Giovanni said. "Is there a problem?"

"She was supposed to meet me at our hotel, but she never showed," Larry said. "Do you have any idea where she might be?"

"I am sorry, I have not seen her since rehearsal."

"I see. Thanks anyway, Maestro."

"Of course. I'm sure you will find her."

Giovanni smiled and closed the door. Larry remained outside, worried and bewildered. He had no idea where to look next and sent a text: *"Julia, I need to know where you are!"*

There was no response. Then he tried calling her cell. And tried again. Still no reaction.

Think, Somers. Think.

He slapped his forehead.

Of course. What was I thinking?

Larry wasn't sure if he could remember how to find the costume shop, but if his memory failed him, he could ask that obnoxious stagehand, Steve. For better or worse, that guy always seemed to be around.

Chapter Forty-Seven

Mille torbidi pensieri mi s'aggiran per la testa:
se mi salvo in tal tempesta, È un prodigio in verità!
A thousand desperate thoughts are whirling in my head:
if I survive such a storm, it'll really be a miracle
—Mozart, *Don Giovanni*, Act 2

Magda's declaration left Julia totally confused. She grasped the locket protectively. "Excuse me?"

"Locket is mine." Magda carefully laid the sword on the worktable. "You will give it to me now." The menace in her expression was unmistakable.

Julia reluctantly unclasped the chain from her neck. She removed the heart, placed it in one hand, and slowly stretched the hand toward Magda, who greedily snatched away the locket. Then Julia carefully refastened the chain to make sure the Star of David remained intact.

Magda held the delicate heart close to her eyes and gazed at it, fingering the zig-zag line dividing the halves. "Buda and Pest, now together at last." She turned the locket over and studied the inscription on the back. "Do you know what it says?"

"N-no. The writing is too small. And it's in…Hungarian."

"But I know what it says. I always have." Magda closed her eyes and recited, "'*Tól Magda hoz Olga. Barátság örökkön örökké*…From Magda to Olga. Friendship forever and ever.' Do you know who was Olga?"

Julia was mystified. The only Olga she knew was…

No. It can't be.

Julia drew in a sharp breath. "My mother?"

"Your mother, Olga, was my best friend in Budapest. We found locket in antique shop when we were girls. We had it engraved, each took one half—she, Buda and I, Pest—and swore eternal friendship. When Olga left for America to live with her sister Zsófia, I gave her my half to take with her. Olga promised to keep it for me until I came to States and we were together again. Then she married your father. But she died when you were five years old."

Magda wiped a tear from her eye. One moment of weakness. Then her steeliness returned.

"After your mother died, your father gave necklace to Zsófia. She gave one half to her Mexican husband, but when they divorced, he moved to Santa Fe and took it with him. He told me when Zsófia died, her daughter gave other half of heart to you. But he would not give his half to me. He insist on selling to gallery."

"So that's why it ended up there." The story and its revelations so intrigued Julia, she momentarily forgot her fright. "Why didn't you buy it?"

"I know your boyfriend Larry would buy it for you. My salary at Opera not enough. I cannot afford to buy locket even when I work extra hours at La Posada."

"La Posada?" The revelation stupefied Julia. "You mean, you were—"

Off Julia's astonished expression, Magda laughed maliciously. "Ghost of Julia Staab."

"The noises, the supernatural activity, my violin strings...That was all you?"

"I sabotage sword to scare you. I try to do everything to scare you away. At opera house. At La Posada. Nothing worked. You are too stubborn, too determined, too smart. Exceptionally so. Like your dear mother." Magda paused long enough to wipe a second tear. Then she went on. "Now you know everything, I have no choice but to kill you."

Julia's terror came crashing back with a vengeance, but she knew she had to quash it. Her only recourse was to placate Magda—and buy herself enough time to think of an escape plan.

* * *

Larry combed the hallways, ascending and descending staircases, trying to find the costume shop. In his current state of agitation over Julia's whereabouts and safety, his pictorial memory, sharpened over nearly two decades of police work, was not serving him, and his usual level-headedness evaded him.

Where could that frigging place be?

Finally deciding he might find Steve in the orchestra pit, which was much easier to locate than the costume shop, Larry found the entrance, leapt up the stairs two at a time, and threw open the door. Once inside, he surveyed the rows of music stands. No one there. It was a dead end.

As Larry had expected, however, Steve was never far away. He was not surprised to come across the stagehand outside the pit with a colleague, hauling a very realistic-looking black-and-red statue depicting a bloodied tangle of writhing bodies to an out-of-the-way corner. The two stagehands grunted from the immense weight and bulk of the piece. Larry could see the statue, which looked like it could have been from post-Vesuvius Pompeii, was a simulation of the real thing. Still, its gruesomeness made him shudder.

When he and the other stagehand had divested themselves of their burden, Steve looked over to see Larry, hovering near them. "Oh, hey. Larry, right? Julia's friend? What's up?" Then he noticed Larry's look of anxiety. "Where's Julia?"

Larry thought of correcting Steve's terminology to "significant other," but he had more important things on his mind. "Here's the thing. She's missing."

"What?"

"Julia was supposed to meet me over an hour ago at our hotel. She never showed. I've texted and called her. No dice. Seems like she vanished into thin air." Larry scowled. "So many damn hiding places in this theatre."

"Did you check the pit?" Steve asked.

"I just did. There's no one there," Larry said. "I even busted in on the maestro in his dressing room. He hasn't seen her since rehearsal ended."

"That's not good. Do you have any idea where else she could be?"

"All I can think of is the costume shop. But I'm damned if I can find it."

Steve wiped his grimy hands on his cargo pants. "Follow me," he said and strode off.

Larry, close behind him, frantically texted as he walked: "*Stella. Julia missing. Meet me backstage at theatre ASAP.*"

Chapter Forty-Eight

Ah...soccorso...son tradito!...L'assassino...m'ha ferito
Ah...help me...I am betrayed!...The assassin's blade...has pierced me
—Mozart, *Don Giovanni*, Act 1

Julia struggled to come up with a way to appease Magda. "But, Magda, surely you wouldn't kill your best friend's daughter? You're better than that."

"It is true Olga was my best friend. But Olga had everything I did not. Sister to sponsor her in America. Safe passage on tourist ship. Money to establish herself here. And then husband and daughter," Magda said. "But I...I had to escape through streets of Budapest, with armed soldiers lurking everywhere, and Sándor holding on to me for dear life. We had no money, no jobs, no family to keep us, take care of us."

Magda placed the heart locket in a small pouch of her apron, reached over the worktable and grabbed hold of the sword. "First time in rehearsal I only scare you. This time I finish job."

Julia backed away, furtively eyeing the exit door, as Magda inched toward her, the glinting tip of the sword pointed toward Julia's chest. Julia desperately tried to think of a way to impede Magda's momentum.

"Door is locked, Júlia," Magda said. "Do not try to escape. Delaying inevitable."

"Larry will be looking for me," Julia said. "He'll find me."

Magda's sword was a mere inch away from Julia's torso. "He will be too late. You must be punished for interfering with me. I will bury your body far away in desert, in Sangre de Cristo Mountains. Grave already dug and waiting. No one will ever find you."

Julia felt a shiver of dread vibrate through her body, but she spoke calmly. "I think you've lost your mind, Magda."

"No, Julia, no. You are afraid. I understand fear. We women grow up believing we are defenseless. Do not be afraid. It will be quick, I promise you."

But at that moment, a familiar voice resonated next to them.

"No, no, my sister. *Nem, nem, lánytestvér.*"

* * *

The moment Stella got Larry's text, she grabbed Constantin by the arm, raced with him out the door and into their squad car, and sped off to the opera house.

"Text Larry we're on our way," she told Constantin.

Constantin tapped hurriedly into his phone. Larry's response came immediately: *"Headed to costume shop. Meet there."*

Stella skidded to a stop in front of the security gate, brakes screeching. She and Constantin flashed their badges to the guard and raced inside. When they reached the backstage area, they found Larry and Steve striding toward the back of the theatre.

"Do you know where you're going?" she asked Larry.

"No," Larry said, pointing to Steve. "But he does."

The trio followed Steve's lead, threading their way through dark hallways, dodging countless pieces of equipment, props and segments of scenery, until they reached the entrance to the costume shop.

Steve jerked on the door. "It's locked."

"I'll kick it in," Stella said.

"Not a good idea. It's pure steel," Steve said. "Easier to head around to the emergency exit in the back of the shop. They never lock it."

"I hope you're right," said Larry.

The quartet rushed off, out the loading dock door, toward the back of the theatre, where they could access the back door to the costume shop. On the way, Steve grabbed an axe hanging near a fire alarm.

*　*　*

Magda clutched the sword more tensely. "Sándor, do not interfere."

"I hear everything you say, Magda. About Emilia, and Adam. How could you?"

"Emilia was evil. And Adam…I am sorry, but your career comes first. Nothing more important, more precious to me than you."

"Nothing is more precious than human life, Magda."

"Not all human life is precious, my brother."

Magda inched the sword closer to Julia, aimed at the space between Julia's ribs and her heart, just below her breast, where the satiny material was at its thinnest. Penetrating the fabric, the tip of the rapier pierced Julia's skin, drawing a tiny drop of blood. Julia winced with pain.

"Magda, no! You must not harm her," Sándor cried. "I love her."

There was a deafening banging noise as the exit door was assaulted.

"Julia! Are you in there? Open the door!"

Julia recognized Larry's voice, but she was too stunned to move and too breathless to reply. There came an earsplitting crash, as Steve's axe penetrated the exit door, which splintered into jagged metal shards. Steve, Larry, Stella, and Constantin burst in and assessed the scene.

Stella pointed her Glock at Magda. "Drop the weapon!"

Larry started toward Julia. Stella restrained him. "Careful. One more centimeter, and she could do serious damage."

"Stay back, or she is dead!" Magda kept the sword trained on Julia. "I am sorry, Sándor. She knows too many things. I cannot let her live."

"And I cannot let her die."

With a sudden lurch forward, Sándor grabbed for the sword. Julia drew back, gasping for breath, and watched, horrified, as Sándor and Magda struggled over the weapon. Suddenly Sándor cried out. The sword had punctured his chest. He doubled over and crumpled to the floor.

"Sándor!" Magda, seething, lunged at Julia. "This is all your fault!"

With Magda charging at her again, Julia panicked, desperately trying to think. Suddenly, the swordplay instruction she had gotten from Sam came hurtling into her mind. What was it the fight director had told her...?

"*...Nudge his shoulder with your sword arm...Super important...Be careful not to hit too hard, you can jar the nerve and make his arm go numb.*"

With every fragment of her strength, Julia thrust her body's full force at Magda's shoulder, exactly as Sam had warned her not to do with Larry. Magda cried out in pain from the impact. Her arm went numb, and the sword tumbled out of her hand, crashing to the floor.

Seizing her opportunity, Stella surged forward, throwing Magda down and cuffing her in one swift movement.

Julia rushed to Sándor and knelt by him. "Sándor, you saved my life. I'm so grateful to you," she said. "Sándor, Sándor. Can you hear me?"

Larry darted to her side. He leaned over Sándor, examining the wound and listening to his chest. "He's breathing, but he's losing blood fast."

Stella swiveled her head in Constantin's direction. "Call an ambulance."

Julia lifted her face toward Constantin. "Please, we've got to save him."

"The paramedics are on their way," Constantin said.

"Sándor, can you hear me? Hang on," Julia said. "Please! You've got to hang on!"

Chapter Forty-Nine

Qui sait de quel démon j'allais être la proie!
Who knows of what demon I was about to become the prey!
—Bizet, *Carmen*, Act 3

T he opening night of *Salome* was a gala affair. With the prospect of a glittering post-performance party for the patrons and stars, the atmosphere was electrified. Onstage, the wind blowing from the mountains seemed to play with the pleats of the tunic-like costumes, giving the singers an ethereal, sculpture-like eeriness.

Julia decided not to wear the costume Magda had chosen for her to the opening night party. Somehow, the associations were more discomfiting than she could handle. And though the dress had been cleaned and the bloodstains rubbed out, it would not have coordinated at all with the swanky cowboy boots Larry had gifted her, the exact ones she had drooled over in the shop window on Santa Fe Plaza. He had insisted she wear them for the opening: it was his way of making sure she officially fit in with the most seasoned opera patrons.

But with her locket returned to her and the loan from Marin of a black velvet jacket festooned with sequined bling, Julia felt as regally operatic as the English Queen in Rossini's *Elisabetta, Regina d'Inghilterra*.

Julia had been thrilled to learn that Marin would be playing the part of the Page of Herodias in *Salome*. It was not as prominent a character as Geschwitz in *Lulu*, but at least Marin would be able to re-establish her worth as an artist with the company.

Now that Magda had been incarcerated and Julia felt safe and secure in her position as leader of the orchestra, she experienced a renewed sense of confidence in her violinistic abilities. Thus, despite the fact that Stewart was watching and listening from the back of the pit, Julia did not waver in her rendition of the violin solos in the opera.

At one point, after she had tossed off a particularly demanding solo passage, Matt spoke *sotto* to her. "Blatchley gave a nod of approval when you finished your solo."

"How do you know?"

"I looked back there. He's grinning like a Lewis Carroll feline."

She fleetingly turned her head, confirmed Matt's assessment, and bumped fists with him.

As the drama progressed relentlessly toward its gruesome finale, Julia took a cursory glimpse skyward at the cloak of stars draped above the theater. She felt part of something that even the majesty of the New Mexico mountains could not transcend: the greatness of the art form that was being performed under that starlit firmament.

There was no place like Santa Fe.

* * *

Backstage in the wings, Larry watched the action with Sándor. The tenor, his chest taped, wearing a sling, and seated in a wheelchair, still had a long way to go on his road to healing. But he had confided to Larry that he was content to be alive.

"Bet you wish you were out there onstage, though," Larry told him.

"Oh. I think I can wait," Sándor said. "In my current condition, I would hardly manage deep enough breath to sing one note."

Larry had turned his attention to the soprano onstage as she launched into her sensuous, depraved Dance of the Seven Veils.

"Great Austrian soprano Leonie Rysanek once said sopranos who take on this role characterized in one of three ways," Sándor said. "'Those who can sing it, those who can dance it, and those who should be shot.'"

236

Larry grinned. "I would say this one has two out of the three covered."

Unlike the original Met Opera *Salome* premiere in 1907, which was so abhorrent to the sensibilities of wealthy New York patrons that the rest of the run was canceled, the Santa Fe production was received with wild enthusiasm. Giovanni acknowledged Julia with a generous gesture from the stage during his curtain call. She felt thoroughly gratified.

"You see? It was worth all your ordeals after all," Matt told her.

"I'm not so sure," Julia said. "What I've been through goes way beyond suffering for one's art."

* * *

For the gala celebration, Stieren Hall was transformed into an Old and New Testament biblical wonderland. Seven glowing orbs representing Salome's veils were suspended from the ceiling on golden ropes. Realistic-looking *faux* palm trees lined the walls. At one end of the room, principals of the cast and crew sat along a lengthy rectangular table under a massive, glittering crystal chandelier, as if posing for Leonardo's iconic Last Supper. In the middle, a cylindrical cage hovered over a shimmering circle in the floor, representing John the Baptist's cistern.

On their way in to join the revelers, Julia, Larry, Katie, and Sándor passed by Stella and Constantin, who were availing themselves of the luscious-looking fare laid out on a huge table.

Stella winked at Julia. "'Such stuff as dreams are made on.'"

Julia smiled in response but cringed when she saw Lenny hovering by the entrance. She girded herself for one of his usual disapproving scowls. But he surprised her by coming up to her, beaming at her genuinely. "Great work on the solos, Julia. Congratulations."

Julia had her suspicions as to the motivation for his sudden change of attitude, but she decided to take it at face value. "Thanks, Lenny, that means a lot, coming from you."

Julia leaned over Sándor and whispered, "By the way, did you ever figure out what was written on that scrap of paper I gave you?"

"*'Hívja azonmmal a rendörséget!'*?" He smiled. "It means 'Call the Police!'"

"What?" Julia was bewildered. "Who could have written that? And why?"

"I think it was Emilia," Sandor said softly. "She was only other person in company beside Magda and me who knew Hungarian. She might have worried Magda would do her harm. If true, regrettably, she was right." His expression saddened. "I thought of giving it to police. But I think it should remain our secret, yes?"

Julia nodded. They held each other's gaze until Katie and Larry each slipped an arm through one of Julia's. "Forgive us if we kidnap her for a moment," Katie said.

Followed by Sándor, the group moved on, stopping by the cast table to give Marin some hugs. Julia raised her eyebrows when she saw Giovanni's arm draped around Marin. She shot an inquisitive look at the mezzo-soprano, who smiled slyly and leaned over to whisper to Julia.

"In case you're wondering, he was very happy with my work in *Salome*. And I certainly was happy with his."

"I see." Julia smiled her approval and whispered back. "So you and the maestro…?"

"What can I say? He's smart, unmarried, and Italian-hot. And he appreciates me."

"Then I'm truly happy for you."

"Thanks. I'm happy for me, too."

"Can we steal you away from your adoring colleagues for a toast?"

"I'll be there in a minute," Marin said.

Julia didn't notice Marin's wink at Larry, which he returned. But when Julia swiveled away from Marin, she found herself face-to-face with a horrendous sight: Sándor, holding the bloodied head of St. John the Baptist on a platter in his lap.

"Seriously!" Julia shrieked. "Are you freaking kidding me?"

"Come on, Jul, can't you appreciate some ghoulish humor?" said Katie.

"Take a closer look, Julia," Larry said. "This one was created especially for you."

Flashing a look of out-and-out menace at Larry, Julia leaned over the contorted lump and realized it was a cake in the shape of the prophet's head. Inscribed along the forehead in red frosting were the words, "To Julia, with love, from Jochanaan."

She burst out laughing. "I give up. This guy is going to haunt me for the rest of my life."

"Lucky him," Sándor said.

"Shall we start with the hair?" Larry said. "I know how much Julia loves licorice ropes."

"I say we eat the lips first," said Katie. "That's what started all of Salome's problems."

"Ugh," Julia said.

The party of five plucked flutes of champagne from a passing waiter.

"I'm back, singing." Marin lifted her glass. "And I have you to thank, Julia."

"To Julia, who rocked as usual," said Katie.

"I second that," said Larry.

The group raised their champagne glasses and clinked. Only Katie noticed that Julia did not drink from hers.

Epilogue

Wer hat sie nicht ursprünglich heiraten wollen!
Who has not always wanted to marry her!
—Berg, *Lulu*, Act 2

The trip through the mountains back to Albuquerque Airport took longer than it had when Julia and Larry first arrived in Santa Fe, due to Julia's need to stop periodically to throw up.

"Morning sickness sucks," she said to Larry after one especially dreadful bout.

"Poor baby. But it'll all be worth it in the end," he told her. "At least that's what my mother told me."

"She might take it back if she could see you now."

Larry chuckled. Julia turned a pallid shade of green and clutched the red stone her Navajo friend Miles had given her after their vision quest high up in the Sangre de Cristo Mountains. Once she had overcome her current wave of nausea, she regarded the mountain views through her window. She was going to miss their stark beauty once she got back to the city's concrete canyons.

"It's magical. No wonder people keep returning here year after year to play," she said. "Do you think we'll come back, Larry?"

"It all depends on what kind of kid Junior turns out to be."

"With any luck, she won't be as much trouble as you are."

"I love you, too."

* * *

Julia was not accustomed to being offered a seat on the New York Subway, especially the IRT uptown train, which always was packed. But she figured it was the sight of her burgeoning tummy that elicited sympathy from her fellow passengers. A burly Hispanic guy wearing a Yankees baseball cap and toting a humongous boom box, who seemed eager to share his CD of *Swan Lake* at top volume with the rest of the subway patrons, freely volunteered his seat.

"Even that dude feels sorry for me," Julia said to Larry.

As Larry helped her struggle into the proffered seat, Julia spied a familiar face on the bench opposite her. The man, whose gaze had never left the giant-sized sketchbook balanced on his lap, looked up when Julia shouted his name over the subway car's clacking noise.

"Sam!"

"Julia, Larry! How great to see you!" Sam had to holler to be heard above the subway clatter. "I see you've been busy."

Julia shrugged. "Must have been all those chile peppers in Santa Fe."

"Red or green?"

"Give *me* a little credit here, will you?" Larry said.

They all shared a laugh.

Julia nodded at Sam's sketchbook. "What are you up to there?"

"Diagramming next season's Santa Fe opening," Sam said. "A fight director's work is never done."

"I have no doubt," said Larry.

"Which opera?" Julia asked.

"*Don Giovanni,*" Sam said. "That's a huge one for me. Lots of major swordplay. I never get tired of it."

"Nor do I." Julia shivered slightly as she remembered the fateful Zerlina costume from the opera that almost heralded her undoing. "Were you at Santa Fe when the Statue of the dead Commendatore appeared onstage exactly at the same moment as a colossal thunderclap?"

"I was. A spectacular moment, the kind that only can happen at Santa Fe

Opera, of course."

"Of course," Larry said.

"How did you feel about your first experience at Santa Fe, Julia?" Sam asked. "Offstage violence and sudden fearsome weather patterns notwithstanding?"

"Impressive," Julia said. "I'm amazed at what they can achieve there every summer, in a few months."

"That's noteworthy, coming from a Met Opera veteran and native New Yorker."

"I'm not a veteran yet," said Julia. "But, yes, seeing what Santa Fe Opera can do almost makes me feel unsophisticated."

Larry chuckled. "Better keep that under your hat when you're at the Met."

"There's no other place like Santa Fe. You never forget it," Sam said. "When will you be back?"

"It could never be too soon," Julia said.

* * *

Preist mit hoher Freude Glut Leonorens edlen Mut!
Praise with high blazing joy Leonora's noble courage
—Beethoven, *Fidelio*, Act 2

A Note from the Author

In my 21 years as a violinist at the Metropolitan Opera in New York, I witnessed deadly accidents, suicides, onstage fatalities, and any number of nefarious goings-on behind the scenes. At times, the level of drama backstage far surpassed what took place onstage. What occurs behind that "Golden Curtain" can be as startlingly dramatic as any opera plot.

I was convinced both opera lovers and mystery novel aficionados would be fascinated by an insider's view of the egos, rivalries, and astonishingly ill-mannered behavior of individuals who made the opera house tick. I discovered that the potential for murder and mayhem at an opera house is virtually limitless. It's always "dark and stormy"—at least figuratively—at the Metropolitan Opera. But at the Santa Fe Opera's spectacular outdoor theatre nestled between two mysterious mountain ranges, "dark and stormy" literally can happen in the blink of an eye.

With the help of my wicked writer's imagination, I toss my unsuspecting violinist protagonist, a rising young star in the orchestra pit, into the fray: first at the Met, then at Santa Fe, and *voilà*—an "Opera Mystery" series is born. Readers will be dying to know where our intrepid amateur sleuth will be fiddling next.

Also by Erica Miner in the Julia Kogan Opera Mystery series:

Aria For Murder (Level Best Books, released Oct. 2022):

Excitement mounts as the moment arrives for brilliant young violinist Julia Kogan's debut in the orchestra of the world-renowned Metropolitan Opera. But the high-stakes milieu of this musical mecca is rocked to its core when, during an onstage murder scene, Julia's mentor, a famous conductor, is assassinated on the podium. Thrust into the investigation when her closest colleague in the orchestra is named chief suspect, Julia teams up with opera-loving NYPD detective Larry Somers to solve the murder. In the process, they are shocked to discover the venerable opera house is rife with a web of secrets, intrigue, and lethal rivalries. But all bets are off when Julia suddenly finds herself the real killer's prime target.

Acknowledgements

I would like to thank the following colleagues, both writing and operatic, for their valued contributions, support and inspiration:

David Holloway, Santa Fe Opera Director Emeritus of the Apprentice Program, longtime friend and colleague, who provided me access to the Santa Fe Opera house and its artists

Award-winning writers James Ziskin, Aaron Paul Lazar, Gabriel Valjan, Lori Robbins and Trudy Kempton Dana, for their loyalty and support throughout this process

Arthur Makar, for inspiring me to write a project set at this amazing opera house

Baritone Richard Stilwell, for his undying appreciation of my writing, and for sharing his many authentic, intriguing stories about Santa Fe Opera

Iconic tenor George Shirley, whose unique Santa Fe Opera experiences inspired key parts of this story

Mezzo-soprano Jennifer Larmore, whose insights on Alban Berg's *Lulu* were an enormous help

Santa Fe Opera Costume Director Missy West, for her valuable insider's view of what makes the costume shop tick

Santa Fe Opera Wig and Makeup Director David Zimmerman, for his indispensable, detailed information about the technical aspects of his craft

Santa Fe Opera Music Director, Maestro Harry Bicket, for sharing his insights on the Santa Fe Opera Orchestra

Jean Devine of Garcia Street Books in Santa Fe, for her enthusiasm about my book

Allison Buchsbaum Barnett and Ivan Barnett of Patina Gallery in Santa Fe, for their continuing interest in my work

Special thanks to my publisher, Level Best Books, and to my LBB "primary," Harriette Wasserman Sackler, for her faith in, and enthusiasm for, my work Stephanie Osser, for her huge help with Hungarian translations

About the Author

After 21 years as a violinist with the Metropolitan Opera, Erica Miner turned to her lifelong love of writing as her creative outlet. Based in the Pacific Northwest, she is now an award-wining author, screenwriter, arts journalist, and lecturer. Her debut novel, Travels with My Lovers, won the Fiction Prize in the Direct from the Author Book Awards, and her screenplays have won awards in the WinFemme, Santa Fe, and Writers Digest competitions.

Erica continues to balance her reviews and interviews of real-world musical artists with her fanciful plot fabrications that reveal the dark side of the fascinating world of opera. *Aria for Murder*, published by Level Best Books in Oct. 2022, the first in her Julia Kogan Opera Mystery series, was a finalist in the 2023 Eric Hoffer Awards. The second in the series, *Prelude to Murder*, finds the violinist in heaps of trouble in the desert at the Santa Fe Opera. The next sequel takes place at San Francisco Opera.

When she isn't plumbing the depths of opera houses for murderous mayhem, Erica frequently contributes reviews and interviews for the well-known arts websites BroadwayWorld.com, us.Bachtrack.com, and LAOpus.com. Her writings also have appeared in *PNWA Magazine, Vision Magazine, WORD San Diego, Our City Istanbul,* and numerous E-zines.

Erica also is a top speaker and lecturer. In the music world, she has presented pre-concert lectures for the Seattle Symphony at Benaroya Hall; Osher Lifelong Learning Institute at the University of California San Diego and the University of Washington; the Creative Retirement Institute at Edmonds College in the greater Seattle area; and Wagner Societies in Boston,

New York, the Bay Area, Los Angeles, San Diego, North Carolina, and New South Wales (Sydney, Australia).

As a writer-lecturer, Erica has given workshops for Sisters in Crime; Greater Los Angeles Writers Conference; EPIC Group Writers; Write on the Sound; Fields End Writer's Community; Savvy Authors; and numerous libraries on the west coast.

SOCIAL MEDIA HANDLES:
   https://www.facebook.com/erica.miner1
   https://twitter.com/EmwrtrErica
   https://www.instagram.com/emwriter3/

AUTHOR WEBSITE:
   https://www.ericaminer.com

Also by Erica Miner

Aria For Murder

Travels With My Lovers

Fourever Friends

Printed in the USA
CPSIA information can be obtained
at www.ICGtesting.com
JSHW022057190923
48548JS00001B/44